Counting The Cost

Faircourt Friends Series Book Two

Alexandra T Armstrong

PARABLE PRINT

PARABLE PRINT

This book is lovingly dedicated to
my dear mother-in-law,
Lois Ann Armstrong
Thank you for decades of consistently modeling every virtue of a godly
Christian woman.

You are a blessing and a treasure to me, your family, and so many others.

Whoever does not bear his own cross and come after me cannot be my
disciple. For which of you, desiring to build a tower. does not first sit
down and count the cost, whether he has enough to complete it.
Luke 14:27-28 (ESV)

CHARACTER RECAP

FRIENDS

Ava and Marcus Van Zant: Interracial couple pushed out of a long-term pastorate before they were financially prepared. They are the parents of three daughters: Marley, Mia, and Marit. Angered by their parent's decision to move to Faircourt, Mia and Marit cut off communication with their parents. This was devastating, especially to Ava, who suffered a breakdown over it. Marcus is known for asking direct and penetrating questions.

Grant and Marie Renniger: The parents of twin sons, David and Daniel, the financially secure couple, lacked purpose in their retirement and traded it for inclusion in the "hippie commune," as Grant initially called it. Marie is forthright, competitive, and not easily intimidated. Grant, a food fussbudget, gets his dream job as a golf starter to indulge his passion for the game.

Cal and June Sherman: A childless couple living on a rollercoaster of Cal's health challenges. They are 20-year friends of the Rennigers and brand-new friends to the Van Zants and Elodie. Cal has a habit of blurting out the wrong thing but is a private prayer warrior. June is kind, a great baker, and above all – a peacemaker.

Elodie Ford: A single black woman known for speaking her mind and childhood friend of Ava and Marie. She refuses to call Cal by his correct name, which is a cover for the soft spot she has for her medically fragile housemate. Elodie is a force of nature in the household: feminine but tough, suspicious but loyal.

NEIGHBORS

The Norman Family: Very recently widowed dad Micah has a son, Chase (13), and daughter, Lovie (7). Lovie has a special attachment to June and a mischievous streak. Chase is the only saved member of his family. The entire family has been enveloped and loved by the household of friends who recognize their vulnerability and minister to their grief.

Christine Williams: 70-something well-to-do neighbor who lives alone across the street and tends a prize rose garden. Her go-to move to get her way is threatening others with legal action. She's a loner and likes it that way.

Bobby McBride: A handsome 70-year-old widowed black man with a cat named Rover. He lives across the street from the friends and co-owns a car business with his sister. Bobby visits his daughter's family in Florida every year for 2-3 months and has a son serving time in prison. He's a regular at Garage Cave Night, and Elodie does not like him.

Jonathan Jefferson: The Pastor of Grace Fellowship Church, married to Kesha, and the father of four young sons. His best friend since high school is Bobby's imprisoned son, DeShawn McBride.

CHAPTER ONE

"Where are you going all tarted up?" Marie asked as Ava breezed into the kitchen for breakfast, wearing a light blue sweater set, navy slacks, and navy kitten-heel pumps.

"Tarted up? I'm wearing mascara and tinted lip balm, Marie. That hardly qualifies as evidence I'm on the path to moral ruin and damnation," Ava responded, amused.

"Besides, you paint your face with a fire hose every day!"

"Touché!" Marie snickered at the hyperbole returned upon her head and drained the last of the coffee pot contents into a white ceramic mug matching the household dinnerware.

"But if you must know, I have a job interview."

"What? Where? Why?" Marie stammered in surprise.

"Pastor Jefferson mentioned to Marcus that the church's part-time secretary gave her two weeks' notice. So, I'm interviewing because I need something to occupy my mind and because a little mad money would be nice. Have you seen my green thermal carafe?" Ava asked as she looked through the cupboard.

"Yes, sorry. I moved all the thermal mugs and bottles to the lower cabinet after my "World's Greatest Grammy" mug – the one Georgia made me when she was five – it fell from the shelf and smashed on the countertop. There were so many bottles, mugs, and glasses! Everything was crammed and precarious, and..."

"Oh! I'm so sorry about your mug. Those precious things are irreplaceable!" Ava consoled.

"I'm not going to lie. I almost shed tears over it. But it's just stuff, right? Better that I still have my Georgia than that mug."

"Yes, it's much better to have your granddaughter," Ava affirmed.

"Oh, I've stepped in it! Just tear off my arm and beat me with the bloody end of it. I know how much you miss your little Emily and her brothers. Of course, I was only thinking of my situation. Here, let me start you a fresh pot," Marie chastised herself and refilled the coffee maker.

Ava stepped toward Marie and encircled her friend in a side hug at the sink, wanting to soothe both of their hearts. She put her head on Marie's shoulder.

"In three weeks, it'll be a year since I've seen Jordan, Luke, Emily, and their parents. And next week is Marit and Robby's first anniversary. If someone had told me early on that the estrangement from my family would last a year...well, I'm glad nobody told me. But having a part-time job for distraction would be nice." Ava sighed.

"Oh, I hope you get it! Are you aware of any competition? I'll send Grant to bust her kneecaps, or better yet, Elodie!"

Ava released Marie and chuckled. "Yeah, Deacon Fowler's 18-year-old daughter, Emma, just graduated from high school and hasn't figured out what she wants to do with her life."

"Did I hear my name? You best not be takin' it in vain!" Elodie announced as she entered the kitchen and the conversation.

"Yes, you're on deck to bust the kneecaps of a kid," Marie answered with a straight face. Then after a second she added, "It's for Ava."

"Say no more and consider it done," Elodie responded, equally poker-faced.

"I can't decide if I have the world's worst friends or the world's best," Ava said, rolling her eyes and creasing their corners with a smile.

"Best or worst, we're what you've got, girl," Marie chuckled.

"Not that it makes any difference, but who is my intended victim?" Elodie asked as she reached into her gold linen dress pocket and pulled out her phone.

"Emma Fowler," Ava and Marie answered in unison.

"I know that girl! She and I had nursery duty together just last week. She seemed nice, a little chatty for me, but nice. What'd she do to our Ava?"

"She's competing with Ava for the part-time secretarial job at church," Marie scowled.

"It's not that I'm not willin', but you don't need me to mess her up. When we were rockin' babies, I learned her momma was four months pregnant with her when she married Deacon Fowler. Also, this past summer, the police arrested one boy in the youth group for shoplifting, and after 23 years together, the Scruggs are taking their marriage to divorce court. There's no way Pastor's gonna hire that girl. She couldn't keep a secret in a vault!"

"If that's the case, I feel better about my chances. So, you might not need to take her out after all. But the thought counts, and I appreciate it, El," Ava said, going along with her friends' ridiculous proposition.

"I'm here for you," Elodie answered. She sat at the kitchen table and soon engrossed herself in the sports scores on her phone screen.

"The coffee's ready," Marie beckoned to Ava, who retrieved and was holding her green carafe in anticipation.

"Anybody else having any?" Ava asked, picking up the pot.

"Nope. The rest of us killed the first pot, so this is all yours," Marie answered.

As she poured, Ava wondered aloud: "I didn't hear June playing hymns this morning. Are the Shermans gone?"

Elodie looked up from her phone and answered. "Ole Calcify had some tests scheduled at the hospital early this mornin'. June told me last night she was taking him."

Elodie kept close tabs on Cal in the few weeks since they'd learned his cancer was back - in a lung this time. She'd cried when June shared the news at Thursday Meeting, and her tears shocked Ava and Marie. In the 50 years they'd known Elodie, they'd only seen her cry twice – at her little brother's and mother's funerals. She put the "stow" in stoic, keeping expressions of sorrow carefully contained.

Elodie later brushed off her rare tears to Marie, attributing them to a combination of inconsistent sleep and a hormone cream she was prescribed. But the others noticed she began to hover over Cal. She asked if the house was warm enough or if he needed a sweater. She'd cook his favorite beef stew or chicken pot pie when it was her night to cook, disregarding Grant's criteria that vegetables never mix with meat. And she allowed June to leave the house by offering to sit with Cal, even learning his complicated medication schedule. Altogether, it was an unfamiliar side of Elodie on display. Neither Ava nor Marie were sure of what to make of it.

"Well, I'm off to my interview. See you girls later." Ava picked up her purse from the counter and fished out the car keys. She looped one arm through the handle, picked up her carafe, and was out the door.

Marie washed out the coffeepot, then inspected her day face in the reflection of the stainless-steel toaster.

"El, do you think I wear too much makeup?"

Elodie looked up from her phone once more.

"No, I don't. I think a lot more might help you out." She gave Marie a wicked smile before returning her attention to her phone screen.

Chapter Two

I t was a perfect night for football: cold, windy, and rainy outside. But inside was inviting, friendly, and full of goodies. Plus, the Bears were playing the Bengals.

Grant, Marcus, and Cal had prepared. They'd backed off their feed at dinner, bought plenty of soda and chips, ran Thursday Meeting like a horserace, and invited Bobby and Micah over to watch the game.

It was handy having Shelby living next door with her brother now. She could mind her niece and nephew while Micah left the house for a bit and let his hair down. He was losing the shell-shocked expression he wore in the first months since his wife's sudden death, and he enjoyed the company of his older neighbors, who steadied his outlook on his new reality.

The men gathered in the living room and closed the heavy pocket doors at the hall and dining room entrances. Despite this measure, the ladies were sure to hear their whoops and hollers wherever they settled in the house for the evening. Grant, Cal, and Bobby were Chicago fans, while Marcus and Micah rooted for Cincinnati.

Because Marcus didn't grow up with football in Aruba, he wasn't as invested in it as the others. He didn't know a Bengal from a billy goat, but he knew Grant liked the Bears, so Marcus declared himself a Bengals fan for the evening. The Thanksgiving Cowboys game was the only game of the year he did not insist on being contrary. Of course, they both despised the Cowboys, but Marcus insisted he had learned to loathe them from his seminary roommate, certainly not from Grant.

"Well, girls, how shall we amuse ourselves while the guys are watching football?" Ava clapped her hands together as she asked.

"How about gin rummy?" Marie enthused.

The others, recalling the last time they'd played cards with Marie, rendered their verdict.

"I'd rather not," June demurred.

"Don't think so," Ava winced.

"Forget it," Elodie refused.

"You girls wouldn't mind playing if you didn't lose all the time. You simply have to focus!" Marie insisted.

"Yeah, that's not the problem at all," Elodie shot back.

Sensing conflict about to erupt, June deflected it with an alternate proposal: "How 'bout we have an old-fashioned pajama party and watch a movie! Elodie can make us her specialty popcorn."

"I like it," nodded Ava.

"It has to be in El's room because she has the king-size bed," Marie pressed.

"That's fine. I just don't want to be rolling in popcorn kernels in my sheets tonight," Elodie cautioned.

"Every princess needs a pea!" Marie laughed. She stopped when Elodie glared at her over the top of her glasses.

It took just 20 minutes for the ladies to assemble themselves on Elodie's giant bed. On the far side next to the window, Marie wore a blue floral satin pajama set. Next to her, June had on a red flannel nightgown with white lace trim on the collar and cuffs. Elodie wore a dark purple t-shirt with paisley print shorts because she still suffered from occasional hot flashes. She claimed the other end of the bed in case she had to throw off the covers. Ava, the last to arrive, had to climb over Elodie to take the open spot between El and June. She was wearing a long-sleeved, cream-colored fleece pajama set that said "Baby It's Cold Outside" across the front of the top. A wide pink headband kept her short red locks off her face and out of a thick application of green facial goop.

"What?" Ava asked, noticing the looks the other women gave her upon her entrance. "It's my night to deep-moisturize."

Marie held the remote and pointed it at the 49" wall-mounted television opposite the bed. She scrolled through the stations and squealed when she saw Pride & Prejudice was starting.

"Please, I beg you all. Can we agree on Pride & Prejudice? It's been years since I've seen it. I love it, and you'll love it, too. It's got period costumes, dancing, and British accents. It's like they made the movie just for senior citizen pajama parties!" Marie pleaded.

June, Ava, and Elodie exchanged looks, and no one seemed to have an objection or alternative.

"On one condition." Ava recognized when she was in a position to negotiate.

"What's that?" Marie asked, tossing the remote to Elodie, confident of her willingness to meet any challenge.

"You make us all biscuits and sausage gravy for breakfast."

"Done!" Marie agreed. There was a reason she wasn't on the cooking rotation with the other ladies, but she could make biscuits and sausage gravy like a Southern Me-Maw.

"Turn up the volume now, El," she directed.

"I love the dancing!" June mused at the first ball scene. "Though there seems to be an awful lot of hopping. That's a dance for youthful knees."

"Pass the popcorn bowls, El!" Ava requested.

Elodie got out of bed and retrieved from her vanity top four bowls filled with her custom blend of microwaved kettle and extra-butter popcorn. She passed them down the line of women in her bed, and they all commenced nibbling.

"That Mrs. Bennett is too much!" June remarked.

"I once aspired to influence my daughters' choices as much," Ava confessed.

"Oh, we're all control freaks; let's face it. Of course, we want the best for our children and think we know what's best. But then God, in His sovereignty, overrules us," Marie admitted with a chuckle.

Hiccup!...Hiccup! "Stink, I've got the hiccups," Elodie moaned.

"Oh, look! Another ball!" June enthused. "Now, this dancing looks more elegant than at the last soiree. If people still danced like this, even Baptists could do it!"

"Mr. Darcy needs to buy a personality if you ask me," Ava groaned in complaint. "Oh, can we pause this for five minutes? I need to wash this mask off before it moisturizes my brain. Be right back!" she said as she crawled back over Elodie, who was searching for the remote.

"Make it quick," Elodie ordered. Hiccup! Hiccup!

Ava climbed back over Elodie, reclaiming her spot ten minutes later, and the movie resumed.

"Oh, Charlotte, don't marry Mr. Collins!" June wailed. "I suppose there needs to be drama, but she's throwing her life away. Well, maybe there'll be dancing at their wedding. I do love the dancing scenes. So much beauty!"

"Let's hear more of Elizabeth's dialogue and less of ours," Marie encouraged, eyes fastened to the television.

They continued munching their snack as the plot progressed through Mr. Darcy's proposal (hiccup), Elizabeth's refusal (hiccup), and her inevitable regret.

HICCUP! "Oh, that was a loud one, sorry," Elodie apologized.

"She's not going to throw herself from that cliff, is she?" June worried.

"A stiff wind could blow her off; she's so tiny," Ava responded.

Elodie continued to hiccup through the runaway sister scene, Jane's reunion with Bingley, and the confrontation with Lady Catherine.

Finally, Marie took the pillow from behind her head, swung it over the heads of June and Ava, and whacked Elodie squarely on her noggin.

"Owww!" Elodie bellowed.

"I dare you to hiccup now!" Marie shouted.

A worried look passed across June's face, and she looked to Ava for help.

"It's okay," Ava whispered to her.

"Hey, they're gone! My hiccups are gone," Elodie said, amazed.

"You're welcome," smiled Marie.

Ava leaned over to June. "Saw her do that to Grant once. Scared the hiccups out of him, too."

"Oh," June relaxed and leaned back into her pillow. "Aww, it doesn't seem likely we'll get another dancing scene. There's the credits."

Elodie turned the television off and insisted they search her sheets for stray popcorn before dispersing.

"Good grief! What do you have in this blanket at the bottom of your bed? Rocks?" June asked as she diligently searched for stray kernels under the fleecy covering.

"It's a weighted blanket I use to help my restless legs. Don't know what they put inside – might be rocks," Elodie answered with a shrug.

"Cal needs one of these! He kicks like a mule some nights," June declared. "You should see my shins!"

"How come romance movies don't show that side of life?" Ava wondered aloud.

"Imagine the sequel! Mr. and Mrs. Darcy take their honeymoon, and she comes back with bruised shins and soured on being a wife," Elodie laughed. "But I have to admit it wasn't an awful movie. Not my normal genre, though."

"June, I'm glad you loved the dancing," Marie said as an idea formed. "I did too, and I think we should learn to do it!"

"Yes!" cried Ava, catching the vision. "We can plan a ball and assimilate our guys into the event by assuming their willingness to participate.

Surely we can learn these dances from the internet. How hard can it be?"

"I don't want to be the accompanist, though. I want to dance! Just want to be clear about that," June insisted.

"And we wear Regency-era gowns! The best part for me is the dresses. We're not doing this in our street clothes," Marie ordered.

Elodie laughed out loud. "In my wildest dreams, I do not see myself in one of those gowns. Do you?" she asked no one in particular.

"Yes!" came the unanimous and synchronized response from Marie, Ava, and June.

Chapter Three

"All dis is deader dan week-old roadkill," Marcus observed, pulling the frost-damaged tomato plants up by their roots, showering his blue jeans with dirt.

"I heard this was early for a killing frost in Faircourt. It rarely happens until after Halloween. Let's just put everything we pull up in one gigantic pile in this garden quadrant. Between now and spring, we ought to get some pretty compost out of it if we break it up a bit," Ava directed.

Marie, Elodie, and June, obeying her instructions, assisted in pulling up the ravaged vegetable plants and heaping them up while Grant chopped at them with a spade.

"I'm gonna miss the taste of these tomatoes when we're eatin' store-bought until next summer," Elodie lamented.

"You're not kidding!" Marie agreed.

"I won't even bother to make a BLT until August," Ava grumbled.

"But we have pasta sauce and salsa put up from the garden. I hope it will last us until then," June wished aloud.

"May they multiply in our cupboard like Jesus' miraculous loaves and fish!" Grant chimed in.

They continued to work until all the plants were pulled up and deposited in the designated area.

"Look who's here!" Marie announced as she bent down to pet Bobby McBride's cat twirling around her legs. "Hello, Rover. Who's a good kitty? Did you come for a visit? Are you looking for catnip?"

At that, Rover scampered off in the direction of the Norman house.

"Cats don't like to be interrogated, Marie," Elodie chided, and Marie frowned.

"Marcus, how would you like to take a turn with this?" Grant asked, holding out the spade in his direction. "My arms are about to fall off!" he confessed, kneading the biceps under his black sweatshirt.

Marcus accepted the tool and began chopping the pile. "I have a question to ask," he stated as the others watched him. "Since Ava mentioned Halloween, and it's next week, and it's da first since we're in dis house, are we taking part in handing out candy to da kids? I don't know what you all tink about it."

Grant and Marie looked at each other, wondering what to say. Although they'd known these friends for decades, they'd never spent a single Halloween together. Marie tried to remember but couldn't recall the Shermans, whom they had gone to church with for the last 20 years, ever attending the annual Reformation Day church supper.

"I never gave out candy at my apartment. All the kids went to the neighborhoods anyway," recalled Elodie. "But our church had "Trunk Or Treat" where we decorated our cars and gave out candy and New Testaments in the parking lot. I did do that."

"What did you do, Marcus?" June wanted to know before she answered.

"We were never home for Halloween. My church celebrated Reformation Day instead of Halloween. I taught someting about Martin Luther or the 95 Theses, and we'd have a fellowship meal afterward," Marcus answered.

"Same with us," Grant offered.

"Come to think of it, I don't remember seeing anything in the bulletin at Grace Fellowship about an upcoming Reformation Day service," Ava recalled.

"Or a "Trunk Or Treat" event," Elodie added.

"Well, if nothing is happening at church, do we just turn the house lights off and pretend we're not home?" Grant wondered aloud.

"But we will be home," June said softly, her head lowered.

Ava looked at her husband and back at June. "June, what do you want to do for Halloween?"

"I like to see the children dressed in costumes and so excited to collect candy from neighbors. Cal and I always gave out candy to the trick-or-treaters." She looked around at her friends to gauge their reaction to her admission. "Do you all think we're horrible?"

Marcus stopped chopping the dead plants and leaned on the spade. He was about to say something when Elodie jumped in.

"I don't see any difference between giving out candy in a church parking lot versus giving out candy on our porch," she stated her opinion emphatically.

"If there's no Reformation Day observance at church, what if we did one at home?" Marie suggested.

"If we participate in secular Halloween, are we promoting a pagan celebration of spirits and wickedness?" Grant asked plainly, avoiding eye contact with June.

"Marie, remember when we used to go trick or treating together as kids? It was fun, right? It's not as if we returned home later, drew a pentagram on the basement floor, and sacrificed a chicken. We were just kids dressing up and collecting candy and homemade popcorn balls," Ava reminded.

Marie shuffled her feet, kicking at some dirt clods. She didn't answer Ava's question.

"Okay, I have another question den," Marcus said. "If we keep da house dark and don't answer da door, will dat communicate love to our neighbors?"

"If we participate in this, will it communicate love to God?" Marie rebutted. "And, aren't our neighbors supposed to notice that we're different?"

Grant held his fist out to give her a congratulatory bump before realizing from his wife's horrified expression it was inappropriate. He morphed the action into an awkward head scratch.

"We don't have to give out candy if you all believe it's wrong," June conceded. "Would anyone be offended if I made up two little treat bags for Lovie and Chase? I'll even bring them to their house."

"I've got an idea," Elodie offered. "June, you and I could go to the Norman's house and give out our candy there. That way, everyone does what their conscience allows. We have fun with the kids, and the old people stay here holed up in a dark house," she mocked the Rennigers with a wink.

"Now, wait a minute. Do we have to decide this right now? I haven't had to consider about this issue for a number of years," Grant interjected. "We always went to Reformation Day service because it was available and preferable to us. I want some time to really think through my convictions about Halloween. I'm not promising I'll change my mind, but I'd like to mull it over."

"I tink dat's a wise idea, Grant," Marcus complimented him. "I'm just surprised dat it came out of your mout!"

"Well, even a blind squirrel stumbles upon a nut now and then," Grant retorted.

"Halloween is Friday. We should decide by Thursday Meeting at the latest if we want to buy candy," Ava suggested.

"Can do," Grant replied.

"I guess the ladies are finished here. Marcus, give that pile a few more chops, please. And Grant, could you get that piece of clear plastic sheeting in the garage and cover the heap? A few rocks will hold it down and keep the heat in, helping it break down faster. We'll go check on Cal and get supper going," Ava instructed as the ladies headed to the house.

"Ooo, what's for supper tonight?" Grant shouted after them.

"Witch's Brew Stew," Elodie replied, still in a mood to mock him.

"Oh, den you'll be boiling your socks, I take it?" Marcus hollered, returning her spunk in Grant's defense. He stretched out his arm in Grant's direction, and they exchanged a fist bump as Grant belly-laughed.

"They'll be your momma's socks!" Elodie yelled over her shoulder, walking past the winterized Chicken Bowl Kiddie Pool and disappearing into the house.

Chapter Four

"Good mornin', Caliper! Nice to see you up and makin' coffee instead of slackin' like you've been gettin' away with," Elodie greeted Cal in the kitchen. Elodie noted he wore gray wool trousers and a pink, long-sleeved button-down shirt.

"Mornin' yourself, El Camino!" he responded cheerfully. "You'll be pleased to know June was baking last night and restocked us with scones. She made maple pecan and chocolate cherry. There's a platter on the table there," he added, pointing toward the kitchen table.

"Why don't you go have a seat, and I'll bring the pot over when it's ready. Just go, get comfortable," she encouraged him.

"Actually, I don't mind standing here. I've spent too much time horizontally lately. As a matter of fact, I'm feeling pretty good and planning to go to church with you all this morning," Cal responded to Elodie's surprise and delight.

"Well, isn't that something? Guess I'll sit myself down if that's the case."

Elodie sat at the kitchen table and watched Cal as he minded the small stream of coffee slowly filling the pot. She crossed her legs and restlessly pumped an imaginary brake with her dangling foot. The man before her eyes had a death sentence invading his body, and there was nothing she could do about it.

He'd become her friend in the seven months they'd lived under the same roof. And although she'd only known him a tiny fraction of the time she'd known Grant and Marcus, Elodie was as loyal to Cal as she was to them. He was her brother in Christ and her brother in this household. He, simply and complicatedly, had become her brother.

She told herself she'd gotten used to him and didn't like change. That much was true. What she couldn't admit to herself was the agitation she felt was, in reality, fear – fear of loss and the aching hurt that would surely follow. She'd lost her only brother and sibling to cancer when he was 16 and she was 19. Although it was uncomfortably familiar, Elodie hadn't realized the illness of her new brother was reaching back through the decades and, like an electric shock, stimulating and resuscitating the pain of losing her little brother, Calvin Darius Ford.

Elodie only knew it seemed much easier to manage Cal than to manage that unidentified anxiety. So, she observed him as he stood watching the coffee, looking for signs of fatigue and ready to assist at the first sign of weakness.

"My people!" Marie came bounding into the kitchen, the flared skirt of her red corduroy dress swishing and her arms open wide, seeking a body to hug. She looked at Elodie, who returned a glare over the top of her glasses, indicating she should choose elsewhere. So Marie rolled her eyes, shrugged, and headed to Cal, who braced a hip against the countertop to prepare for her onslaught of affection. Marie pinned his arms to the sides of his body and squeezed.

"What did I do to deserve that? Er, I mean, thanks, I guess," Cal stumbled over his response as Marie released him.

"I'm just happy it's the Lord's Day, and we get to worship together!" Marie gushed. "And it looks like you're going with us from how you're dressed, Cal. I'm so glad you're stronger today, my friend! And look at this," she said, noticing the loaded platter on the counter. "Scones! This day keeps getting better!"

Grant followed his wife into the kitchen, flipped on the electric kettle switch to heat water for his tea, and sat beside Elodie while he waited.

"Why's your wife so happy this mornin'?" Elodie quizzed him. "Wait! I don't wanna know. Pretend I never asked," she smirked at him in a way she knew would embarrass him.

Sure enough, Grant blushed and flustered. "And why do you have to be so irritating this and *every* morning?" he countered.

"It's kinda my hobby," she chuckled.

Grant shook his head, stood, and repositioned himself two seats away from her.

"She's not lying, dear," Marie said as she placed a jar of honey and the platter of scones on the table. "Can you think of another hobby she has besides irritating you and Marcus?"

"She's certainly committed to it. And she needs a life," Grant muttered, reaching for a chocolate cherry scone.

"My people!" Ava pronounced cheerfully as she and Marcus entered the kitchen and headed to retrieve coffee mugs.

Afraid the greeting forewarned an impending bear hug, Cal poured his coffee and shuffled as quickly as he could to seat himself at the table.

Ava giggled, "I heard Marie say it when we were on the stairs. Thought I'd give it a replay. Didn't mean to scare you, Cal. We haven't seen you move that fast for a while."

Cal reached for a scone and took a bite to spare Ava any expectation of a reply.

"Here, June, you can have da rest of dis pot. I'll start anoder," Marcus called out to her as he saw her close their first-floor bedroom door, steps away from the kitchen.

"You're so kind," June thanked him as she reached for the steaming mug Marcus extended to her. She wore pink boot-cut denim pants topped with a fluffy gray tunic sweater that reached mid-thigh. In terms of fashion, she coordinated but was the opposite of Cal, who wore pink on top and gray on the bottom. June enjoyed coordinating outfits for church with her husband. She liked being an identifiable couple.

"June, you spoil us all with your baking. This chocolate and cherry scone is delicious," Grant complimented her. "Would it be piggish of me to try the maple pecan, too?" he asked.

"Go right ahead and help yourself," she responded, pleased.

Grant reached for the scone and avoided looking at his wife, who had been encouraging him to monitor his white flour intake. And his sugar. Carbohydrates in general. Really, any joy derived from food at all.

Spurred by his comrade's success in being allowed, albeit not by his wife, another scone, Marcus also helped himself to seconds.

Marie and Ava exchanged helpless glances. Ava had encouraged Marcus to adopt a healthy eating mindset and met similar resistance.

"Maybe instead of walking to church this morning, we should run," suggested Ava.

"Ok. Yeah. Whatever," Marcus agreed dismissively as he ate.

"I'll be drafting right behind you," Grant pictured the scene of running in Marcus' wake and laughed with a mouthful of scone he hadn't swallowed. In the next second, it lodged in his throat.

Grant was never one to instigate a scene, so he tried to cough without drawing attention to himself. He was horrified to discover he couldn't cough. Grant looked to Marie, who was asking June if she'd ever used a sugar substitute in her baking. He grasped her arm to get her attention. Annoyed, she looked at her husband and saw panic in his eyes.

"Are you alright?" she asked.

Grant shook his head. His eyes widened, and his face was reddening.

"Grant!" Marie shrieked, getting everyone's attention.

He pointed to his throat to indicate he was choking, and Marie laid five successive karate chops hard between his shoulder blades to no avail. At length, Grant's face turned a dark purple.

Elodie vaulted her 5'9", 210-pound frame from her seat so fast she nearly flipped the table. Every mug turned over and spilled whatever contents they held. Scones skittered across the table, and a few landed on the tile floor. She jumped behind Grant's chair, threaded her arms under his, and clasped her hands across his chest. Then, with a single upward jerk, she pulled him to his feet, and with another, she dislodged the food that flew from his mouth.

Everyone heard the crack. With the adrenaline-fueled strength of a man, Elodie broke a rib in the process of her Heimlich maneuver to save Grant. Perhaps two.

CHAPTER FIVE

"How's the patient doing?" Ava asked as Marie descended the staircase late Sunday afternoon.

"Much better since the pain meds kicked in. The only thing he's moaning about now is missing the last few weeks of his job and its perks at the country club. The ER doctor showed us two ribs were broken clean through and told Grant he had to lie low for three weeks and couldn't golf for six, Marie answered wearily.

"I'm sure that crushed Grant harder than Elodie did. Had any lunch?"

"Not a bite, and I'm starved."

"There's leftover pizza from lunch in the fridge. I'll keep you company," Ava offered.

They headed to the kitchen where Cal and June sat at the table, sipping iced coffees they'd brought home from the Main Street coffee shop, Latte Da. Ava poured herself a glass of filtered water from the fridge and joined the Shermans at the table while Marie heated a slice of pizza in the microwave. As she waited for it to warm, she asked: "Anyone know where El is?"

"She's in her room," answered June somberly. "After the drama with Grant and you all rushing to the emergency room, Elodie realized she'd done something to her back when she pulled Grant up. She didn't go to church with us. Instead, she stayed home to soak in a hot Epsom salt bath."

"I stayed home with her," Ava picked up the narrative. "I helped her navigate climbing the stairs, bathing, and getting into bed. You should have heard her holler when I put an icepack on her lower back! The neighbors probably thought someone was being stabbed."

"Oh, I'm so sorry she's hurt too," Marie lamented, joining her friends at the table.

"I'll tell you what. It sure is nice not to be the one down in bed. It's good for someone else to have a turn," Cal remarked in a chipper tone.

June frowned at him.

"I should not have said that out loud, right?" he asked, lowering his head.

"It's alright, Cal," Marie assured him. "You've had weeks of bad days. You enjoy this good one you're having. Grant and El would gladly take more turns if it could spare you."

Ava nodded her agreement. "Marcus is in bed too, but he's only taking a late nap. So it doesn't count as being down in bed."

She noticed Marie had nothing to drink and offered to get her some water. As soon as she reached the refrigerator, the doorbell rang. Ava looked over her shoulder and saw Lovie's face in the front door window at the end of the main hall.

"You've got company, June!" she informed her.

"Lovie?" June guessed hopefully.

"None other."

June's eyes scanned the counter and spied two leftover scones in the glass-covered serving dish. She grabbed one, wrapped it in a paper towel, and headed toward the 7-year-old neighbor girl she adored waiting at the front door.

"Yes, mam? Can I help you?" June teased as she opened the door.

"I came to visit you, Miss June! It's been a long time since we've seen each other," Lovie reminded her.

June did not need reminding. The most she'd seen of Lovie in the past four, if not five weeks, was waving at her as she came off the school bus that dropped her off in the afternoons. Of course, Lovie would wave back, but it wasn't like it was before when she'd run up to the porch, plop her backpack on the floor, and climb up on the porch glider next to June and prattle at length about her day at school with her friends, Addy and Lena. Now she skipped past June, eager to get home where her Aunt Shelby, who was living with the Norman family, was waiting for her. But Lovie was here now, and June would soak her up.

"I know it's a bit cool outside, but let's sit on the porch to catch up. We have three people napping in the house, and we don't want to wake them up to be grumpy, do we? And look what I have for you – a chocolate cherry scone to nibble on!"

Lovie sat close to June's left side on the glider, unwrapped the treat she'd been given, and took a big bite.

"Be careful, Lovie! Maybe take smaller bites," June warned. She told her what had happened to Mr. Renniger that morning when a big bite got caught in his throat. If a little fear of what could happen moderated the size of the bites Lovie took, June was okay with that.

"Did he almost die?" Lovie asked after she'd chewed and swallowed the bite, her blue eyes wide with concern.

"Oh no! I went too far!" June fretted as she remembered it hadn't been a year since Lovie had lost her mother unexpectedly. *"How stupid of me not to think of that!"* she scolded herself. But it was too late to gather her words back. Instead, she considered how to answer Lovie's question for a long moment.

"Yes and no," she finally said.

Lovie's expression turned to puzzlement. She scooted away from June and turned her body to face her more directly as if she needed the entire surface area of her face and chest to absorb an explanation, not merely her right ear.

"The 'yes' part is because when Mr. Renniger was choking, he couldn't breathe. That's very dangerous and very scary. Our bodies need to breathe. So all of us need to be mindful of that and careful when eating," June answered calmly.

"Why did you say there's a 'no' part?" Lovie pressed.

"Well, the 'no' part is because of something God tells us in His Word. He said that before we were born, He'd planned and written down all the days appointed for us. And do you understand why that's a wonderful thing?"

Lovie shook her head and raised her shoulders, indicating she had no clue.

"It means all of us live the exact number of days God planned for us all along. Nobody misses a single day that God intended them to have. The problem for us is God doesn't tell us how many days we get or how many days our loved ones will get. And when that number is smaller than we expected, we're sad and disappointed. But God must have more days for Mr. Renniger because He put Miss Elodie at the table this morning to help get the food unstuck."

Lovie absorbed June's words thoughtfully and applied them to her nearer concern. "So, Mommy lived all the days God planned for her?"

"She didn't miss one."

Lovie turned her body and scooted back to June's side. They swayed back and forth on the glider while Lovie finished her scone with careful bites.

"It's like we all have an invisible milk date," Lovie said at last.

June chuckled as she translated 'milk date' to 'expiration date.' "That's a good way to put it, Lovie. We all have an invisible date, and God wants us to know and remember only that much so that we live our days carefully."

Chapter Six

"Well, tomorrow's Halloween," Marcus began Thursday Meeting. "We've all had several days to tink it over and examine our consciences, so I suggest we take a vote and let the majority rule. Can we agree to dat?" he asked.

"Let's face it. Marie and I were the only ones who had reservations about participating," Grant began, sitting stiffly in his chair. "But this week, the Lord gave me a lot of time to be still, look into His word, and pray. I want to share that Marie and I landed on participating in Trick or Treating. It seemed to us a lot like the ancient church's issue of eating meat sacrificed to idols – some people were scandalized, and some people didn't think it mattered because the gods weren't real. The difference was their experience and association with idols. Marie and I know Satan is real, and that's true every day, not just on October 31st. But our experience and association with Halloween aren't related to exalting him; therefore, our consciences can be free. So, they are free."

Marie sat close to Grant on the couch, her hand resting on his thigh, and added to her husband's comment: "This was a good spiritual exercise for us, but it humbled us too. The Lord showed us we harbored some pride in our hearts. One reason we were lazy about searching the scriptures on this topic for so long is that we enjoyed the appearance of holiness and sacrifice – as if we gave up something dear to us. The truth is, it costs us nothing to give up handing out candy to kids since ours have been grown and gone a long time. So we want to apologize to you for our spiritual snootiness and ask your forgiveness."

"We forgive you," June and Marcus' words spilled over each other in unison.

"I forgive you, too, but I think we should impose a penance. You have to buy the candy this year!" Elodie needled.

"That's harsh! But I'll go to Big Mart first thing after breakfast," Marie promised.

"Anybody interested in dressin' up?" Elodie suggested with her question. "I have a Raggedy Ann costume I was going to wear for Trunk Or Treat last year, but I got diarrhea and couldn't go. So I could break that out."

Ava cocked her head to the right. "To clarify, would you be breaking out the costume or the diarrhea?"

Grant chuckled and regretted it as a sharp pain stabbed his torso.

"See, you're not right in the head. Get some help!" Elodie scoffed at Ava.

"I think dressing up will be all you, El," June demurred.

"I'd like to see that!" interjected Cal.

"Then you will!" Elodie pronounced.

"Are we ready to move on? I have some other news!" Ava was animated. Whatever she had to share was obviously good news. Seeing no objection, she continued, "You all are looking at the new part-time secretary of Grace Fellowship Church! I'll work six hours on Tuesdays, Wednesdays, and Thursdays. Nine o'clock to three o'clock, and I start next week. Pastor Jefferson called me this afternoon to tell me I got the job!"

"Oh, Ava! I'm so glad for you. There was never any doubt that you were the best candidate. I'll help you pick out your outfit for Tuesday," Marie offered her immediate, heartfelt, enthusiastic support.

"It's my first day at a new job, not my first day of high school, Marie,"

Ava chided her.

"I wouldn't give a nickel to be in high school these days," Elodie retorted, drawing them all into a conversational tangent on the state of teenagers and public education.

Marie heard the melded sound of their chatter, but Ava's curt rebuff hurt her feelings. She'd helped Ava choose every mother-of-the-bride dress she'd worn and helped her choose a 20th-class reunion dress and 25th wedding anniversary dress. And yes, she helped Ava select her outfit for her first day of high school. Junior high, too. Helping Ava dress for special occasions was what she did.

So, she wondered why Ava had slapped her down for offering to be involved now. As she struggled to find an answer, she felt the top of her head growing hot and her throat tightening. She knew the next thing that would happen if she didn't get a grip. Tears would pool in her eyes, and then, God forbid, one might fall. Marie had to get out of the room without making a scene.

She coughed, as if there was an irritation in her throat, and stood to announce: "I've got to get a drink of water." Then she retreated to the kitchen and poured herself a glass of filtered water she didn't need. She sipped it anyway as she stood before the kitchen window, looking across the colorless, leaf-strewn yard in the faint evening light. She noticed a light rain, making dots on the glass pane.

If Elodie had spoken the exact words Ava had, Marie knew she would have laughed them off. Probably would have asked her if she even went to high school because, unlike with Ava, teasing was a significant dynamic of her relationship with Elodie. On the other hand, if June had said those words...well, Marie couldn't imagine sweet June saying something like that. Anyway, why couldn't she chalk up Ava's words to Ava having a lousy day – make it Ava's problem and not hers? And where was her typical thick skin? It took more than an offhand comment or slight to hurt her feelings. She'd often told people through the years, "If you're trying to hurt my feelings, you're going to have to spell it out because it's not my default assumption."

"*Maybe,*" Marie thought, "*I'm just getting old-lady sensitive. Great. The entire household will love this new twist in my personality.*"

The heavens opened up just then, and the light rain became a heavy downpour. Marie focused outside the window on a sodden row of leaves that had migrated and piled up against the Chicken Bowl Kiddie Pool fence. And to her memory came the pungent aroma of wet, crusty leaves.

It was a smell she'd known from childhood when she'd slip out of the house after dark and walk across damp autumn leaves to her grandparent's house next door because her mother and father were drunk and fighting over whose fault it was that they were saddled with this unexceptional kid. And it was the smell of the rainy November evening when she was 20 that the boy she'd married at 18 told her he didn't love her anymore and wanted a divorce. It was the smell of rejection.

As Marie studied the fallen leaves and smelled them from memory, she understood why Ava's words had wounded her. They felt like rejection from someone she loved at a vulnerable time of year.

CHAPTER SEVEN

Marcus and Cal cheerfully cleared away the pizza boxes, paper plates, and plastic cups from the dining table and deposited them into a trash bag. As far as they were concerned, this was the best thing about Halloween. There'd be no pots, pans, or dishes to rinse and load into the dishwasher tonight because the trick-or-treaters, they'd been told by Micah next door, would start pounding the doorbells at 5:30 pm. So, dinner was necessarily a quick affair.

Ava, Marie, and June settled on the porch at 5:25 pm, awaiting the parade of costumed children. Grant had taken himself for his usual post-supper walk through the neighborhood, and Elodie was upstairs putting on her Raggedy Ann costume and makeup. It had drizzled all night but cleared up mid-morning, so the roads and sidewalks were dry. The air was pleasantly chilly, and the women wore cozy sweaters.

"Would you look at the size of these candy bars," Ava observed, picking one out of the enameled roasting pan pulled into service as a giant candy bowl with handles. "They're minuscule! I could eat three at once."

"That's all Big Mart had," Marie was defensive.

"Remember when we'd go trick or treating when we were kids, Marie? People gave out full-sized candy bars. We'd eat three or four before we got home and make ourselves sick. I always got out of my costume and went to bed, and then rotten little Rae Jean would steal any Dots candy I'd collected in my pillowcase bag," Ava reminisced, referencing her younger sister.

"Um," Marie acknowledged with the bare minimum response.

"Don't tell me you're our first trick-or-treater! You've made no effort on your costume at all," June needled their neighbor, Bobby McBride, as he approached their porch wearing his regular work clothes.

"Well, that wasn't the intention of my visit. I came to verify we weren't having Garage Cave night since it's Friday and Halloween. No one ever said. But could I stick my hand in this marvelous tub of chocolate if I said the magic words?" he laughed.

"I'm sorry; there are no Garage Cave activities tonight since we're all doing this. But you're welcome to our treats," answered Marie, appreciating his admiration of the candy.

"Don't you participate in Halloween, Bobby?" June asked him.

"Oh, there's candy to be had at my house. I brought my sister home with me this evening 'cause she likes to hand it out. She lives in a secure condo, and they don't get kids coming to their doors. So she always buys a mountain of Twizzlers to give out so she can take leftovers home. The kids know my house for the Twizzlers. And that's why I'm happy to come across some chocolate here," he explained as he reached into the roasting pan and selected one piece.

"Maaagic wooords," June offered in a singsong reminder.

"Ha! Caught me. Trick or treat!" Bobby responded gamely. He opened the tiny wrapper and popped the candy bar into his mouth.

"Looks like the house across the street won't be handing out candy," Marie said as she observed Christine Williams moving from room to room and closing blinds in the windows of the pristine white clapboard house. The van of her cleaning help was pulling away from the curb on the Tamarack Street side of her house.

"Never has in 40 years," muttered Bobby. "Nor the gray house beside her, across from the Normans. Lots of turnover in that one – all renters, I think," he added.

"Grant's back and in his usual rush," Ava snickered as they all turned to see him hustling up the walkway toward them.

Marie did not find her comment as amusing as Ava seemed to. "At least he tries to take care of himself," she answered, again on the defensive.

This time, Ava picked up on her friend's tone and tipped her head sideways with a puzzled expression. Marie did not satisfy her with an explanation or further comment.

"Hey, Grant!" Bobby greeted him as he scurried to the front door.

"Hey, Bobby, I'll be right back," Grant shouted over his shoulder and disappeared into the house.

"Call of nature," Marie explained so Bobby wouldn't think her husband was rude.

"I'm familiar," Bobby chuckled.

Suddenly, from inside the house, they heard Grant emit a startled "Aaarrrgh!"

The group on the porch exchanged questioning glances. Then, in the next moment, the front door opened, and it was Bobby's turn to be startled.

"Hell's bells!" he yelped spontaneously at the sight in the doorway.

Elodie had arrived to join them on the porch dressed in an extra-large adult-sized Raggedy Ann costume complete with a calico dress, white apron, red striped stockings, and a pigtail wig of bright red yarn. Unfortunately, her makeup had run off the rails. She'd applied a pale powder all over her face and drawn a triangle on the tip of her broad nose, which she'd filled with red lipstick. She used the lipstick on her mouth, which she'd extend into a wide smile with the addition of a thick black line radiating from each corner to the middle of each cheek. Her eyebrows were redefined into heavy black arches, which created an expression of perpetual surprise. And whether Elodie innocently failed to draw prominent eyelashes with the liner, intentionally smudged them, or merely grew tired of the whole effort, was uncertain. But the outcome was that her eyes appeared like sunken, lifeless spheres.

"Miss Elodie, is that you?" Bobby asked as he steadied his nerves.

"Holy terrifying rag doll!" Marie winced and shook her head.

Ava rose from her chair to get a better view, but she and June remained speechless, mouths agape.

Marcus and Cal, done cleaning up in the dining room and kitchen, were now trying to get past Raggedy Elodie, who stood fixed in the doorway with her back to them. She turned her body to let them through but didn't move her feet from their position. Both men were annoyed she wouldn't step out of the way, but they managed to squeeze through the space between her and the door frame. Once on the porch, they greeted Bobby and then turned back to look at what was holding his attention.

When he saw Elodie's face, Marcus drew a breath in sharply. Cal began to laugh and snort, becoming a contagion the others caught. When Bobby laughed, Elodie shouted at him, "You can go home!" Then she spun around – quicker than she should with a back that was still sore - and returned inside the house, closing the door like she was protecting herself from a swarm of bees.

"Uh oh. We've embarrassed her," Bobby said, still laughing.

"Did she say she was going to be a scary doll? Do you tink she meant to look like dat?" Marcus wondered aloud.

"She rarely wears makeup. Maybe she didn't realize..." Marie left her comment unfinished.

"We shouldn't have laughed at her," June said.

"I was laughing at Cal laughing," Ava insisted.

"I thought she was a perfect scream. All the kids would have loved it!" Cal tried to justify his reaction.

"Speaking of kids, here come our Lovie and Chase," June said, pleased to see them coming up the walkway from the sidewalk.

Lovie dressed as Queen Elizabeth II, wearing a white granny wig, a powder blue coat and matching pillbox hat, along with a strand of costume pearls and pearl clip-on earrings. On her arm, she carried a small black pocketbook she would use to collect candy and then dump it into a large plastic bag carried by her big brother. He was dressed as a Queen's Guard in black trousers, a white-belted red jacket, and a mammoth black fur hat that his Aunt Shelby bribed him to wear, unbeknownst to Lovie, with $20 cash.

"Trick or treat!" Lovie shouted enthusiastically, holding open her purse in expectation.

"You guys are darling!" gushed June.

"Aunt Shelby made our costumes. We went to the thrift shop and found things she fixed up for us," Lovie explained.

"Of course she did," June thought to herself jealously.

Just then, Grant came out of the house and, seeing the soldier standing on his porch, threw him a sharp salute.

Chase reddened. "Come on, QE2," he said to his sister. "We've got a big neighborhood to cover." And he turned to go with a tug on Lovie's arm.

"Happy Halloween!" Lovie bid them goodbye.

"That's two embarrassed off the porch so far. Let's see if we can keep this going!" Cal suggested mischievously as a small group of costumed children approached their house.

CHAPTER EIGHT

"Anyone seen Marie?" Ava asked as everyone cleared their breakfast dishes from the kitchen table.

"She's cleaning out the chicken coop. I would have helped her, but, you know, doctor's orders," Grant said, gently patting his ribs with a sly smile.

"That's okay. I'll help her. But first, I have to run and change into some nasty-chore pants."

Ava darted upstairs and down again two minutes later, wearing paint-spattered blue jeans and a thick, dark purple sweatshirt. She headed out the back door, walking quickly past the vegetable garden toward the coop at the back of the Garage Cave.

Marie was nowhere in sight. The access door to the henhouse was unlatched, and the chickens eagerly pecked at scratch grains in their run below it. A red-painted wire egg basket containing six dirty white eggs sat in the grass a little distance from the coop. Ava stood, hands on hips, wondering where her friend could be.

Just a half-minute later, Marie, pushing an empty wheelbarrow, came around the far side of the Garage Cave. She wore a pair of navy wide-leg jeans tucked into brown rubber ankle boots and a yellow plastic rain jacket that reached mid-thigh. Her hair was pulled back into a nubby ponytail at the nape of her neck, and a white dust mask fogged the bottom half of her glasses' lenses.

"There you are! I asked the hens where you were, but they wouldn't give up your location," Ava joked.

Marie smiled under her mask. Ava could see the corners of her eyes slightly crease from the change in expression.

"I came out here to see if you needed any help," she offered.

"I'm done with the worst part. But if you want, you can drag a bag of wood shavings from the garage out here and help me spread it."

"I'm on it!" Ava said, disappearing into the garage. She quickly retrieved the bags and took direction from Marie on lining the hen house and nesting boxes with the shavings. When they were finished, they closed the large access doors and sat on the grass to catch their breath.

"You wouldn't think spreading wood shavings was anaerobic activity, but I'm winded," Ava confessed.

"I think it's being bent at the waist to reach in the coop and holding your core muscles taut that saps your energy. I feel it, too," Marie agreed.

They sat next to each other in silence for a minute before Ava asked the question she'd sought her friend to ask.

"Marie, are you upset with me? I'm sensing some tension between us, and I hate that."

Marie considered her answer. She understood Ava was healing but still raw in places from the estrangement with her daughters, Mia and Marit. However, she was indeed upset and inclined to avail herself of the opportunity Ava was giving her.

"Let me ask you a question first. How much bluntness can you handle on a scale of one to ten?" Marie inquired.

"Hmm. Eight, I guess. I want you to be honest but not mean."

"Fair enough," Marie began. "My feelings were hurt the other night at Thursday Meeting when I offered to help you pick out an outfit for your new job, and you said this wasn't high school. And yesterday, you mocked Grant for having bathroom issues, which also touched a nerve. How could I not be hurt for him when I know he's been shamed?"

"I apologize from the bottom of my heart for my careless words, which hurt your feelings, Marie. Please forgive me," Ava replied sincerely, making no excuses whatsoever.

Marie laughed out loud. "What in the name of perfect apologies is that? Don't you even want to go 'round and 'round about it first? You're just going straight to 'forgive me'?"

Now Ava laughed. "Yes, I am. I'm sorry too if that's unsatisfying for you."

"Well, it does take the wind out of my sails if you're still looking for honesty," Marie retorted candidly.

Ava scooted her bottom closer to Marie until they were elbow to elbow, and she put her arm around Marie and her head on her shoulder. "I love you," she said quietly.

Marie inhaled and exhaled deeply. "I love you, too."

"Friends, again?" Ava asked.

"We will never not be friends," Marie replied, lowering her head against Ava's.

"You don't have chicken lice or anything like that in your hair, do you?" asked Ava, suddenly concerned.

"I guess you'll find out soon enough," Marie chuckled.

They sat side by side, heads touching for a minute before Ava asked: "Marie, on a scale of one to ten, how much were your feelings hurt?"

"Bout a six or seven."

"Okay. And on a scale of one to ten, how important were the things you were upset with me about?"

"Probably not more than two or three." Marie straightened quickly as she realized Ava's point. "My feelings were out of proportion to the offense," she admitted with embarrassment, lowering her head.

Ava smiled. "We all do it. I think the question we never ask is - why? Was there more to it?"

Marie hesitated a few seconds before turning her body to face her friend. "I smelled the wet leaves," she answered.

Ava understood the cryptic explanation. They'd lived in the village of Liverpool, New York, as children, saturated with giant, hundred-year-old trees that carpeted nearly every square foot of lawn with leaves in the Fall. In those days, each homeowner was obliged to rake them into piles at the edge of the uncurbed streets for disposal in the leaf-vacuum trucks that came on the second and fourth Saturdays of November. The piles awaiting collection and dampened by rains produced a moldy, acidic scent that hung low like a spirit reluctant to leave its corpse.

Ava could recall the aroma in her memory as clearly as Marie. And she knew her friend's association of it with fleeing to her grandparent's house and the disappointment of her failed teenage marriage in which Ava had participated as maid-of-honor. Marie's shorthand acknowledgment of smelling leaves was all that was necessary to communicate in a friendship in its seventh decade that she felt abandoned.

"Funny how ancient hurts find their way to our hearts through certain smells," Ava hugged her friend tightly and released her.

"It's annoying. The smell of wet leaves wrecks me. But you're right; those hurts are ancient. I hate that they won't stay in the past where they belong. God has blessed me so much since the long-ago Liverpool years. I wish there were a smell that would remind me of that. If blessing were a scent, I'd buy the perfume, the candles, and the car freshener!" Marie confessed as she subconsciously fiddled with the gold chain bracelet on her wrist.

"Hmm. If blessing were a scent, I think it would smell like June's pound cake," Ava took up the idea.

"Or Elodie's fried chicken," Marie chuckled.

"Or a new leather Bible," Ava remembered.

"Or the lawn after Grant mows," Marie smiled.

"Or Marcus' man soap," Ava giggled.

"Or sheets hung on a clothesline on a warm spring day," Marie closed her eyes and inhaled deeply.

"Or," Ava hesitated and laid her head back on Marie's shoulder. "Blessings can smell like friends with chicken poop on their boots."

Chapter Nine

"Where's everybody else?" Chase asked, bounding down his porch steps as he zipped his navy hoodie to join Marcus and Ava on their walk to Grace Fellowship Church.

"We're the only walkers today. The others are driving, but they'll be along," Ava answered cheerfully.

The narrow sidewalk in the old neighborhood would not accommodate three people walking side by side, so Ava dropped back to let Marcus and Chase chat with one another. Since Chase started eighth grade and made the basketball team in his final year of middle school, they didn't see much of him.

"So, you're on da top of da heap at school dis year. You're enjoying dat, right?" Marcus commented on an assumed fact.

A slow smile spread across Chase's face, and he nodded his response.

"Tell me about your friends," Marcus requested.

"I've actually made a bunch of new friends this year because of being on the basketball team and all. Do you know I grew almost three inches just over last summer? Dad says my feet also grew three inches, but that's not true. I only went up one shoe size. But anyway, the guys on the basketball team are really cool. We all eat at the same lunch table besides having practices together. Coach Robbins says it's important to have camaraderie off the court."

"Oh," Marcus said as he stepped over a large crack in the sidewalk produced by a thick tree root visible underneath. "Are you able to keep up wit your friends from last year? Do you spend time wit Silas?"

"Silas doesn't play basketball," Chase answered defensively. "But I see him at church on the weekends he's at his dad's!" he brightened.

"I see. Do your new basketball buddies know Jesus?"

"Well, we don't really talk about that. I'm not sure. But they're good guys. Trevor is our best player and is pretty cool. He even has a girlfriend. I like him."

"Whoa, a girlfriend! Do you have a girlfriend?"

Chase was caught off guard by the directness of the question and gave a nervous laugh. Finally, he answered, "I have a few friends who are girls but not a girlfriend."

"Well, dere's plenty of time for dat in da future."

Chase laughed nervously again. They walked the remaining block, looking ahead and watching a steady stream of vehicles pull into the church parking lot, including the Renniger's black sedan stuffed with the remaining household members.

When they entered the vestibule of the 80-year-old red brick building, Chase waved to Miss Elodie, peeled off to the staircase, and headed to the second-floor junior high boys' Sunday School classroom. He opened the classroom door and scanned the room warily. There were only ten junior high boys, including himself, and he was relieved to see Silas was not among them this week.

Being around Silas had become a liability. Trevor said Silas was a nerd, and people who hung with him got nerd juice on them. Chase couldn't afford to have nerd juice on him when he'd just won acceptance with the cool crowd. So, he'd stealthily dodged his former friend at school and half-heartedly acknowledged him at church. He told himself they hadn't been that close to begin with, reminding himself they'd only known each other since beginning sixth grade, just a little over two years ago. Still, he felt a twinge of guilt when Silas was at church, so he was glad that unpleasant sensation wouldn't bother him today.

Downstairs in the multigenerational men's class, Will was teaching a lesson contrasting the general call of God as seen in Matthew's parable of the wedding banquet in chapter 22 with the effectual call of God that Paul presents in Romans 8. After presenting the contrasting passages, he encouraged the men to debate the meaning of Jesus' words in Matthew 22:14: "For many are called, but few are chosen." The rule in Will's class was if you stated a position, you had to back it up with Scripture. He insisted the men think biblically and trained them to do so.

"I don't think 'chosen' means God chooses who He will save because 2 Peter 3:9 says God is not willing that any should perish, but that all should reach repentance," Lefty Schneider, a church deacon, asserted.

Tom Farmer, the church's part-time maintenance man, responded: "To what do the words 'any' and 'all' in that passage refer? Any redhead-ed toddlers? All Roman citizens under four feet tall? Grammatically, those words refer back to the word 'you.' So, we can insert that antecedent and read it as 'God does not wish that any of *you* should perish, but that all of *you* should reach repentance.' So then, who does the word 'you' refer to? You left-handed nose-pickers? You web-toed teenagers? The antecedents that identify who Peter is talking to are found in verse 1 of chapter 3, 'the beloved,' and verse 1 of chapter 1, 'those who have obtained a faith of equal standing with ours.' The 'you' are believers! Therefore, Peter is not saying God isn't willing for unbelievers to perish – because they do. Instead, Peter is saying that God is not willing for any believers to perish – and the chosen elect won't because Jesus said all that the Father has given him will come to him."

"None of us, including Lefty, believes that 2 Peter 3:9 is a proof-text for universalism. It doesn't mean that everyone will be saved. But John 3:16 says, 'whosoever believes in Him will not perish,'" interjected Cal. "That means anybody can be saved, right?"

"Theoretically," Grant replied. "But in Colossians 2 somewhere – I can't remember the exact verse – Paul says we were spiritually dead in sin until Christ made us alive. We weren't spiritually sick with just enough strength to call on the name of the Lord, but we were dead without the ability to take a single spiritual breath. So, God effectually called us from deadness just as Jesus called Lazarus from the tomb. The 'whosoever' of John 3:16 has to be whosoever God gives faith to by His prior effectual call. Isn't that right, Will?"

Will just smiled and shrugged, indicating the guys should keep drilling into the Word.

"Lefty, I want to go back with you to the word 'chosen' as Will asked us to discuss," the local funeral home director, David Cowman, chided his classmates' lack of focus. "But I'm not going to agree with you because Paul writes in the first chapter of Ephesians that God did indeed choose His believers. And he writes God did it even before the world's foundations were laid."

Marcus observed his fellow class members rising to the challenge of relying on Scripture for their discussion points and sensed a wave of jealousy wash over his heart. He looked back on his own ministry tenure and regretted not having instituted the same policy in the Sunday School classes of Delaware Street Community Church. Why hadn't he thought of it? Such a simple precept: think biblically before speaking. He had missed a significant opportunity for spiritual formation with his 350-person congregation that his mailman had capitalized on with his tiny class of eight men.

Jealousy was an uncommon temptation for Marcus. A far more frequent enticement was the allure of believing himself superior to others.

Pride was his nemesis. He knew it, hated it, and had preached regularly on the subject as much for the exhortation of his own soul as for the church members. He often cited C. S. Lewis, who wrote: "Pride is the mother hen under which all other sins are hatched."

"Tink about it," he would elaborate for his congregation. "Doesn't every sin begin wit pride? Coveting, murder, gossip, adultery, telling lies, stealing what's not yours - every sin starts wit da idea dat we indeed deserve what God has said we do not. Dat is pride at its core."

Marcus recognized his budding jealousy of Will's teaching success and felt ashamed before God. While the lively class conversation swirled around him and he wore an outward expression of interest, internally, he prayed for forgiveness and the Lord's help to resist further pettiness. He asked God for protection from wallowing in self-reproach for the past he couldn't change and for the grace to rejoice in the gifts God gave to others for building up His Church.

"You seemed distracted today, Marcus. I'm sorry if the lesson didn't challenge you – I always worry about that. I know you have high standards, and I confess I'm a little intimidated by you in the class," Will said as he left the classroom with the man he respected.

"On the contrary," Marcus admitted, clapping Will on the back. "I found it quite challenging."

Chapter Ten

I t was late Sunday afternoon, and every household member was napping except June, who would treat them all this evening to an Italian Crème Cake she was making. She'd once made one for a church supper in Michigan and remembered Grant and Marie raved about it. Grant was still sullen about missing his last few weeks of seasonal work at Grassy Hills Country Club, and she thought the cake might brighten his day.

The doorbell chime filled the quiet house, and June, wiping her hands on the citrus-print apron that covered the light-yellow tunic she wore over black leggings, hurried to the front door before it rang again. Through the large oval window in the door, June could see a tall woman with shoulder-length strawberry-blond hair standing on the other side. She recognized Shelby Norman immediately, though they'd never formally met.

"Hello, can I help you?" June answered the door with an unusual reserve for her competitor for Lovie's affections.

"I hope you can," Shelby smiled. "I'd like to speak with June Sherman."

June's cerebrum lit up like a fireworks display as she processed the simple request in her mind. *"She doesn't even know who I am. What could she want to see me about? Maybe she doesn't like my being friends with Lovie! What do I say about that? Wouldn't Micah vouch for me? This visit can't be good!"* She felt her heart race as quickly as her thoughts.

"You are speaking with June Sherman," she answered at last, returning Shelby's smile.

"Oh, good! I'm Shelby Norman, Chase and Lovie's aunt, and I'm staying next door with them for a while," she said, explaining everything June already knew. She continued, "I'd like to talk to you about Lovie if you have a few minutes."

"Nope. Not today," June imagined herself saying and slamming the door. Instead, she answered: "I'm just getting ready to put a cake in the oven. I can also put the teakettle on if you'd like to come in. We can chat in the kitchen." She opened the door in invitation, and Shelby stepped through, following June to the kitchen.

Surveying the abundance of ingredients on the island's white quartz countertop, Shelby asked casually, "What kind of cake are you making?"

"Italian Crème," June replied. "Just give me a minute to turn the teakettle on and get this cake where it needs to go. Please, have a seat," she said, nodding toward the kitchen table.

Shelby sat and watched June as she moved deftly about the kitchen, filling and starting the electric tea kettle, sliding the cake pans into the oven and setting a timer, and finally, retrieving two mugs and a variety box of herbal teas from the cupboard, placing them on the table in front of her guest.

June sat kitty-corner from Shelby and plunged into the conversation she already dreaded. "You said you wanted to talk about Lovie?" she asked with forced lightness.

She noted Shelby wore no makeup and had no need for it. Freckles dotted her fair complexion across the bridge of her straight Grecian nose. Her light green eyes had long eyelashes framing them, and her lips were the color of youth itself. She was, June had to admit, a natural beauty.

"Lovie said you told her that her mother – my sister-in-law, Dahlia - lived every day that God intended her to live. Is that true?" Shelby asked directly.

June hesitated, and the switch on the tea kettle flipped off, indicating the water was ready, to her great relief. She stood up and walked across the kitchen to bring the kettle to the table, giving her a much-needed half-minute to think about her answer. Of course, she wouldn't consider lying. She had, indeed, confirmed that bit of information to Lovie. But why was Shelby here asking about it? Did she disagree and come to argue theology? Did she think it was inappropriate or overstepping for June to discuss her mother's death with Lovie? Was she there to deliver a reprimand or consequences? June couldn't help but think the worst. She feared losing Lovie like last summer over the feared drowning incident at the Chicken Bowl Kiddie Pool.

"One of our friends in this house had a serious choking accident and suffered broken ribs. I told Lovie about it to encourage her to chew her food carefully, and she asked if he almost died. Part of my answer to her acknowledged that God is sovereign over the length of our lives. She asked me if that applied to her mother, and I said it did," June answered, providing context to her conversation with Lovie. She braced for Shelby's disapproving response.

"Oh," Shelby responded, lowering her gaze to the mug in front of her, which held a tea bag but no water.

"I'm sorry. Let me pour some water in there," June said, following Shelby's non-verbal cue.

Shelby dunked her teabag a few times and left it to steep. June was surprised to see tears clinging to the rims of Shelby's eyes when she looked up again.

"Dahlia was my best friend before she became my sister-in-law," Shelby spoke slowly. "She was the closest thing I had to a sister since we were in second grade – Lovie's age now. I hardly remember life before she was in it. Neither of us had other close friends because we didn't need any. All through school and even college, it was the two of us. We always teased Micah that she married him just so we could be actual family," she added with a quick smile crossing her mouth and crinkling her eyes, forcing a tear to lose its grip and fall.

Shelby continued, "I've been drifting since we lost her last January. I tried throwing myself into a new job in Nashville this summer, but the new scenery didn't take away the old hurt. I realized what actually helped was being close to Chase and Lovie. So, I came back. Micah told me what a blessing you and everyone in this house have been to them since you moved in. The kids adore you all, but Lovie speaks especially highly of you, June. I've been trying to figure out a way to meet you, so I decided I'd just come over. I'm sorry it wasn't completely true that I only wanted to talk to you about Lovie. I wanted to ask about what you said to her...about Dahlia. Is it true? And how can you be sure?"

June listened, and Shelby's candid confession utterly disarmed her. She hadn't expected to be Shelby's counselor, but here they were.

June took a deep breath and began earnestly. "Well, God's word says in Psalm 139 – and I'm paraphrasing here - that we are all fearfully and wonderfully made and known by God as He knits us together in our mother's womb. He sees us there and writes in a book all the days He has planned for us before we're born. Shelby, God wants us to know Him, and He gave us the Bible to tell us these things about Himself and ourselves, too. I've been reading and following it since I was 15, and it has always told me the truth, even the hard truths. Sometimes, I would have preferred my ideas of truth. But when our heads are on the pillow at night, we all understand there can only be one truth, right?"

Shelby nodded in affirmation and took a sip of her tea. Another tear fell, this one dropping in her cup, and she laughed self-consciously and wiped away followers on her cheeks with slender fingers. June waited for her to speak, not rushing to fill the expanding gap of silence with further explanation.

At last, Shelby set her mug on the table and spoke. "I understand what you said. That Psalm, 139 did you say? God sets our time on Earth, and that's comforting to know. It helps me concerning Dahlia. But..." her voice wavered, and she propped her elbows on the table and lowered her head into her fingertips, obscuring her face from June's view. "At the same time, it also tells me the truth about myself. Several years ago, I was pregnant with twins. My boyfriend told me they weren't really babies yet. And I told myself that the whole time I was in the procedure room at the family clinic." She lifted her head, looked June in the eye, and repeated June's conclusion: "But there can only be one truth, right?"

June reached across the table and clasped her neighbor's hand, wordlessly affirming Shelby's comprehension of the two-edged nature of Scripture and empathy for the conviction that prompted her confession.

Shelby stood quickly, saying, "I should get back home. I'm not sure what got into me, unloading all that on you. I'm very sorry. Please forget it. Thank you for your time, June." She hurried down the center hall and out the front door.

Left alone at the kitchen table with her tea, June could not forget it. She remembered her misery as a young woman desperate but unable to conceive and was distressed by Shelby's confession.

"It's no use to condemn her when it's so obvious she condemns herself," June reasoned. *"I've preached Psalm 139 to Lovie, then to Shelby, and now, I guess, it's time to preach its comforts to myself."*

CHAPTER ELEVEN

"How was your first week on the job at Grace Fellowship, Ava?" Elodie asked, wrapping a multi-colored, crocheted shawl around her shoulders as Thursday Meeting began.

"I was overdressed for it; I can tell you that!" Ava exclaimed from her seat on the couch, kicking off a black leather pump to tuck a foot under her bottom. "Pastor Jefferson runs a very casual office. But the work isn't rocket science, and my computer skills are adequate, so I think I'll be okay. Discovered utilities, insurance, and other monthly payments were never automated, and the membership rolls have never been purged. So, I'm going to suggest those for projects right away."

"Really? Dey never purged da membership? We might belong to a mega-church and not even know it," Marcus joked.

"I just want to go on record...Is anybody making records of our meetings? No? Well, I want to say you're missed around here when you're there," Marie lamented.

Ava blew a kiss across the room, and Marie turned her cheek to catch it and pat it in place.

"Cal already knows about this, but I've been keeping back something that happened a few days ago – pondering on just how much to share," June changed the subject, sensing they were done with the previous one. "On Sunday afternoon, while everyone was napping, I had a visitor. Shelby Norman came over to ask me about something Lovie told her I said. It seems she was quite close to Dahlia and has taken her death harder than we would have imagined. Her foray to Nashville last summer was hoping that a change of scenery would change her sorrow, but it didn't work. The long and the short of it is she's hurting, and I think she's spiritually sensitive. We all know that's often how God prepares us for a work of His Spirit. So I'm asking you all to pray for her - that her heart might be softened to the Gospel. And let's pray for ourselves that any of us might share it with her when she's ready," June finished, keeping Shelby's intimate confidence about her abortion to herself.

"What did you tell Lovie that she asked about?" Marie asked directly.

"I told her that God's word says He ordains all our days before we're born," June answered, just as direct.

"You told little Lovie that?" Grant raised his substantial eyebrows in surprise.

"Well, how old should one be to learn theology, Grant?" Marcus rose to June's defense.

Grant sputtered. "There's no...I'm not saying...I just wouldn't have thought to say that to a seven-year-old," he finished and looked to his wife for backup.

Marie shrugged her shoulders in response. No help at all.

"June says things to children and adults I'd never think of," admitted Cal, rescuing Grant, who appreciated it.

"Thank you for sharing about your visit with Shelby," Ava pressed forward. "Since we haven't seen much of her, I honestly hadn't thought much about her. I'm glad you've brought her forward as someone we should pray for."

Heads nodded in affirmation.

"Anybody have anyting else to share?" Marcus inquired of the group.

"As a matter of fact, I do," Grant said as he sat forward in his chair and wiped sweaty palms on his blue jeans. "There's just a couple of weeks till Thanksgiving, and I'm assuming we're all staying here." His statement had a question in its tone.

The friends looked from one to another and, with silent expressions, confirmed they were all staying home for Thanksgiving. They hadn't discussed the upcoming winter holidays and whether anyone would travel to spend them with relatives or other friends. But now they decided, at least for Thanksgiving. They'd spend it together.

"Well, I was wondering if it would be okay with everyone if Marie and I invited G-Lu to spend the long Thanksgiving weekend here."

There was a spontaneous eruption of whoops, laughs, and "Of course!" in reply. They all knew and loved G-Lu, Grant's 94-year-old mother, Louisa Jane Renniger.

G-Lu was an abbreviation of Grandma Lulu. Grant's twins, David and Daniel, had given their grandmother the moniker when they were teens, telling her it was her gangsta-thug name. Grant's mother, to no one else's surprise but Grant's, loved the nickname and used it to refer to herself, forcing her son to adopt it, too. Years later, the boys tried to tell her that gangsta-thug was out of style, but G-Lu wasn't having it. She said it was all the better that no one else was using it. It would make her unique. That was her reckoning anyway.

"You know, if I weren't already married and if she weren't 20 years my senior, I'd want to marry your mama, Grant," Cal snorted. "She's a firecracker!"

This was news to June, who retorted: "She can have you right now! I won't stand in your way."

"Ooo, sorry, Dumplin'. I forgot you were sitting next to me." Cal stretched out his arm and put it around his wife's shoulder, giving her an affectionate squeeze.

June pinched his cheek and asked, "Does this help you remember?" Then she laughed and turned to Grant. "Despite the recent revelation that she is a rival for my husband's affections, G-Lu is most welcome to come for Thanksgiving."

"I always feel like a white-robed saint when G-Lu's around," Elodie chuckled.

"She's got absolutely no filter!" Ava recalled, shaking her head and grinning.

"But she loves da Lord," Marcus credited her.

"Well, we'll do our best to rein her in, but you know..." Grant didn't complete the sentence. After decades of acquaintance with Grant's mother, they all knew.

"Okay, den, we've got tree weeks to brace ourselves for G-Lu. Are we done here?" Marcus was wrapping up Thursday Meeting.

"Not quite," Marie countered. "We've got Thanksgiving worked out. Are we all here for Christmas, too?"

After another round of nodding heads gave confirmation, Marie reached down to retrieve the laptop resting against her chair and opened it.

"There's something we ladies would like you gentlemen to see."

She turned the computer screen to face the men and played a clip of a Regency dance scene from a Jane Austen movie she'd cued up. It was 18th-century dancing to 18th-century music by people in 18th-century costumes.

"How long does this go on?" Grant asked after ten seconds.

"Is there a car chase scene when they get done dancing?" Cal mocked.

"No, I've seen dis before. Da candles blow up and ignite da punch-bowl, and den dere's a car chase!" Marcus laughed.

"Glad you are amused because on Christmas Eve, we're having a costumed Regency Ball right here, and every Saturday evening between now and then, we'll be learning dances. Cal, we realize your knees won't take dancing, so you'll be our caller. As Miss Austen might say: 'We take our leave and bid you good night,'" Marie announced. Then she and the other ladies stood and retreated from the living room.

Grant, Cal, and Marcus remained seated in stunned silence for a minute that felt like ten.

At last, Grant spoke. "We may be old men, but we're still men, right?"

"Was last time I checked," Cal responded.

"We are certainly dat!" Marcus agreed. "Dis meeting was not adjourned." He rose from his seat, walked to the kitchen where the ladies were making decaf coffees, and asked them to return for the conclusion of Thursday Meeting.

The ladies exchanged puzzled glances and traipsed back to the living room to reclaim their seats.

"We've been tinking Saturday evenings from now until Christmas Eve should be spent sitting on nests of fire ants and stabbing toothpicks under our fingernails. Sound like fun?" Marcus asked with sarcasm, making his point while wearing an expression that communicated the opposite of fun.

Ava hadn't seen that expression on her husband's face in a very long time, and it set her back. She understood the answer to his rhetorical question should be silence. The other women understood it, too.

Grant continued for the men. "No one asked us if we would like to participate in this activity you've legislated. That's not how healthy marriages operate, nor does this combined household. And if you would have asked us, we would have politely declined. We are declining now. Does anyone have anything to say?" he asked, looking squarely at his wife.

"We should know better," June spoke first, embarrassed.

"We got carried away," Ava offered.

"We're sorry," Marie apologized and began playing nervously with her chain bracelet.

"There aren't any fire ants in Faircourt. We'd have to make a road trip," Elodie sassed.

Chapter Twelve

Christine Williams sat alone at the glass-topped, chrome kitchenette set, eating her usual breakfast: a cold, hard-boiled egg, one slice of toasted rye bread barely touched with margarine, and a cup of coffee the same shade as her blonde hair for all the skim milk she added. She cooked a half-dozen eggs at a time in a small egg steamer and kept them in the refrigerator, ready-made for breakfast. And sometimes lunch.

It was the same breakfast her mother, Vivienne, had eaten all her adult life. "Eat small meals to stay thin," she'd told Christine. "You must stay thin if you want to keep your man," she drilled her while dragging on cigarettes. Vivienne stayed thin and kept her man, Faircourt title attorney Edward Hall, until she died of throat cancer at 48.

Christine was 26 years old and had been married to her college sweetheart, handsome Clarkson Dean Williams, for a year and a half when her mother died. The loss of the woman she respected for her self-control and admired for her beauty and standing in the community devastated her. But only three months after her death, Edward introduced Christine and her younger brother, Luther, to his new wife, Margie, and her two teenage sons, who were doppelgangers for Edward and Luther.

Christine wrapped herself in a jacket of anger and zipped it tight with bitter hate. She raged at her father for his betrayal. And he, awkwardly trying to defend himself, stupidly admitted Vivienne had discovered his cross-town family several years earlier. Christine hated her father all the more when she realized her mother did not live in ignorant bliss but in paranoid shame, desperate to hold on to her marriage and protect her children.

In hindsight, she could see it in the things her mother told her before she wed Clarkson: "There are worse things than arguments, dear." "Children change everything in every way." "A smart woman keeps a secret purse." Of course, her mother knew.

And so, her father's confession was gasoline on Christine's emotional blaze, transforming it into an inferno. She knelt on her mother's grave and, in appreciation for all Vivienne had absorbed to spare her and Luther small-town shame, vowed to destroy her father's new family. Not literally, as she may have liked, but figuratively with devastating ruin.

Following in his father's footsteps, Luther was finishing his first year of law school. He couldn't be of much help and probably wouldn't help, even if he were able. Luther felt resentment towards his father, but he wasn't spiteful. He'd told Christine he imagined that after some time had passed, he and Dad would patch things up and move on. She berated him for disloyalty to their mother and dismissed his charitable outlook as naiveté.

Alternatively, Christine recruited her reluctant Clarkson to aid her mission. Clark, as she called him, enjoyed a warm relationship with his father-in-law, Edward, and genuinely liked him. Like Luther, he understood his wife's anger but was inclined to imagine things would eventually calm down. However, Christine demanded he choose sides, and the marital bed was getting cold while he vacillated, trying to placate her.

Once he relented and committed to her team, the first step was to pick the low-hanging fruit. Clark owned an expanding printing business on the edge of town, purchased after college with investment help from his paternal grandfather. They discovered his third-shift supervisor – Joe, the sole support of his own family – was Margie's brother. He was fired for his unfortunate connection and was unemployed for five months before he found a lower-paying maintenance job at an apartment complex. He was fired from that job after his first week when Clark called in a favor from a fraternity brother who managed the complex. With a clear understanding of his situation, Joe moved his family out of Faircourt and across the state to Ashland, KY, where his wife's family lived.

Christine and Clark spent several weeks digging dirt on Margie's parents, George and Millie Fleur, who owned the downtown bowling alley and lived in its spacious, second-floor loft apartment. But they found nothing: no previous family scandal, fudged income tax reporting, or disgruntled former employees. They were long-time faithful members of Grace Fellowship Church and had run their business with integrity for 38 years.

However, Christine discovered a vulnerability with the help of a cousin who operated a local insurance agency. Because Millie was recovering from hip replacement surgery, she overlooked the Faircourt Lanes commercial property policy, leading to its cancellation for non-payment. Christine shared this information with Clark, who in turn shared it with local ne'er-do-well Buzzy Smith. Shortly after that, the bowling alley building burned to the ground. The Fleurs escaped injury but lost the asset meant to fund imminent retirement plans. They had to move in with their son's family in Ashland.

It was trickier to get to Margie herself. She didn't work outside the home - the home she'd invaded with her boys - that used to be Vivienne's home and where Christine lived until she married. But Christine figured she might get to Edward, as she now referred to her father, and Margie if she could get to their illegitimate brats. It took her almost a year to figure out the means and another few months to arrange the method with help from a relative of Buzzy's.

On Saturday nights in Faircourt in the summer of 1974, the back rows of the now-defunct Palace Drive-In Theater were filled with the high-mileage Mustangs, Beetles, Tempests, and Caprices of the local high schoolers. The drug dealers were there too, pushing marijuana, cocaine, quaaludes, and LSD. Most of the kids could only afford gas, admission, and concessions. But Edward Hall's boys took weekly LSD trips because, strangely, they never had to pay for it.

Their minds were wrecked for academics when school began again in August. Their SAT scores were abysmal; neither would attend college or trade school. They struggled with addiction and petty crimes to support it, and within a few years, frustrated Edward insisted they move out of the house. The boys moved, all right. They moved across the country to Southern California, living as vagrants in the California sunshine, who were never seen in Faircourt again. Margie was devastated and furious with her husband.

Christine's 5-year campaign seemed a success to her. Everyone important to her father, save Christine's brother, Luther, was miserable. Unbeknownst to Christine, this also included her Clark.

Forcing Clark to support her mission and do her vindictive bidding had debilitated him. The tenderhearted man she'd married, who taught her to cultivate roses, lost his love for his wife and any shred of self-respect. And she'd been so consumed with her objective she hadn't noticed the shift.

Clarkson Dean Williams left her and this world on December 1, 1978. Christine maintained the printing company and roses he left behind with obsessive devotion, and her endeavors resulted in wealth and State Fair ribbons. But she never escaped the habitual rut of managing offenses against her with retaliatory vigor. And she never stopped loving and missing Clark.

She thought about him now as she sat at her kitchenette, looking at the crumby remains of the breakfast her mother said would help her keep her man – the blue-eyed, sandy-haired man who would never age beyond

32 years old in her memory. She swept the table with her arm, letting the plate, mug, and utensils shatter and clatter to the brick-tiled floor. Then she folded her arms on the table, set her elegantly coiffed head down upon them, and wept.

Chapter Thirteen

"I brought wine!" Bobby laughed as he entered the Garage Cave holding two six-packs above his head.

"Oh, good! Let's try dat," Marcus replied, knowing it must be the Cheerwine soda Bobby told them about after they'd confused Ale-8-One for beer.

"Now that Bobby's here, I'm going to put the garage doors down and turn on the space heater," Grant said, moving toward the automatic door buttons.

"June baked us up some spicy Chex Mix. All the ladies are trying extra hard to be considerate after we called them out for trying to railroad us into those dance lessons. I didn't have the heart to remind her spicy doesn't sit well on my stomach with these treatments," said Cal as he emptied the zippered bag into two large plastic bowls.

The guys settled into chairs, and Grant pulled the heater close to their table. Marcus dumped dominoes on it, and they all helped turn them face down before selecting 15 each.

"How are you feeling these days, Cal?" Bobby was genuinely interested. It had been nearly 18 years since he'd lost his Julia to cancer, but he still winced when he recalled the awful side effects she suffered from the treatments.

"I've felt better, to tell you the truth. Don't have a lot of energy, seem to forget more than I remember, and get the bubble guts daily. But I don't have much pain, so I'm grateful for that. And I'm glad to be out here with you all this evening. This distraction is medicine for me, really."

"Glad to hear there's not much pain for you, buddy," Bobby was empathetic.

Grant, sitting on Cal's other side, reached out and, in silent man-speak, gave his shoulder a light squeeze. He remembered Cal bruised easily now.

"Bobby, you go first," Marcus directed. "We're starting with double eights to get Cal back in the house at a decent hour."

Bobby arranged his dominoes and put one down, asking, "So what's this about being railroaded into dancing lessons?"

"Oh, da women announced we were having some fancy dress-up ball at home on Christmas Eve, and we had to learn dese 250-year-old English dances. We told dem dey should have asked us, and we weren't doing dat," Marcus explained and played his turn.

"Why not? I mean, yes, it's nicer to be asked than told. But you don't like the Jane Austen-style dancing?" Bobby inquired.

Marcus, Grant, and Cal looked from one to another like Bobby suggested they open a restaurant selling beef eyeballs on burger buns. "I don't think we can be friends with him," Grant said, shaking his head.

"Too late!" Bobby laughed.

Cal and Grant placed their dominoes and considered Bobby's question, figuring he was halfway serious.

"So, you'd like to dress up in a frilly shirt and short pants?" Cal asked.

"Maybe. For the right cause. My daughter and her girls also like those British period dramas with fancy dancing. I sat through a few of them when I visited the family in Florida last winter. And here's what I learned from watching them watch these movies: women want a man who's the total package. They want a hero, a lover, a provider, a smart and funny man, and someone they can respect. And they want to dance with him. If my Julia were alive, I'd dance that woman off her feet – in short pants, tights, anything!"

Marcus pushed away from the table and sat back in his folding chair, thinking. "It's possible dat we may revisit dis subject sometime." He looked at Cal and Grant, who avoided eye contact with him by paying rapt attention to the domino tiles remaining before them.

They finished the round and the next one in relative silence before Grant remembered he wanted to ask Bobby: "So how's it going with DeShawn? You've gotten to see him twice now, right?"

"It's going good, it's going good," Bobby repeated mechanically, nodding. He played his tile and added more honestly, "But it's not great."

The other guys gave him their full attention.

"I mean, it's so good to have him back in my life. I'm thankful for that. But DeShawn's a grown man now, not the boy I remember. He's changed so much, outside and inside. Some things about him are familiar, but he's almost a stranger in other ways. 'Course, from the look on his face when he first saw me with this white hair, he realizes I've changed over the years, too." Bobby raked the fingers of his left hand through his hair self-consciously. "We're getting to know one another again, and I can see it will take time. I thought it would be more like old friends who pick up where they left off, but that's not the case. I wasn't expecting that."

"What's changed da most about him?" Marcus leaned into Bobby's observations.

"He's really religious now!" Bobby didn't have to think. "You guys would like him. Get this: he wants to be a preacher when he gets out of prison! He doesn't want to be a chef anymore."

"Does that bother you?" Marcus prodded.

Bobby's eyes scoured the garage floor as if he might find his answer lying somewhere on it. "It was good when he wanted to make food because I like to eat and talk about food. But if he wants to preach about God...well, as you know, that's not something I can relate to. So, yeah, it bothers me. I can't talk to him about God."

Before Marcus could follow up with something pastoral and profound, Cal, hanging on Bobby's every word, simply asked, "Why?"

Bobby sat upright as a soldier and answered with a bit of volume added to his voice. "You're supposed to love God, and I don't! I don't even like Him! He's hurt me, destroyed my family, left me alone. I got by all these years on my own, so I got no use for God!" He sat there, nostrils flaring, breathing hard, hands hanging ridged by his sides like he was ready to chop boards in half with them.

Marcus looked at the agitated man and distilled his words: "So you believe in God, but you don't understand Him? Dat's da same as my Ava at da moment."

Bobby cocked his head and looked at Marcus, letting the tension in his hands ease. He relaxed in his chair again and steadied his breathing, evaluating Marcus' discerning comment.

With decades of pastoral experience, Marcus could easily have launched into correcting Bobby's misunderstandings of God. However, he knew of another man who could build two bridges at once – one to God and one to himself. So instead, Marcus selected a domino, and before he placed it down, he said: "Dere's a very good chance DeShawn was also once angry wit God. Dat would give you someting to talk about wit your son."

Chapter Fourteen

"Looks like we got ourselves an Indian Summer day," Marie announced as she walked into the kitchen, dressed for church in a gray and black-striped shirtwaist dress, 2" black sling-back pumps, and a pearl earring and necklace set. Her salt and pepper hair was pulled neatly back into a French roll secured with a black comb.

"Yup. It's gonna be a pretty one," Elodie confirmed from her seat at the breakfast table. "Too bad Calvinator is down today. I'm staying home with him so June can go to church," her pronouncement explained why she was still wearing her bathrobe.

Nobody asked her to stay home, and June would have gone to church anyway since Cal was only worn out and tired, but Elodie needed to mother Cal to avoid turning into a twitching mass of anxiety over leaving him home alone. Marie, Ava, and June realized Elodie's insistence on hovering over him was rooted in her fears for herself, regardless of how she played it off.

"Aww, I'm sorry it's not a good day for him," Ava said as she turned to June, standing next to her at the coffee station, waiting for the pot to finish brewing. Before June could respond, Ava had an idea. "Say! Would you like to walk with us if he's not coming to church? It's just three blocks. I always walk by myself since Elodie started driving with you and Cal. Marie walks with Grant, and Chase elbows me out to walk with Marcus. I'd love your company!"

"Why not?" June answered. "Have to warn you, though, you might find me a bit pokey. We'll get there but won't set any land speed records." She wanted to manage expectations, knowing their pairing was akin to a tortoise and a hare.

"Ha. No worries, girl," Ava reassured her.

***

"I'm bringing a visitor!" Chase dashed down his front porch steps toward Marcus. The group of friends stopped on the sidewalk in front of the Norman house as Shelby quickened her pace to catch up to her energetic nephew.

"I hope you all don't mind. Chase invited me to come to church with him. I'm Shelby Norman, Chase's aunt," she explained shyly. She dressed casually but put-together, wearing slim khaki ankle pants, a light green blouse embroidered with khaki strawflowers on its Peter Pan collar, and nude flats on her feet. She tied her strawberry blond hair back into a loose ponytail with a few escaping tendrils, and she applied subtle makeup. Taupe eyeshadow, mascara, and a neutral pink lipstick were all that were discernible.

"Finally!" Marie stepped forward to greet Shelby. "We're so glad to meet you at last. I'm Marie Renniger, and this is my husband, Grant. Here, we have Marcus Van Zant and Ava, his wife. And I believe you've already met June Sherman," each friend demonstrably delighted to make her acquaintance as Marie introduced them.

Shelby reddened at the last introduction. She wondered how much information accompanied Marie's knowledge that she'd already met June. Had June shared *everything* about their meeting? She was also caught off guard because Chase told her that June didn't walk to church with the Rennigers and Van Zants. She didn't expect her to be there.

June glanced at Ava and mouthed, "Sorry," then guided Shelby to walk beside her, leaving Ava to walk again without a companion.

She hurried to put Shelby at ease. "I made the others completely jealous when I told them you'd stopped by last Sunday afternoon, and we had tea and talked about our sweet Lovie while they were all napping. As you can see, they couldn't wait to meet you." June paused and offered a warm smile. The deep red blotches of visible embarrassment on Shelby's neck began to fade.

While June welcomed Shelby to their walking party, Ava's mental wheels turned. They would arrive at church for Sunday School hour. Surely, Shelby didn't belong in the same senior ladies' class they attended. She could participate with them; it wasn't illegal or anything. But it wasn't optimal. Shelby needed to make friends with women in her life stage with whom she'd have more in common. Ah, Kesha Jefferson! Shelby was probably just a few years older than the pastor's wife. Ava would try to connect the two when they reached the vestibule.

When they reached the church, Marcus opened and held the door for the others. He noticed as Chase rushed past Silas, standing alone at the bottom of the stairs leading to the youth room. When he was out of sight, Marcus saw Silas trudge, dejectedly up the stairs himself.

"Hey, Mrs. Boss!" Ava said when she spied Kesha standing next to the welcome center with little Jalen wrapped around her leg. She hurried toward her.

"Hey yourself!" Kesha replied with a broad smile for her husband's new part-time secretary.

"We have a visitor with us I'd like you to meet. She probably belongs in your Sunday School class."

"I'd love to meet her, but I'm a little handicapped at the moment with this guy who will not let me go."

Ava reached down to greet Jalen with a smile and a tickle in his ribs. When he giggled and let go of his mother's leg, Ava scooped him up and started walking to the nursery with him. She stage-whispered over her shoulder, "Green blouse with June."

"You're a lifesaver, Ava!" Kesha replied as she went to welcome the pretty woman standing with June.

"I like your church," Shelby admitted to June as they walked home after the worship service. "The people certainly are friendly, the music was lovely, and the pastor gave me a lot to think about during his sermon. He sure isn't hesitant to tell people there's a price to be paid for sin both in this life and the afterlife," she said, adding a tiny nervous laugh at the end.

"It would be malpractice if he were," June responded, slowing her already leisurely pace as she spoke. "My husband is at home because he's wiped out from his cancer treatments. Imagine if his oncologist was afraid to tell him his actual diagnosis and, instead, told him he was just fine as he was and to go home and have a pleasant week. That might be what Cal wants to hear, but it's not what he needs to hear. He needs to know the hard truth to seek the appropriate treatment, right? It's no different if we want to be spiritually healthy. The starting point is knowing our true condition and prognosis."

"Hmm," was all Shelby said in response.

Marcus and Chase walked ahead of the others with an ever-widening gap. "I was wondering someting," Marcus began an earnest conversation after a block's worth of chit-chat. "I saw dat you ignored Silas today. I was wondering if you'll do dat to me if your basketball friends tink I'm not cool. And we bot know I'm only just barely cool."

It was a brief conversation because Chase was at a loss for an answer. He merely hung his head and continued to walk.

CHAPTER FIFTEEN

Cal reclined in his bed on the mountain of pillows June had propped behind him before she left for church. There were so many pillows behind his back and head he was nearly sitting upright. A plate of dry toast and a soft-boiled egg sat cold and untouched on his nightstand beside a half-drained cup of cold herbal tea. He'd drunk just enough of the tea to get his meds down, meds which were supposed to be taken with food to prevent nausea. But the thought of biting into the egg or toast was enough to induce queasiness, so he skipped them.

He reached next to the plate, retrieved his eyeglasses, and put them on. He wasn't sure why he did that; he didn't feel up to reading. But with his glasses on, he caught a focused glimpse of his reflection in the bathroom mirror opposite his position in the bed. June had left the door wide open to facilitate quick access to the commode should the need arise.

"Great Caesar's ghost!" he exclaimed, bending forward for a closer inspection.

In the mirror, he saw a wrecked and rumpled man. His white hair sported a disturbing case of bedhead and, with thin locks dipping below his earlobes, it was longer than he'd ever worn it. Since his cancer returned, he hadn't made it to Director's Cut, the Main Street barbershop he and Marcus frequented. He had shaved four days ago, but now his jaw and upper lip were covered with a patchy, silvery stubble visible with his glasses at a distance of 15 feet. Cal's wan complexion looked even paler in the gray t-shirt he wore. And the arms that poked out of the short sleeves seemed distressingly wimpy, wrapped in loose, crepey skin.

"Maybe an ear stud would draw attention away from all this," he mused half seriously. His barber, Keith, had one, and Cal's eyes were always riveted to it. That, and his man bun, which Cal deemed absurd on a man in his late fifties.

The sound of someone rinsing something in the kitchen sink and adding it to the dishwasher interrupted his consideration of an ear stud. Elodie, no doubt.

He'd asked June recently why Elodie was constantly babysitting him, not that he didn't like the attention. She responded by asking him what it meant when they used to go on driving trips, and she'd ask if he was hungry.

"When you asked if I was hungry, it meant *you* were hungry!" he laughed.

"Bingo," she verified his conclusion. "When she watches over you, Elodie tells us that's what she thinks should be done. It's what she'd want for herself in your situation. She fears being sick and alone, so she won't let you be sick and alone."

That made sense to Cal even though it meant Elodie's attentions weren't purely motivated by the fact that he was a terrific guy. He forgave her for the component of self-interest in her care for him. The Lord knew Cal had plenty of self-interest of his own.

When the kitchen sounds ceased, Cal laid back on his pillow mountain. He couldn't be at the worship service, and he couldn't read his devotional book or Bible just now, but he was able to pray. And he could try, as he did so, to be deliberately disinterested in himself for the sake of others.

Gracious God, Thank You for the assembly of believers gathered this morning at Grace Fellowship Church. Please count me among them in spirit even though my body is weak in this bed. I ask that through the preaching of Your word and the ministry of Your Spirit, You give them wisdom and understanding so they may live honorable and fruitful lives for the glory of Christ. May my brothers and sisters patiently endure their trials so the world may see that You are valued by Your people above the cares of this life. We bless You, Lord, for sustaining and sanctifying us in all our difficulties.

Father, I pray for any visitors coming into Your sanctuary today. Refresh the weak ones and regenerate the lifeless. As they hear Pastor Jefferson proclaim salvation in Jesus' name, I pray Your Holy Spirit would show them the reality and danger of their sin and lead them to repentance. Restore believing ones to fellowship with You and give eternal life to any who will run to Jesus for salvation from Your righteous wrath. Thank You, Lord, that You offer mercy and complete forgiveness to rebellious sinners. What a wonderful demonstration of Your love!

Lord, I think of my neighbor and new little brother in Christ, Chase. I pray you will help him be a shining light in his home to his unsaved family. But to do that, he will have to hunger and thirst for righteousness, and there are so many distractions and temptations for a boy his age. Help him grow in the knowledge of Your will for his life and to be obedient to Your commands. Help him, dear Lord, to recognize and resist our Enemy and become a Kingdom warrior.

And Gracious God, I'm excited that Bobby admitted to us and himself that he believes in You even if he doesn't think he likes You. His head is full of wrong ideas and expectations about You, which, of course, You know all about. I pray You will reveal Yourself to him. Show him You are good, kind, and always wanted more for him than he wanted for himself. I pray you would prepare DeShawn to be a conduit of Your grace in his life. Please help them bridge the distance the years apart have created. May their healing be a monument of praise to You.

Finally, Father, I pray for Christine Williams. You have instructed Your people to love our neighbors as ourselves, without exception. So, I pray you will show Your grace and kindness to her. Tenderize her heart toward those willing to be her friends and ultimate Friend. Give her the gift of faith in Your Son. Call her, as You called Lazarus from his physical grave, from her spiritual death to everlasting life. For Your glory and honor and the joy of the angels in Heaven, hear my request from Your throne and answer.

I ask all these things as your humble servant and grateful son, in the name of my dear Savior Jesus. Amen.

Chapter Sixteen

"You'd have thought in the half-century since we graduated, somebody would have thought to pad school bleachers," Ava complained to Elodie as she shifted uncomfortably on the ribbed metal benches.

"I carry my own," El chuckled, patting her naturally cushioned hips.

Marcus, Ava, Elodie, and June were at Faircourt Middle School for a special Friday evening basketball game. Chase had come to their house after school to invite them to the 7 pm game, breathless and bursting with information that he would be a starting player tonight because Ryan Wiggins had the flu. Grant and Marie stayed home, wanting to go to bed early to prepare for an early Saturday morning departure to pick up G-Lu from her retirement village in Champaign, IL. They would also be there if Cal needed them, to Elodie's satisfaction and relief.

"Look who's here, Lovie!" As they walked into the auditorium, Shelby directed her niece's attention to their neighbors sitting on the bottom row of the bleachers. Lovie waved and beamed, following Micah and Shelby into the row above them.

Then she frowned, turning to her daddy, saying, "I'd really like to sit up high in the bleachers – on the top row."

"Do you know that's what every fidgety little girl has said just before she fell off the top bleacher and broke her arm? What a coincidence!" Micah said with a pointed finger, indicating she should plant herself next to him on the second row.

With an alternate suggestion at the tip of her tongue, Lovie countered: "Well, can I sit down there with Miss June?"

"Go ahead," he relented.

She put a pink-sparkled sneaker'd foot on the bench between June and Elodie, stepped down to the floor, and then sat between them, scooching into June's side.

"Hello, my sweet friend!" June side-hugged her. "Are you warm? Do you want to unzip your jacket and take it off? When Lovie nodded affirmatively, June helped her with the task and passed the coat back to Shelby for safekeeping. Lovie reclaimed her snuggle spot.

Marcus turned around to chat with Micah. "Big night for your son as a starter," he said, sharing in Micah's delight.

"Yeah. He's pretty nervous, though. Wouldn't eat much supper," Micah admitted.

"I'm sure he'll make up for it after da game."

"That's what I would do when I played basketball in high school – eat after the game and go to bed with a food rock in my gut," Micah laughed at his memory.

As the men continued the conversation to which she had nothing substantial to contribute, Ava stood and walked in front of her friends to claim a seat on the second row next to Shelby.

"I was out of there at 'food rock in my gut,'" Ava whispered conspiratorially in Shelby's ear, eliciting a slight chuckle.

"I don't blame you one bit," she sympathized, smiling. Looking over at Ava, she noticed the bleachers were now near capacity.

"I'm so glad we've finally met and broken the ice. You know we adore your niece and nephew, and even Micah when he's not recalling the digestive upsets of his glory days."

"He says your entire household has been a God-send," Shelby said in a tone that conveyed her gratitude.

"Good! It's nice to think we're not so old that God can't make us a blessing to our neighbors," Ava responded.

The dimming of the gymnasium lights interrupted their conversation. The home team starting players were introduced and spotlighted with an ancient apparatus discovered in the back of the school's dusty equipment closet.

"Hey, dey make dem look professional!" Marcus exclaimed to Micah.

"The home team, anyway. It's not so nice for the visitors," he warned.

Sure enough, the lights were turned back up, the spotlight removed, and after each visiting team starter and their position was announced, the siblings of the Faircourt players would shout: "Who's he?" "Don't care!" "Big deal!" "Go home" and "P-U!"

Since Ava was behind him, Marcus looked to Elodie, who shared his expression of disapproval with furrowed eyebrows. "Hmm," she noted succinctly to him.

All the starting players met at center court for the tip-off, and Ava spotted Chase wearing the blue jersey of the Faircourt Falcons and looking nervous. Although he'd grown over the summer, he was still one of the smaller players on his team. Trevor Allman was the tallest kid Faircourt had and played center. He was also the best shooter the Falcons had, and he knew it.

As the game progressed, it was clear Trevor was a persistent ball hog who only felt obligated to pass the ball at the sound of his coach's loud and insistent direction to do so.

It took about five minutes of play before Chase could touch the ball. He got past his defender, but his shot rimmed out.

"Awwwww," his cheering section in the front rows lamented in unison.

"Good effort! You'll get the next one!" Micah encouraged his son.

And he did. Chase made his next two shots, contributing 4 points before the half-time buzzer. The Falcons had 24 points on the scoreboard,

12 of which belonged to Trevor. Unfortunately, the visiting Cougars had 35 points.

When the second half resumed, the tip-off landed in Chase's hands. He was dribbling toward his goal when the ball hit his shin and rolled into the hands of a Cougar, who converted the turnover into two points.

"Idiot!" muttered Trevor, loud enough for Chase and a few teammates to hear it.

The Falcons found some momentum as the half progressed and closed the point differential. Of course, it was Trevor who mostly closed it. When Chase was fouled and had the opportunity to shoot two free throws, his nervousness got the better of him, and both shots were air balls – never touching the net, rim, or backboard.

"You suck!" Trevor yelled at him in frustration.

Micah and Marcus shook their heads in disbelief. Elodie's hand flew over her mouth to keep her unsanctified words from spilling at Trevor.

"The coach has nothing to say about that?" Shelby was indignant, and Ava patted her shoulder in sympathy.

The game continued, and with nine seconds on the clock and the score tied, a Cougar guard let the ball get away from him and roll out of bounds near Chase's contingent of supporters.

"Chase, you inbound it to Trevor and let him take our last shot," Coach directed.

Chase meant to inbound the ball over the outstretched arms of the Cougar defender, but the boy leaped, and the ball went straight into his hands. He, in turn, lobbed the ball to a forward standing under their basket, who made an easy bank shot for the winning points.

Trevor stomped over to Chase and let loose a roaring string of profanity in his face. Micah jumped to his feet and was halfway between Marcus and Elodie, ready to defend his son, when a pink-sparkled sneaker sailed from the front row, smacking Trevor in the head. Lovie beat her daddy to it.

Chapter Seventeen

"Who goes there, friend or foe?" the woman's hearty voice rang through the tiny speaker built into the modern, three-story brick building.

"It's me, Mom," Grant answered into the speaker, shaking his head at Marie, who grinned as she stood beside him.

"So it's foe, then! Is Marie with you?" G-Lu wanted to know.

"I'm here too, Mom," Marie answered for herself.

"In that case, I'll let you in!" she guffawed at her own silliness.

A buzzer rang, indicating the electronic lock was released, and Grant and Marie entered a side entrance of Pleasant Pond Retirement Village's Building Four. It was one of five independent living buildings on campus, which also boasted assisted care, memory care, and skilled nursing facilities.

Grant's mother had lived here for the past four years, moving in the week of her 90th birthday. She'd been a widow for 30 years and told her sons, Grant and Gerard, that she wanted to find the companionship that seemed unavailable in her declining Presbyterian church and stuffy patio-home community. They assumed she meant female friends. She meant a boyfriend, possibly even a husband "if he was the right kind of Presbyterian, had a strong pulse, and was in his right mind."

Grant and Marie took the elevator to G-Lu's second-floor apartment. They walked down the spacious hallway, noticing a new name on the door before Mom's – Dottie Battles. Marie was about to ring G-Lu's doorbell when the door opened wide.

"Hello, kids!" she greeted them, hugging Marie and Grant into her tiny frame as she welcomed them inside. She was five foot nothing and weighed 90 pounds, fully dressed, including her wig of short brown curls. Today, she wore her traveling outfit: black orthopedic shoes and a lime green windbreaker set with two hot pink vertical stripes down each arm and leg that she bought in 1988 and "still had plenty of life in it."

"New neighbor, Mom?" Grant asked, pitching his head toward the neighbor's door. "What happened to Ruthie?" he followed up in rapid succession.

"She's gone on to her reward," G-Lu answered.

"I'm so sorry," Marie sympathized earnestly. "She was a sweet lady."

"Oh, she didn't die! She moved over to assisted living, where they don't have to do their own housekeeping or laundry. We call that "your reward" here, G-Lu corrected with a cackle. "Her replacement is a tramp named Dottie."

"Mom!" Grant interjected, attempting to correct her unkind characterization. "It's true! She's been married five times and wears push-up bras and low-cut blouses that put all her goods on display like a dime-store window. Even I stare at them! And she's only 79."

Marie looked away so Grant would not see her grin. She loved her mother-in-law and her bluntness. Now. But for the first two years of her marriage to Grant, G-Lu's plain speaking intimidated an insecure Marie. She dreaded the day it would be aimed at her. But she'd been gentle with Marie and only let loose after she'd birthed Grant's twin sons and felt solid in the Renniger family. After a few more years, Marie found a bit of her own plain-speaking voice, though never in G-Lu's league, to Grant's great relief.

"You ready to go? I'll grab your suitcase." Grant lifted the large avocado-green case from the sofa where his mom had packed it.

"I'm ready, but do you want to use the bathroom before we leave?"

"I'm good." Grant took a few steps toward the apartment door and put the suitcase down. "On second thought, I guess I'd better." He went into the bathroom and closed the door.

Marie smiled at G-Lu. "Always a mother, right?" she asked.

"Always," she smiled back.

"We didn't notice the swans out front when we drove by the main entrance," Marie commented on the signature feature of Pleasant Pond.

"Oh, there's a story there!" G-Lu took a few steps toward her kitchenette, beckoning Marie to join her. She whispered to avoid further correction from her son on the other side of the bathroom door.

"Neighbor Dottie wasn't here a month before she landed the attention of the big man on campus, Jonah Fineman. He's nearly my age and fit as a fiddle with plenty of money. On the first warm day of Spring, Jonah asked Dottie if he could show her around the pond and such – take a tour of the grounds. He was pointing out where the swans' nest was when one bird came charging after him, flapping its wings in a big to-do. Dottie high-tailed it, but Jonah decided to play the hero and act like the alpha male. He called the bird's bluff and stood his ground like a man. Well, the critter nipped his manhood and dropped him fast. Then he couldn't run!" G-Lu made a quick opening/closing beak motion with both hands to supplement her narrative before continuing.

"Dottie hollered bloody murder and threw handfuls of landscaping stones at the thing, and it backed off. Several residents said they saw the whole thing through their windows. Anyway, she dragged Jonah by his ankles across the grass to the edge of the parking lot, and he got an ambulance ride for his trouble. The swans were relocated after that. And we haven't seen much of ole Jonah either since then."

"Oh my!" Marie gasped, imagining the scene.

"Yeah, we all blame her for taking the prime candidate out of our meager dating pool," G-Lu said somberly. "What a way to be literally taken down," she added, shaking her head.

And then they both giggled and worked unsuccessfully to stifle themselves.

"What's so funny?" Grant asked, coming out of the bathroom.

"Just girl stuff." Marie brushed the question away, the remnants of laughter in her voice. "Let's get on the road!" She diverted her husband's attention by opening the apartment door.

Grant picked up the suitcase once more and stepped into the hallway. "Mom, we have a houseful for Thanksgiving dinner, and you will be in your element!" he said brightly.

G-Lu pulled her apartment door closed behind them and rattled the knob to make sure it was locked. She threaded her arm through Marie's, and the two of them walked down the hallway several paces behind Grant. They looked at each other as they passed Dottie Battles' door and giggled again.

"Who's the alpha male now that Jonah Fineman has retreated in disgrace?" Marie asked in a whisper before they reached Grant standing at the elevator.

"I don't know. It's probably Deaf Donald. He's 86 and has a pretty good halo of white hair around the sides of his head. He wears hearing aids but can't remember to charge the batteries. Still, the ladies like him because he smiles and nods a lot."

"Is he going to be Grant's new Daddy?" Marie goaded, squeezing her mother-in-law's thin arm gently.

"Probably not," G-Lu sighed. "Not my kind of Presbyterian."

CHAPTER EIGHTEEN

"Snack time, Calamine?" Elodie asked chipperly as she entered the kitchen to check the progress of the yeast rolls she'd started a few hours earlier. Cal and June sat at the kitchen table dipping apple slices in peanut butter just an hour before dinner.

"What can I say? June is always pushing food at me," he answered sheepishly.

"I've got no problem with that. You eat whatever and whenever you want," Elodie encouraged.

Elodie walked to the sink, turned the water on, and pumped the soap dispenser. As she washed her hands, she noticed a figure standing at the chicken coop, but she couldn't make out who it was because of the distance and her poor eyesight.

"Hey June, can you tell who's standin' out by our coop?" she beckoned her friend to come to the window.

June came to Elodie's side and peered through the glass in the late afternoon light. "It's Chase," she answered confidently. "I'm going to let Marcus know he's outside. I'm sure he'd like to talk to him after what happened at last night's ball game." She disappeared down the hall and, in less than two minutes, was back in the kitchen with Marcus trailing and zipping his jacket.

"Say a prayer for me, guys," he said to his friends as he walked out the kitchen door and across the backyard toward the coop. Marcus believed prayer paved the ministry road and he relied on divine help for his abilities.

"Miss Elodie says if you cluck at dem, dey will cluck back to you. Have you tried dat?" Marcus asked as he strolled beside Chase and feigned interest in the plain white birds he considered scrawny for laying hens.

"Nah. She can be the chicken chatterer," Chase muttered.

They stood silently for a bit, watching the birds doing nothing notable. Only one was pecking the ground, and that was without genuine interest.

Marcus had never known Chase to visit the coop since he helped relocate the birds and their habitat from the Brewer's place last summer. He suspected Chase might have wanted to be discovered here. So, he waded into the subject that seemed pressing.

"Your friend believes in speaking his mind." There was no need to specify whom he was talking about.

"He's not my friend!" Chase retorted hotly.

"Hmmm. Dat's okay. Not everyone should be our friend," Marcus affirmed.

Chase turned to face Marcus, surprised by his comment. "Really? I thought you would say we have to love everybody or something like that."

"Oh, we do. But I tink we need to define some terms here. Love is a commitment we make to act in da best interest of oders. For instance, you know your dad loves you when he pays da bills, takes you to Latte Da for a treat, or when he comes to watch you play basketball. But it's also love when he disciplines you for doing wrong because it's in your best interest, even dough you may not appreciate dat. Your dad might not even be happy wit you when he has to discipline you, but love is not a feeling. Love is doing what's best for oders, even if da good feelings aren't dere. Do you understand dat?"

Chase nodded his head, fully engaged in Marcus' explanation.

"Jesus tells us to love our neighbor as ourselves, and our neighbor is everyone. So we are to do what's best for everyone. It's noting to do wit feelings. So now let's talk about our friends. Friends are the people we are close to, da people we spend time wit, and wit whom we share our troubles and confidences and our hearts wit. Da Bible tells us to be careful about who dose people are. Dat's why I said not everyone should be our friend."

"Good, because I don't want to be friends with Trevor anymore. But if I was crazy and wanted to, why shouldn't I be friends with everyone?" Chase challenged, trying to understand.

"Because dere's danger. Some danger we can see, and some danger we can't see. Let me ask you a question. Are dere guys at school who drink dere parent's alcohol or get drugs from older broders?"

"Yes," Chase admitted.

"I'm guessing your dad wouldn't like you hanging out at dere houses, right?"

"No, he's talked to me about that already."

"Your dad is right to warn you about dat danger. But dere are oder dangers dat are not so easy to see. Sometimes, da pressure is not to *do* someting bad but to *tink* someting bad. It's a more subtle danger, like a slow poison working in our minds. I have anoder question: Did Trevor influence you to stop being friends wit Silas?"

Chase hung his head and answered, "Yes."

"Was dat in Silas' best interest? Did Trevor's influence help you obey God's command to love Silas?"

"No," came the whispered reply.

"Da Apostle Paul told da people in da Corinthian church, 'Do not be deceived, bad company ruins good morals.' What do you tink dat means, Chase?"

"It means bad people leave their bad influence on good people, and if you don't think that's true, you're mixed up. Is that right?"

"Dat's exactly right. We want to tink dat we can be a good influence on bad people. But the Bible is clear; it doesn't work dat way. It works da opposite. Dat's why, even dough I'm a grandpa, I'm still careful about who my friends are. Da Bible doesn't say dis stops being an issue just because we reach a certain age. Dis is true for all our life."

"But aren't you friends with Mr. McBride? When I helped him clean out his garage last summer, he told me he had no use for God. So why do you still hang out with him?" Chase continued to challenge Marcus.

"Do you see me hanging out wit him by myself?" Marcus asked.

"No," Chase admitted.

"Dat's right because I don't. I want to love my neighbor and be available for God to use me in Mr. McBride's life. Dat's in his best interest, right? Though, I'm also cautious to make certain I have support so I'm not tricked or influenced in a negative way."

"I get it! It's not love your neighbor *or* don't be deceived about bad company. It's both at the same time."

"Exactly right!" Marcus clapped the boy on his back.

Chase grinned but grew solemn. "Do you suppose Silas will want to be my friend again?" he asked.

"I don't know. But you should find out," Marcus encouraged.

Chapter Nineteen

Marie threaded her arm through G-Lu's as they stepped off the porch and began the three-block walk to Grace Fellowship Church. Both wore wool winter coats – Marie's powder pink and G-Lu's cherry red – since the November air had a bite this Sunday morning. June had offered G-Lu a ride in the Sherman's F150, but she declined, saying she needed the exercise. The truth was, she couldn't imagine what kind of team effort it would have taken to hoist her slight but fragile frame into the truck. Nor did she want to risk a broken hip tumbling out of it upon exit. Walking was easier. Besides, she could ask Grant to chauffeur her in his sedan if she wanted a ride.

The walking party comprising Marie, G-Lu, Grant, Ava, and Marcus enlarged in front of the Norman's house where Chase and Shelby, for her second week, joined them. After a slower than usual walk to accommodate the 94-year-old among them, they arrived at the church door just as Cal pulled into the parking lot with his passengers, June and Elodie.

Marcus held the door open for the first wave of walkers and followed them in. Standing at the bottom of the staircase, he spied Silas and watched Chase approach him. He took a few steps in their direction and managed to hear the quick exchange that passed between them.

"I was a real jerk," Chase confessed.

"Yeah, you were!" Silas agreed, letting the past tense stand. He grinned and threw a pulled punch at Chase's arm. Then he got a two-step head start, dashing up the stairs before Chase ran after him.

Will walked up behind Marcus, putting his hand on Marcus' shoulder. "Thanks for the text to encourage Silas to be receptive to reconciliation. He was angry with Chase, but he missed him too."

"So, what did you say to him?" Marcus inquired.

"I shared Proverbs 17:17 with him: 'A friend loves at all times, and a brother is born for adversity.' Told him the best friendships are those that are tested and survive."

Marcus nodded, and together, they ambled toward their classroom.

"By the way, I notice you've brought that visitor with you again. What's her name?" Will asked, trying to sound casual.

"Shelby Norman, our new neighbor," Marcus divulged.

"Micah's sister?" Will was thinking out loud. "She must take after the better-looking side of the family.

The Senior Ladies' Sunday School class at Grace Fellowship had been in disarray long before the female residents of 306 Cedar Street started attending. There'd been a succession of three teachers in the past year who'd tried and failed to fill the shoes of the dearly departed Fonda Lee Farnsworth. Fonda Lee was a formidable woman who ran the class like a benevolent sergeant of the Lord's army for 18 years before she passed in her sleep last year at 87.

When no one within the class stepped up to take her place, 43-year-old Faith McAdams was recruited by Kesha Jefferson to try her hand at it. Faith lasted eight weeks before calling it quits. She found the older women intimidating.

Next was Karen Schneider, the 67-year-old wife of deacon Lefty

Schneider and the teacher when Elodie, Ave, Marie, and June started attending. She stayed on the job for six months until she suffered a debilitating stroke that impaired her ability to speak clearly.

The most recent teacher was 59-year-old Anna Cramer. It was Marie's fault she quit, though Anna's stated reason was that she needed to devote more time to her husband's ailing mother.

Two weeks ago, Anna was teaching a lesson on Psalm 92 and presented the idea that oil is a metaphor for the Holy Spirit in the Old Testament. She asserted that where verse 10 states, "you have poured over me fresh oil," it meant God fills Sabbath worshippers with the Holy Spirit.

"Shouldn't we follow some basic rules of hermeneutics and understand the Scriptures like the original audience would have understood them? No way they would have concluded anyone other than prophets, priests, or kings could be filled with the Spirit of God!" Marie blurted.

Anna reddened and tried to defend her conjecture with evident frustration.

The following week - last week, Anna's lesson was in the safe zone of the much-studied second half of Proverbs 31. After reading the verses pertaining to the woman's exemplary industry and accomplishment, she commented empathetically: "I know it's discouraging when we compare ourselves to the Proverbs 31 woman. It makes us feel bad about ourselves."

"Maybe that's why God put her there!" Marie's knee-jerk reaction flew out of her mouth, and several women in the class responded with tittering laughter.

"Maybe," Anna retorted, tightening her lips. She was finished.

This week, Kesha Jefferson stood before the class and announced Anna's decision to step down to be more available for her mother-in-law. Kesha would serve as a fill-in until a new teacher could be recruited.

"Marie should be the teacher!" G-Lu suggested, unsolicited. That she was a first-time visitor did not impede her participation in the affairs of

Grace Fellowship Church or anywhere else. "Really, she's smarter than she looks," came her reinforcing follow-up.

Marie turned sharply to face her mother-in-law seated next to her. She turned her eyes upward, shook her head from side to side, and smiled with a what-am-I-going-to-do-with-you expression.

"I second the motion!" Ava chimed in with a mischievous grin on her face.

Sensing an opportunity, Kesha responded quickly, "All in favor, say aye."

A chorus of 'ayes' rang out, the loudest voice belonging to Anna Cramer. Kesha was eager to rejoin her own class with newcomer Shelby Norman and dispensed with asking for opposing votes. Fortunately, there was no parliamentary procedure policeman to object.

And that's how Marie became the Senior Ladies' Sunday School Class teacher.

CHAPTER TWENTY

"That tasted so good I could eat it all over again!" G-Lu exclaimed, dabbing the corners of her mouth with a napkin. Then she wadded it up and tossed it playfully at her son.

"Glad you liked it, Mom," Grant responded with a chuckle. "Elodie makes miracles with chicken. Her fried chicken is everyone's favorite, but this piccata is right up there, too."

"Is Marie taking notes?" she shot back from the seat of honor at the head of the table.

June feigned a sudden and intense interest in the sleeve of her tunic printed with autumn leaves and picked at nonexistent fuzz. Marcus looked to Grant to see if there'd be a defense of his wife forthcoming.

"I most certainly am not!" Marie brushed off the minor insult she accepted from her mother-in-law as good-natured teasing. "If you live with Michelangelo churning out masterpieces regularly, why take up sculpting?"

Elodie beamed, sitting back in her chair at the dining table, absorbing the Renniger's appreciation and compliments. "Lord, don't let me get a big head!" she said, subconsciously adjusting the crown of braids on her head.

They all sat back in their chairs, sated from the heaviness of the angel hair pasta and chicken smothered in lemon/wine sauce and capers. Marcus was in no hurry to wash dishes. Nor was Grant, who'd taken up Cal's part of the dinner clean-up operation.

"So, what's the final headcount for Thanksgiving dinner? Marie and I are grocery shopping for beverages and a few last-minute items in the morning," June asked.

"We're confirmed for 14," replied Ava. "Bobby said his sister would spend Thanksgiving at her daughter's house. So, she's out. That leaves all of us, Bobby, the Norman family, and Will."

"Somebody remembered to take da turkeys out of da freezer and move dem to da refrigerator, right?" asked Marcus.

"The ladies thought you were gonna' to do that!" Elodie remarked defensively. She cast a glance over her glasses at Ava.

Marcus shot up from his seat as if a firecracker had gone off underneath it. "We can't smoke frozen turkeys! I need dem in da smoker tomorrow!"

Ava laid a hand on her husband's arm. "El's kidding. They've been in the garage fridge since Saturday evening."

Marcus sank back into his chair and glared at a smirking Elodie.

"You should have fainted, Marcus. Would serve her right if you just keeled over and gave her a taste of her own malicious medicine," Grant offered in sympathy.

"I tink I'll just do as da Bible says and do good to my enemy and, in dat way, heap burning coals on dere head."

"Ut oh, Elodie! He plans to kill you with kindness. I wish my adversaries would do that!" G-Lu laughed.

"Why are we not surprised to hear you have adversaries?" Marie found her opportunity to tease her mother-in-law back.

"Touché!" G-Lu granted her a warm smile.

"Ava, how was work today?" June changed the subject.

"It's slow. Everybody's either away or cooking during Thanksgiving week. I got the bulletin ready for Sunday and had nothing else pressing to do, so I started looking at the membership rolls for my purging project.

Oh, you all will find this interesting. Guess who's still a member of our church?"

The friends looked from one to another, but no one ventured a guess out loud. They'd been in Faircourt just eight months, and most of the people they knew were active members of Grace Fellowship Church.

"Christine Williams!" Ava informed them.

"Really?" Marie's eyebrows arched in surprise.

"She was churched?" Cal asked in disbelief.

"It didn't take," shrugged Elodie.

"Who's Christine Williams?" G-Lu wanted to know.

"Dat's our elderly neighbor in da white house across da street. She doesn't like us," explained Marcus.

"She tried to get us evicted by the town for running an unlicensed retirement home," Grant elaborated.

"She grows beautiful roses, though," June contributed some positivity.

"What's her story?" G-Lu asked, genuinely curious.

"We don't know her story. Nobody seems to because she doesn't let anybody close to her. Bobby, our neighbor you'll meet on Thursday, spoke with her briefly this summer. But that was because she was outside having a fit over her roses being vandalized. He just helped calm her down so she didn't have a stroke," Marie answered.

"She lives alone?" G-Lu inquired.

"I guess. We've never seen anyone else over there but a lawn man or cleaning help," Cal offered.

G-Lu looked thoughtful, tapping rose-painted fingernails on the arms of her chair. "We should invite her for Thanksgiving dinner!" she suggested exuberantly.

"When you say 'we,' who do you suggest we sacrifice to send over there on such a suicide mission, Mom?" Grant laughed.

"I'll go myself!" G-Lu responded.

Grant furrowed his thick eyebrows, rubbed his hand over his smooth head, and grew serious. "Mom, I don't think it's a good idea right now. We have other guests coming who would need time to brace themselves psychologically. Seriously. We can't just spring this on them."

"I have to agree wit Grant, G-Lu. Da young boy next door would be particularly nervous because he was da one dat vandalized her flowers. It's not dat we'll never invite her for dinner, but we have to start small," Marcus backed Grant up.

"I understand," she responded. Inwardly, she was hatching a Plan B.

Chapter Twenty-One

June stuck her head in the doorway of the study. "El-O-Dee!" she pronounced each syllable of the name as if it were its own name. "You're never going to guess what Bobby just texted me!"

"Not gonna' try to," El responded, not looking up from the paperback mystery she was reading. She was sitting in one of the crewelwork chairs in the study by a window flooding the room with natural light. Comfortable in her red knit, A-line dress that reached mid-calf and a pair of fuzzy yellow knitted socks, she crossed her legs in the opposite manner they'd been and continued her book.

June marched over to her and snatched the book from her hand. Elodie looked up, astounded at such an aggressive gesture from mild June.

"Okay! What'd he text you?" she gave in.

"He said we can use his oven to bake our pies if we need to! We need to! I must bake in that green-enameled Italian marvel of culinary engineering and magnificence! You, me, and Marie are going over after lunch to get started." June begged and demanded at the same time.

Elodie looked at June, pondering her options. She had no interest in a return visit to Bobby McBride's house, but June was pleading – not only with her voice but with sad blue puppy eyes.

"Well, I'm not gonna' be the one to shatter your dreams," Elodie began.

"Oh, thank you, thank you!" June broke in, getting the response she sought. She bent down and hugged Elodie's head to her bosom.

"This time!" Elodie finished her sentence and chuckled. "Just got one question..."

"G-Lu is going to be home with Cal while we're over at Bobby's and Ava's at work. Besides, Marcus and Grant will just be out back tending the smoker," June answered in anticipation of the question.

"Okay, just makin' sure," Elodie held out her hand for the paperback's return.

Ava trudged up the stairs toward her bedroom, ready to change from her business casual work outfit and into comfortable food-prepping clothes . She saw the guest room door open and a light from inside spilling into the hall. It was only 3:30 in the afternoon, but the sky outside had grown overcast and threatening, making the entire house seem dark. Ava stuck her head in the door to greet G-Lu.

"It's the calm before the storm," Ava said to the tiny woman, dressed in gray stretch pants and a gray and yellow-striped blouse, standing at the window that looked across Cedar Street to Christine Williams' house.

"It does look like rain. Those boys will get soaked tending that smoker," G-Lu agreed, turning from the window.

"That too! I guess I was thinking of the calm before we have a noisy houseful tomorrow," Ava clarified.

"Come in for a little quiet visit then," G-Lu crossed the floor and sat in the pink room's only chair, a cream-colored wingback. She nodded for Ava to sit on the bed and noted the mascara she'd worn when she left the house this morning was now absent.

"Were you left to amuse yourself this afternoon?" Ava asked.

"Elodie conscripted me to babysit June's husband, who's napping at the moment. I don't know why she doesn't get herself a long-range baby monitor to keep track of him. They make those things, don't they?"

"I'll suggest that to her," Ava laughed. "She's vigilant when it comes to caring for Cal. So, where is she and the other girls? I thought they'd be knee-deep in pies by now," Ava wondered.

"They're at the man-with-the-fancy-oven's house over there." G-Lu pointed toward Bobby's house. "Breaking it in, they told me."

"Wow! He was saving the first use for his son, who has six more years of a 25-year prison sentence left to serve. Something changed for him to let go of it after all this time," Ava marveled at the news.

"How about you, Ava? Are you letting go?" G-Lu dove directly into her concern for her daughter-in-law's lifelong friend, whom G-Lu herself had known as long as Grant had been married.

Ava's gaze wandered out the window, and her eyes filled at the acknowledgment of the year-long estrangement from her daughters. G-Lu waited, patient with the silence.

"No one's asked me anything remotely like that in weeks," Ava started, still not looking at the woman who had. "I guess they're hoping that it's much better for me now because I have a job. And it is a little better. I'm grateful for the distraction, but as soon as I get in my car at three o'clock, my mind is drawn like a magnet to Marit and Mia, and the floodgates open. Since it's only a three-block drive home, I take a lot of excursions around Faircourt. I talk to myself like the Psalmist: "Why are you downcast, O my soul...hope in God!" And then I recite all that I have to be thankful for, dry my face, and then I can come home. Nobody here needs to know that."

"Not even Marcus?"

"Especially not Marcus!" Ava turned her gaze to make eye contact again. "He bore the brunt of my...my...I don't even know what to call it.

Breakdown? Collapse? Whatever it was, he tried so hard to take it from me and carry it himself. If such a thing were possible, he'd have done it. He needs a break. I can do that for him. My legs are wobbly, but I can stand on them."

G-Lu pushed her hands into the wingback's arms and stood. She walked to the bed and sat next to Ava, putting a veined, thin-skinned hand on Ava's freckled one.

"I'm glad you're doing a little better. Marie was fearful for you, you know."

Ava nodded and wiped her wet cheeks with her free hand.

"I'm also proud of you for being unselfish and self-controlled enough to spare your man what you can. Too many women act like their husbands are their emotional waste disposals. They fling every little thing at him - as if men don't have their own weaknesses and worries. You're stronger and wiser than you think you are." G-Lu patted the hand she held and continued.

"I won't pretend to understand what you've gone through this past year – are still going through. My sons have never been cruel to me. But I will say I've seen many of my friends at Pleasant Pond going through it in their families. If it's not their heartless children casting them off, their grandchildren do it to their parents. It seems to be a modern epidemic!

In my day, we never heard of such things happening. But now friends regularly cite Second Timothy chapter 3, which says in the last days, people will be lovers of self and money, proud, arrogant, abusive, disobedient to their parents, ungrateful, unholy, and heartless, etc. They just shake their heads and conclude these must be the last days. But I quote Proverbs 30:17 back to them:

"The eye that mocks a father and scorns to obey a mother will be picked out by the ravens of the valley and eaten by the vultures."

"I'm sure you do!" Ava smiled. "I'm sure you do!"

"You understand this situation is God's plan for your good, don't you?" G-Lu turned her body to face Ava squarely and quoted Romans 8:28

"And we know that for those who love God, all things work together for good, for those who are called according to his purpose."

"I know it – deep down under the hurt," Ava answered. After a moment, she shook off her melancholy and offered a playful rebuke to her elder. "But do you realize, it's become unfashionable to quote that verse to anyone in actual pain?"

"I've heard that, and it's poppycock!" G-Lu slapped a hand down on the bed beside her. "If that verse isn't true or needful when we are in agonizing despair, when do we need it? Is the comfort of God's benevolent sovereignty over every situation appropriate only when we misplace our keys or need a good parking spot? Ridiculous! I'd like to meet the fool who first said it's kinder to say nothing to a brother or sister drowning in sorrow than to offer them the truth of God's word which is able to ground their feet and support their burden.

How did that blatantly un-Christian idea become a norm in Christian counsel? Is it because too many of us, in our time of testing, become petulant children wanting to fling away the Scriptures – and God with them, if that were possible? Suddenly, the Scriptures that led us to salvation are characterized as "trite," and anyone who shares them is "bludgeoning." Well, I for one, call that what it is – baloney. The problem is not God's word. The problem is our whiny, childish hearts when we're called to stand firm, and the solution is not to reinforce that nonsense."

After her lengthy speech, G-Lu inhaled slowly and added: "That section of Romans, section 8, tells us if we wish to be honored with Christ, then we must endure with Him. Must! Whose fault is it that we are so unprepared to do so? My prayer for the church is that we may all grow up and learn to suffer well. And this I know: silence in the midst of suffering teaches us nothing."

Ava, who had absorbed the sermon while staring at the graining of the wood floor, turned her head and looked at G-Lu. "You missed your calling as a preacher," she advised her.

"Well, then I would have had to be the other kind of Presbyterian," G-Lu smiled and patted Ava's hand again. "Remember, Ava, God is working in this awful situation with your estranged family for your ultimate good. And since that's true, whatever replaces what you've lost will be of more valuable from eternity's perspective."

"Thank you. Thank you for putting the solid ground of Truth under my feet and not leaving me to flounder and wallow. It's hard to imagine anything more valuable than my family. But maybe that was the problem to begin with," Ava acknowledged and gave her houseguest a lingering, heartfelt hug.

Chapter Twenty-Two

"Don't smile at her," Marie whispered to Bobby. She was the last one to step through the front door, and she dawdled, pretending to struggle with the bag of ingredients she carried, while June and Elodie made their way down the hall to the kitchen at the back of his house.

"What?" Bobby asked, skeptical. "Did Cal tell you to say that to me? Is this another one of his so-called jokes that will blow up in my face like when he told me to call her 'El Camino'?"

"No. Your smile reminds Elodie of slick, smooth-talkers she knew as a young woman in Columbus. She doesn't trust it."

Bobby stuffed his hands into the pockets of his black chinos and looked doubtful.

"Ok. Put it to the test, then. Hold back on the smile and see if she's civilized to you," Marie recommended.

Bobby nodded his head in a figure-eight pattern and rolled his eyes. He had nothing to lose since Elodie already didn't like him. He extended an arm, indicating Marie should precede him into the kitchen.

June and Elodie were already tying on Thanksgiving-print aprons. Elodie tossed one to Marie. "Here you go. You know what this is for, right?" she taunted her.

"Just because I don't cook, doesn't mean I don't clean. They're also worn for that purpose, or wouldn't you know?" Marie was defensive.

Pulling the garment over her head, she muttered, "Though they get soaked when you clean. If they can put a man on the moon, you'd think they could invent waterproof aprons."

"Be right back!" Bobby said and disappeared. A few minutes later, he returned wearing a tall white chef's hat and jacket.

"Would you look at that!" Marie stared at him, amused and impressed all at once.

June and Elodie looked up from unpacking and organizing ingredients and pie plates on the countertop.

"He just leveled up the apron game," Elodie remarked with detached admiration.

Bobby didn't react to the compliment, keeping his expression neutral.

"You are a man of surprises!" June remarked.

"I borrowed it from a trunk of DeShawn's things in his room," Bobby confessed.

"Ahhh," June nodded. "Say, I don't mean to look a gift horse in the mouth, but I have to ask – why are you letting us use DeShawn's oven? Your text that we could use it was a genuine surprise – a welcome surprise."

"Two reasons. One, he said I should put it to use. Two, I got something better to hold on to now," Bobby answered sincerely. He spied a piece of packing material on the floor that he'd pulled out of the stove before hooking up the gas that morning and bent to pick it up.

"There's another piece over here," Elodie pointed out.

Bobby retrieved that one too. "Had this stuff flying everywhere this morning, trying to get the oven ready for you ladies," he explained. "Guess my eyes aren't what they used to be."

"Nobody's are," El added wistfully.

Bobby deposited the crumbling Styrofoam pieces in the lidded trash can at the end of the counter. "How can I help you?" he directed his question to June.

"How do you feel about peeling apples? I have a bag of them here that need doing, and I loathe peeling apples," she answered.

"I'm game. But I'm going to need my apple-peeling music if you need the job done with tempo." He picked up his cell phone from the kitchenette table, tapped on the screen a few times, and 1940s big band music poured from two small white speakers mounted near the ceiling, blending into it.

"My parents loved big band music!" June squealed. "They had to hide it from the sour church ladies at my dad's church, but they closed the drapes of the parsonage and danced in our living room. Oh, this brings back memories!" she yelled over the blaring trumpets.

"Mine loved it too!" Bobby declared. "They taught my sister and me how to jitterbug." He removed the chef's hat, tossed it on the counter, and gave the ladies a demonstration in front of the kitchen door. His arms flailed, legs kicked, and hips twisted with an imaginary partner to the lively tune.

"You need a proper partner to do that right," Elodie admonished. She walked onto his impromptu dance floor, took his left hand, and joined him in the dance – feet flying in sync with Bobby's and the music. It wasn't even apparent she was guarding her back, which hadn't fully recovered from the injury sustained performing the Heimlich on Grant.

June and Marie looked at one another in astonishment at the display of talent previously hidden from knowledge or sight. They watched the couple dance until the song ended, and they both doubled over, hands on knees, catching their breath.

"Where did you hide this skill for the last 50 years?" Marie demanded of Elodie. "How did it never come up that you're a big-band dancing queen?"

Elodie stood up straight and smoothed her apron. "No one asked," she replied, panting.

Bobby reached for his phone on the table and tapped the volume of the music down a bit. "You had an excellent teacher, Ms. Elodie," he complimented her with a neutral expression.

"And you as well." She turned her back to him and focused on making her momma's pecan pie.

Bobby walked over to get the bag of apples from June and whispered to Marie, standing nearby, "Did not foresee that. Sorry I doubted your advice."

Marie smiled at him. "I forgot a can opener to open these cans of pumpkin and condensed milk. Do you have one, Bobby?"

"Right over here in this drawer." He retrieved the manual opener and the peeler he'd need for June's apples. "Here you go," he said, handing the tool to her.

"So, how have your visits with DeShawn been going?" June ventured to inquire. She knew Elodie and Marie were as interested as she was.

"The guys asked me that at a Garage Cave night; they didn't tell you?" he asked, surprised.

The ladies looked at one another, and Marie answered, "Apparently, what happens in the Garage Cave stays in the Garage Cave."

"As it should be!" Bobby started to smile and stopped himself. "Well, I'll tell you myself then. It's not the same dynamic as when he was a teenager 'cause he's a man now, and I've got to get used to that. He talks about God a lot, and that's new to me. But some things are very familiar, like his laugh or the way he drums his fingers on his legs when he's thinking. And something else: the look in his eyes when he's not telling me the truth – or, at least, not telling everything he knows. I feel like he's holding back something. Maybe that's to be expected as we get reacquainted. I don't know what prison is like. Well, on his side of the wall, anyway."

"I've been praying for you and DeShawn – that God would knit your hearts together as father and son and that he would be a joy to you for the rest of your life," Marie shared as they worked shoulder to shoulder.

"Me too," Elodie said as she faced them.

Elodie's simple statement took Bobby aback. He returned a simple nod of acknowledgment and then handed June a peeled apple ready to be cored and sliced. He set his peeler on the counter and said: "All of a sudden, I'm surrounded by God-fearing folk. Do you think it's possible your God brought you to Cedar Street in Faircourt, Kentucky, to make my son's religious conversion less of a shock to my system?"

"It's not only possible; it's probable," June answered.

"It may be one of several reasons," Marie added.

Chapter Twenty-Three

While Ava, Elodie, and June did the lion's share of the Thanksgiving feast's food preparation, Marie focused on transforming the dining room table into a rustic holiday landscape. Over a white damask tablecloth, she laid a narrow burlap runner with fringed edges. Along the length of the runner, she spread sprays of feather reed grass she'd gotten, with permission, from the Norman's backyard, and on these Marie had arranged white mini-pumpkins and colorful Indian corn she'd bought from Big Mart. In the center of the table was a pedestal'd hurricane candle holder with a white pillar candle surrounded by layers of green split peas, red kidney beans, and yellow popcorn.

G-Lu, dressed festively in a bright pink blouse and black slacks, contributed a chart of seating assignments for the meal to ensure guests and household members were mingled. Strategically, she placed herself between Micah and Chase Norman, who she thought unlikely to pay particular attention to an old woman. Today, she was avoiding conversational engagement.

At 2 p.m., Grant turned on the Bluetooth speaker placed on the lower level of the antique bar cart in the dining room. He'd made a playlist of easy-listening instrumental music to add an additional layer of ambiance to the gathering. And just a few minutes after the music began wafting through the space, the doorbell announced guests had arrived for the mid-afternoon meal.

They all nibbled on a large charcuterie board of summer sausage, green and purple grapes, jalapeno pepper jelly, cream cheese, and wheat crackers while June finished the gravy on the stovetop. Elodie and Grant filled water glasses on the table, and Marcus carved the first of the two smoked turkeys, piling the meat on a platter. Cal lit the warming candles under the chafing dishes on the buffet while Marie and Ava filled them with stuffing, potatoes, and mixed veggies. These were besides the cranberry sauce, dinner rolls, and coleslaw in serving bowls already in place.

With everything arranged on the buffet, Marcus instructed everyone to find their place card at the table and stand behind their chair for prayer before they served themselves. Lovie ran around the extended table twice before locating her seat between June and Shelby, but once she was settled, Ava and Marie showed by example they should all join hands.

"Father, we are grateful for da blessing of neighbors who are now our friends, for da provision of abundant food to share at our table, and for Your goodness dat You show us every day. We bless You in return and tank You especially for the salvation of our eternal souls dat You make possible through faith in Jesus. Amen," Marcus prayed.

A chorus of solemn amens responded. Then afterward, plates loaded, and everyone settled at the table; the room filled with chatter, laughter, and silverware clatter – weft upon the underlying warp of music creating a woven covering of sound.

Bobby, to no one in particular: "Hey! This stuffing is terrific! What's in it?"

Grant, sighing heavily: "I've learned to enjoy the food and not ask questions about contents. The ladies are always scamming cooked vegetables into things that shouldn't have them. It's probably kale or beets."

Elodie: "Relax, Grant, it's just a few cranberries and chestnuts to make it festive."

Will: "So Shelby, what do you do for work?"

Shelby answered shyly: "I'm a web designer and graphic artist."

Lovie, making a sour face: "Something smells! Who passed gas?"

Chase: "He who smelt it dealt it!"

Micah, in a low voice: "Guys, behave!"

Ava: "Are you going Black Friday shopping tomorrow, Marie?"

Marie: "Maybe. Hadn't thought about it. But Little Grant and Georgia texted me their Christmas wishes the day after Halloween. I could shop for the grandchildren, I guess."

Marcus, overhearing and mocking: "Cal, do you want to go to da mall tomorrow wit me and 80,000 oder people to spend da first hour driving around looking for a spot to park da car?"

Cal, also mocking: "I was going to wash my hair, but that sounds like fun! What time do we go?"

Elodie: "Calibrate, I'm gettin' more turkey. Do you want some while I'm up?"

Cal: "No, thanks. I'm saving room for pie."

June, looking at the plate Lovie fixed herself: "Lovie, don't you want anything else besides turkey and gravy?"

Lovie: "Nope. Addy, Lena, and me are vegans now. We don't eat any vegetables. But we eat pie!"

Shelby, laughing: "Lov, vegans do eat vegetables, and they don't eat turkey."

Lovie, crestfallen: "Oh."

Bobby, laughing: "I think she's done with veganism."

Grant: "What time do the Cowboys come on?

Micah: "You like the Cowboys?"

Grant, Marcus, and Cal in unison: "No!"

Marcus: "We're anti-fans."

Chase: "Did you see the giant balloon go out of control at the parade on TV this morning? That was cool!"

Bobby: "I saw it! Sure sent that marching band in front of it, scurrying and screaming."

In a low voice to Shelby, Will said: "Latte Da has a new holiday coffee – coconut snowball. Would you like to try it out with me this Sunday evening?

Shelby, flustered and unprepared: "Maybe. I mean, I'm not a big coffee person. But sure, I guess."

Marie, facing the living room window and spying a dot of hot pink on the porch across the street, stood to her feet: "G-Lu's standing at Christine Williams' front door!"

Grant, alarmed: "What?"

Everyone stopped talking and rushed en masse to the living room window. They were just in time to see the front door open, and G-Lu welcomed inside. Then the door closed behind her.

Chapter Twenty-Four

The chime of her doorbell startled Christine, unaccustomed as she was to visitors. Prepared to open her door to an errant holiday guest meant for another address, she had worked herself up to annoyance at the minor intrusion, ready to bark the fool off her porch. She was not prepared to be standing face-to-face with the aged incarnation of Vivienne Hall. Nor could she resist inviting the woman, who bore an uncanny resemblance to her late mother in both face and frame, into her home.

She ushered her unexpected guest into the spacious entry hall, which was papered with an elegant gold-on-vanilla pattern of scrolling leaves and marigold flowers G-Lu guessed to be a William Morris design. Cautiously, Christine accepted the sampler plate of Thanksgiving pies, setting it on a round mahogany table as she pointed the stranger toward the formal living room on the left side of the hall. G-Lu complied, tearing her gaze away from the elegant, sweeping, curved staircase that spilled from the upper story. The banister was stained a rich cherry, as were the stair treads and ornate newel posts that anchored the feature in the hall. The stair risers and balusters were painted a creamy white and contrasted dramatically with the dark wood.

In the tastefully appointed living room, G-Lu stepped onto a colorful Oriental rug in muted hues and sat on one of the two white, traditionally styled sofas facing each other. Christine settled across from her;

a travertine coffee table with brass legs and a neat stack of art books arranged upon it separated them. G-Lu took a moment to take in her surroundings, noting a large portrait above the marble mantelpiece of a handsome sandy-haired man in his prime, seated and dressed in a fitted navy suit. She studied her surroundings and did not notice her hostess studying her.

"I'm sorry, you said your name was..." The unfinished statement sufficed as Christine's question.

"Louisa. I'm Louisa Renniger. My kids live across the street. Well, my son and his wife with their friends. They have so much pie over there; even the buffet table will need a shot of insulin. I thought I'd make some of it disappear before I have to call the paramedics for them all. Your acceptance of this contraband is a service to me."

Christine smiled appropriately but not genuinely. She considered Louisa's association with the overfull house across the street most unfortunate. Still, she was intrigued and remained polite to buy some time with this astonishing maternal stand-in. "And where do you live?" she asked bluntly but without malice.

"Pleasant Pond Retirement Village. It's in Champaign. I've made gobs of friends there, and there's always something to do. Best of all, I have next to nothing to clean – not like you have here, though your home is exquisite."

Christine furrowed her brow at the suggestion she might clean her own home. "I have help," she replied.

"Who's the handsome man who rules the room?" G-Lu asked admiringly.

"That was my Clark," came the grudging reply from one used to asking the questions. "My husband, Clarkson," she corrected her lapse of formality.

G-Lu responded to the past tense of the initial answer, which betrayed a hint of tenderness. "I'm sorry for your loss. Do you have hope?" she probed.

"Excuse me?" Christine recoiled at the audacity of the visiting stranger to probe into personal matters.

"Do you have hope of seeing him again in Heaven? Did he know Christ? Do you know Christ as your Savior?" G-Lu explained with further questions.

Christine turned her head left and right as if looking for another person in the room who might share her disapproval of such an interrogation. The palms of her hands grew hot. Yet, she controlled her swelling outrage at the woman with a face so like her mother's. She dodged the question by responding coolly: "You certainly are direct! Do you find success with this?"

"Not always. But if God has prepared someone's heart, it can't fail. And the only way to find out if He's been at work is by asking. I find that asking directly is best. I don't have time or patience to create a conversational Rube Goldberg machine to get my answer."

Christine cracked an involuntary smile. She related to the last sentiment.

G-Lu took the subtle reaction as an invitation to continue. "I'm a widow for 35 years myself and look forward to seeing my Albert again. I would fuss him over good for leaving me so soon if I didn't accept it was God's best plan for both of us. I didn't always consider God's plans. Early in our marriage, we lived for ourselves. We were young and stupid, thinking we were adults and smart. But God was gracious to us and drew us to His Son. We repented of our sins and asked Jesus to save us from the punishment our rebellious sins deserved. And we knew something real had happened because we suddenly had no taste for the things we'd been doing. Instead, we wanted to learn more about God and be with His people. Godly desires replaced our sinful desires, and we replaced our wild friends with broken and humbled ones.

Christine stared at her visitor in disbelief at the unsolicited, albeit unspecific, confession. She couldn't find the words to respond, so she admitted her inability to speak. "I don't know what to say to that," she remarked with an exasperated sigh.

"Mrs. Williams, I believe I have the answer to my question," G-Lu said, reading Christine's face as much as her words. "Someday, we will join our husbands in the grave. That is certain. And then we must face our Creator and Judge. The question is: Will you face Him with confidence in your own tainted merit or in Jesus' perfect merit and sacrifice in our place?"

"I reject your hypothesis," Christine answered tersely.

"Most people do. But then there's hell to pay," G-Lu responded with a resigned shrug.

She stood, sensing the visit was over, and Christine ushered her to the front door.

"I did not invite you into my house to receive a sermon. I invited you because you bear some resemblance to my late mother." Christine could not resist scolding.

"Then, let me give you a hug from your mother." G-Lu reacted impulsively. And before Christine could stop it, she was enfolded in a loving maternal embrace that pressed into her soul. After several seconds, G-Lu released her with a gentle pat on her arm, and departed without further comment.

Through a sidelight window, Christine watched her walk across the street, stop to pet that nuisance McBride cat, and disappear into the stone house. Then she returned to her living room to sit in the exact spot G-Lu had occupied – overwhelmed by the gesture of affection, which touched something within her, and glum that she had no One to tell.

Chapter Twenty-Five

"Good morning, Callous!" Elodie greeted her friend and noted the plate before him on the table. "Pumpkin pie for breakfast, I see."

"You won't rat me out to June, will you?" Cal asked without looking at her.

"Did I say I saw somethin'? My mistake. These glasses are filthy." She removed them and swiped the lenses with her tattered purple bathrobe sleeve. Replacing them on her face, she poured herself a cup of coffee. Marie appeared at her side, grabbed a mug from the cabinet, and waited her turn to fill it.

"Girl, that terrycloth robe has seen better days. Can't give it up?" she asked.

Elodie put down the coffeepot and the full mug she held, looking herself over. "It's mainly the sleeves that are worn. It still serves its purpose. Besides, nice robes are pricey."

"Of course, it's still perfectly fine!" Marie backpedaled from her comment, regretting she'd brought the robe's worn condition to Elodie's attention. She looked over at Cal, eager to change the subject. "Looks like we're doing leftover pie for breakfast!"

"I know nothin'! I see nothin'!" Elodie reassured the man, trapping crumbs of pie crust between the tines of his fork.

"Dat's Sergeant Schultz from Hogan's Heros!" Marcus, entering the kitchen with his wife, enthusiastically identified the catchphrase from one of the Classic TV shows he had discovered in recent years.

"The topics Elodie knows nothing about are legion, but what are we discussing now? Maybe we can educate our sweet bumpkin," pre-caffeinated Ava was able to tease.

"'Sweet bumpkin' is just mindin' her own business. You should try it!" Elodie shot back with a glance over the top of her eyeglasses and a smirk on her face.

"I tried it once. Didn't care for it," Ava chuckled, giving Elodie a side hug.

"Here, Ava, you take dis cup. I'll make anoder pot," Marcus handed her a steaming cup of coffee. "Is dere any more apple pie in the fridge?"

"I'm getting all the leftover pies out right now," Marie announced.

"We're having pie for breakfast? It's a great day to be alive!" Grant cheered as he entered the kitchen.

"Where's your mother, dear?" Marie asked, concerned.

"Don't worry; I walked her down the stairs. She went into the living room with June."

In the next minute, they heard June begin a boisterous rendition of *Wonderful Grace of Jesus* on the piano.

"That's one of Mom's favorites. June must have taken a request," Grant noted.

"If she paid her a quarter. That's what June charges for requests," Cal joked. Even though he'd finished his coffee and pie, he stayed seated at the table while the others assembled around it with theirs.

"You guys taking G-Lu home tomorrow?" Ava asked, blowing over her hot coffee.

"Just Grant. I have a Sunday School lesson to prepare, thanks to her. Besides, it'll give them some quality time, just the two of them. And she'll make him take her to lunch. She does love that Biscuit Tin!" Marie explained.

Elodie giggled. "I can't believe she told old Christine Williams there'd be hell to pay for rejectin' Christ."

"She's my hero for that! We put too much emphasis on enticing people to Christ with the benefits of being in His kingdom and not enough on challenging them to count the cost. Where's that passage?" Marie asked as she reached for the phone in her trouser pocket to pull up digital Scripture.

Ava, already scrolling news headlines on her phone, tapped her Bible app and found it before Marie. "Here it is! Luke 14:28-30," she answered and read:

"For which of you, desiring to build a tower, does not first sit down and count the cost, whether he has enough to complete it? Otherwise, when he has laid a foundation and is not able to finish, all who see it begin to mock him, saying, 'This man began to build and was not able to finish.'"

"Ava read da verse at da end of dat paragraph," Marcus requested.

"So therefore, any one of you who does not renounce all that he has cannot be my disciple."

"Can you imagine an evangelism program leading off with that?" Grant wondered aloud. "It wouldn't sell ten copies."

Except for the music from June's piano floating through the house, the kitchen was quiet as the breakfasters reflected on Grant's assessment.

"Jesus believed in truth in advertising, dats for sure," Marcus said at last.

"So, now I'm thinking about the rich young ruler who seemed interested in pursuing God until Jesus threw up a roadblock and told him to sell all that he had to test his commitment. He counted the cost and walked away. Well, he's had a couple of thousand years to reflect on his choice. I wonder whether he's torn up with regret or cemented in bitterness and hatred toward God. Either way, it's no good," Marie reflected.

"How did we get so afraid to tell people there's a cost to following

Jesus? He plainly said if people persecuted him, they'd persecute His followers. I guess we're not as truthful in our advertising as Jesus was," Cal lamented.

"That's how we end up with people who drift away from the church," Ava responded. "They count the cost on the back end instead of the front and decide it's too steep for them."

"But what about bein' gentle and lovin'?" Elodie countered. "Is it wrong to ease folks into the deeper truths?"

"If we've made gentleness and truthfulness mutually exclusive, that's another problem," Grant answered thoughtfully. "And how do you ease someone into a lifelong commitment without telling them once they put their hand to the plow, there's no looking back because if they do, they're unfit for the Kingdom of God, as Jesus said?"

The group fell silent again, considering Grant's comment. He was on a roll this morning.

Chapter Twenty-Six

"That was good thinking, Grant, to fire up the space heater early and take the nip off this place." Bobby was chilled from the short walk from his back door to the Garage Cave, and he rubbed his hands together for friction heat. "But I'm still going to leave my toboggan on."

Marcus and Grant exchanged confused looks. "Leave your toboggan on what?" Marcus asked.

"My head!" Bobby answered, befuddled by the question.

"That thing on your head is called a knit cap, and if it's long and comes to a point with a fuzzy ball on the end, it's a stocking cap. A toboggan is a multi-passenger sled you ride down a snowy hill." Grant corrected him.

Will, filling in at game night for Cal again, interjected: "Did I ever tell you about the time a toboggan almost killed me?"

"Did it fall over your eyes and you fell into an uncovered manhole?" Marcus asked, appropriating Bobby's definition and feigning a concerned expression.

Grant spat out the gulp of Cheerwine soda he'd just taken, spraying the floor beside his chair. "You should have let me swallow before you said that!" he sputtered, laughed, and retrieved the roll of paper towels on Cal's workbench to clean up his mess.

"That's what happens when you mock a man's toboggan," Bobby warned, grinning.

"No. Let me tell you what happened," Will insisted. "I was about 14 years old and went on a winter retreat with our youth group to Black Bear Ski Resort in Colorado. We were there to go tubing, not skiing. Anyway, Bucky Mullins and I were trying to impress the older girls and thought we'd do something stupid to show them how clever we were."

"Know what that's like!" Bobby interrupted as Marcus and Grant nodded in agreement.

"The tube shed had an old toboggan hanging on a side wall. We got it off the wall and took it for a run down the hill. Only we did it standing up like it was a two-person snowboard. Well, someone must have waxed the bottom of that old relic. We were probably going 40 miles an hour and headed for a tree line when it dawned on us: we had no way to steer. Geniuses that we were, we hadn't thought that through. I don't remember the accident because I was knocked out cold and woke up in the ambulance, but they told me Bucky jumped and pulled me off the sled with him before it hit a pine tree. We tumbled in the snow before Bucky knocked out his front teeth on my forehead. Look at this!" Will instructed, pointing to the faded scar.

"Your friend wasn't called Bucky after dat," Marcus mused.

"He sure was. He wasn't called Bucky because he had buck teeth. It was short for Buckwald – some family name on his mother's side."

"Buckwald Mullins, Buckwald Mullins," Grant repeated. "Where have I heard that name before?"

"He was Attorney General of Michigan for a term," Will answered helpfully.

"Ha! That's it! I voted for him," Grant recalled. "Marie and I lived in Michigan for 25 years before we moved to Faircourt."

"Yup, he became a successful attorney and politician, and I became a mailman with a useless Ph.D.," Will said matter-of-factly. "I don't know what I was thinking asking Shelby Norman for a coffee date."

"Why do you tink your PhD is useless?" Marcus probed.

"Why do you think your PhD is useless?" Bobby repeated incredulously. "He just said he asked Shelby Norman for a coffee date, and you want to talk about a diploma? Can we park that question while we find out when ole Will jumped in the dating pool?"

Priorities were at odds in the conversation, and it was increasingly clear the Rook cards in the center of the table would go untouched. Marcus deferred to Bobby's question with a nod toward Will.

"Well, you guys are brilliant company, but it's still not good for man to be alone. The divorce wasn't my idea or desire, but here I am. The boys' mom has moved on and remarried, so I wonder if God has another partner for me. But, I have no idea what I'm doing. I haven't dated in 20 years. Am I supposed to be looking for a female to be friends with first, or do guys with some mileage on them, like me, go right to courting? And then I wonder: What do I even have to offer a woman now? I'm more liability than an asset."

"Not to a mail-order bride! I hear there are overseas women desperate for green cards who would marry a four-foot Frankenstein as long as he was an American citizen. Have you considered ordering one off the internet?" Bobby suggested in earnest.

"Not quite that desperate yet, Bobby, but I'll keep that option in my back pocket in case I need it. Thanks." Will couldn't tell if he was serious or joking.

"Now dat your dating issues have been solved, let's go back to why you tink your Ph.D. is useless," Marcus steered the conversation back to more comfortable territory.

"People do it all the time," Bobby muttered defensively before ceding the conversation back to Marcus' control.

"You know my divorce disqualifies me from pastoral positions or any seminary worth working for," Will lamented with a heavy sigh.

"I do know dat. So, don't tink about what you can't do, tink about what you can do," Marcus advised.

"I don't want to think about it! I want to stop thinking about it," Will snapped at him.

Marcus, who'd spent the last year hearing that exact phrase come from his wife's lips countless times regarding their estrangement from their daughters and privately struggling to unshackle himself from resenting being put out to pasture by his former church, was undeterred.

"I understand, Will. It's a painful loss on top of losing your marriage and family life. Who wants to tink about what dey've lost? I'm asking you to flip da coin and consider what you've gained."

Will sat back in his chair and raked his fingers through the crown of his dark hair. He did not want to have this conversation but felt stuck to his seat – too tired for an intense discussion, too tired to walk away. He said nothing, so Marcus continued.

"Proverbs 16:9 tells us: *The heart of a man plans his way, but the Lord establishes his steps.*

Da best and biggest word in dat sentence is da word 'but.' We don't plan our way, *and* da Lord establishes it. We make our plans, *but* God does what He wants wit us because He is sovereign, and we are not. You planned to take your PhD into religious ministry to shepherd da sheep. What if God's plan is for you to take your PhD into secular ministry to convert da goats? Could it be da divorce you didn't want was a means to take you off your track and put you on His?" Marcus let the question hang in the air for a few seconds before he concluded.

"God never promised da sin of oders wouldn't touch us. But He did promise it wouldn't be determinative for our futures because He holds dat right for Himself. Da question you need to answer is: 'Will you trust His plan for you will prove better den your plan for you, and will you bless Him for it in faith before you see da result?'"

Will shifted uneasily in his chair and brushed unseen lint from the blue jeans covering the tops of his legs. "Pray for me, Marcus. I can't seem to get over that hill," he answered.

Marcus nodded to Will, reached for, and unboxed the Rook cards. A somber silence hung in the air until Bobby couldn't take it anymore and, trying to be helpful, said: "The Philippines, Ukraine, Brazil, Vietnam – they're all loaded with women who don't require a man with a Ph.D., just American citizenship!"

"How are you so informed on this subject, Bobby?" Grant inquired.

"I get sports updates from my phone. There are ads," Bobby explained with a sheepish grin.

Chapter Twenty-Seven

"You'll take me to lunch at the Biscuit Tin," G-Lu made the statement with a soft question mark in her voice.

"Yes, Mom. We'll stop at the one off the highway near Pleasant Pond before I take you home. It'll be lunchtime then," Grant reassured as he helped her into his car for the ride home.

"Good. I already know what I'm having!"

"Chicken and dumplings, coleslaw, buttered corn, water to drink, and biscuits, not corn muffins," he recited from memory.

"Exactly, dear!" she smiled as her son tucked her into the passenger seat with a colorful crocheted lap quilt, a gift from Marie.

As they drove toward Champaign, their conversation evolved as quickly as the scenery.

"So, what do you think of our little commune setup, Mom?"

"I wouldn't mind moving in myself if it weren't for the fact I'm enriching my purse on the average of $1.25 per week at the expense of Deaf Donald. He should really give up penny poker, but I think he has the gambling fever."

"Do we need to talk about your gambling fever, Mother?" Grant asked with a side-eyed glance and a raised bushy eyebrow.

G-Lu ignored the question and changed the subject. "Your neighbor Bobby is quite the handsome widower. Has Elodie noticed?"

"I don't believe he's her type," Grant answered abruptly, then added:

"We shouldn't gossip about them behind their backs."

G-Lu scowled. She didn't understand how one complimentary statement and one question of perception added up to gossip and shifted gears again.

"That little Lovie next door is a delightful child. I always wanted a little girl, but the Lord saw fit to bless me with sons, and His ways are best." She was trying to find safe ground.

"I hope Gerard and I haven't been too much of a disappointment," Grant answered with unnecessary defensiveness.

"No. I merely..." She gave up the explanation.

"How are your ribs healing, dear? Have you been using the comfrey root salve like I told you?"

"Mom, we no longer have to go foraging in the woods for medicines. Big Mart and Super Drug sell sterile drugs manufactured in pharmaceutical labs. We also don't have to use phones attached to the wall or bake bread in wood-fired ovens," Grant teased.

G-Lu was not amused and turned to look out her passenger window for a while. Grant was driving, for the moment, in the highway's passing lane, and her attention was captured by a solemn-looking middle-aged man driving a lime green semi-truck next to them. She could see his reflection in the truck's large sideview mirror. He wore a red plaid flannel shirt, a trimmed mustache, and a slack-jawed, forlorn expression that made G-Lu wonder what was pressing on his mind.

As the vehicles came precisely even with one another, the truck driver looked down and made eye contact with her. Impulsively, G-Lu blew him a kiss, and his countenance brightened with a full-faced grin that wrinkled the corners of his eyes and laughter she couldn't hear but which was, nonetheless, unmistakable.

"Mother!" Grant scolded. "What are you doing? Did you just blow a kiss to a strange man? You did; I saw it! I can't take my eyes off you for one second. Mom, this is not 1940. It's not the world you grew up in.

You can't do things like that because people are crazy!" He was animated – voice and blood pressure elevated.

G-Lu didn't say a word. She closed her eyes and pretended to sleep, determined to find a measure of peace lacking in her son's company.

They drove silently for the final 20 minutes before the Biscuit Tin/Champaign exit. Just as Grant signaled his intention to turn on the exit ramp, the front left tire blew, jerking the vehicle into the passing lane. G-Lu's eyes flew open, and she grabbed the passenger door armrest to pull herself back upright, having been flung in her seatbelt restraint toward her son.

Grant managed to slow the sedan, steer it back into the right lane and off the exit ramp, then stop on the road's right shoulder. He turned off the vehicle and let out the breath he'd been holding. They both exited the car and walked in front of it to assess the damage. What remained of the tire was wound around its rim, and an edge of the side front panel was torn from its fasteners. Grant leaned against the hood of the car, collecting his wits.

G-Lu stood before him, looked him in the eye, and did something she hadn't done since he was a teenager. She reached out and grabbed a hunk of his navy sweatshirt and the inside flesh of his upper arm and twisted hard.

"Ooooouch!" Grant yelled. "Mom! I couldn't help that! I didn't blow a tire on purpose to scare you."

"You were not pinched for blowing a tire. You were pinched for being rude and disrespectful to your mother in our conversation. It makes no difference to me you are a grandfather yourself. That's all the more reason you should know that treating your parents respectfully doesn't have an expiration date. Whatever you allow your adult children to say to you, that's your business. But I will not be held up for your critique, patronized, condescended to, or scolded for kindness that you interpret as irresponsibility. Have I made myself clear?"

Grant lowered his head and drew a deep breath. "I'm sorry, Mom. I was just…"

"Aaaat!" She cut him off. "Excuses for the behavior do not accompany genuine apologies. Do you mean to make a genuine apology or excuses?"

He began again. "I'm sorry, Mom. You're right. I was awful and wish I could have a do-over for the entire ride here. Will you forgive me? By the grace of God, I mean never to speak disrespectfully to you again."

"From my heart, I forgive you, Grant," she answered as she reached to give a sympathetic rub to the arm she'd pinched.

Grant flinched when he saw her arm extending, then laughed and let her soothe it. "I guess I had this coming," he responded, nodding toward the mangled tire. "I have a membership with a roadside service to help get us back on the road." He reached for the cell phone in his back pocket to make the call.

"Don't bother. I've got this," G-Lu directed, motioning him to leave his phone in his pocket and relishing his bewildered expression.

With his back to the highway, Grant didn't see the lime green semi with the red-flannelled, still-smiling trucker pulling off the exit ramp and onto the shoulder of the road behind them.

Chapter Twenty-Eight

Anna Cramer smiled coyly from her seat in the Senior Women's Sunday School class. Her front seat. It was Marie Renniger's first Sunday to teach the lesson, and Anna wouldn't let a cloud of murder hornets up her skirt keep her from attending. She intended to show the new teacher what it was like to have a class member criticize and contradict one's lesson. Marie, dressed in a hunter green shirtwaist dress with 2"-heel hunter green pumps on her feet, stood at the front of the class, her notes on a small stand before her. Previous teachers of the ladies' class taught from a seat among the attendees. But Marie found it difficult to manage her Bible and notes while seated. She preferred to teach while standing behind a podium or music stand.

"Today, we're beginning a study of the little book of Ruth," she began.

Anna, who was very familiar with the 4-chapter book, felt delighted. She looked forward to participating in the discussion questions.

Marie began the lesson by explaining the events of the book took place in the 450 years of the Judges – the period between the death of Joshua and Samuel's anointing of Saul as the first King of Israel. She noted it was a low point in the young nation's history where everyone did what was right in their own eyes. In other words, it was practically lawless even though they'd been given God's law through Moses.

"In this bleak period, the book of Ruth takes up the story of a Jewish man named Elimelech, his wife, Naomi, and their two sons, Mahlon and

Kilion, in the town of Bethlehem during a famine. Question," Marie said as a statement. "Isn't this supposed to be the land flowing with milk and honey? Why is there a famine? Were the Jews victims of a divine bait-and-switch ruse?"

Anna wasn't sure how to answer that. Of course, she didn't believe God had lied to His people, but she didn't know how to explain the famine, which was indeed under God's sovereign control. She looked around the room, and neither Ava nor June, who were pretty knowledgeable, had raised their hands.

"Turn your Bibles to Deuteronomy chapter 28," Marie instructed. She pointed out how the first half of the chapter was a list of blessings that God's people would enjoy if they were obedient to Him in the Promised Land. The second half was a list of curses for disobedience. "Let your eyes scan through verses 15 through 24. You'll see that basket, kneading bowl, and the fruit of the ground are cursed if the people are disobedient. And more than that! In verse 22, in addition to drought, blight, and mildew for the crops, physical ailments such as wasting disease, fever, and inflammation will strike the people themselves."

"Okay, so let me ask the question again. Why was there a famine in the land of Israel?" Marie reviewed.

Ava spoke up: "Because the people were disobedient. They weren't obeying God's law, so He did what He promised He would do."

Anna had to admit she hadn't connected the passage in Deuteronomy to the events in the Ruth text before.

"Let's turn back to Ruth," Marie continued. "So, there's a famine in the land, but it's worse than that. Ruth and Elimelech's sons are Mahlon and Kilion. Isn't that sad?"

The class attendees exchanged glances of puzzlement.

"The name Mahlon means 'sickly,' and Kilion means 'wasting away.' These boys were unhealthy from birth and suffered the promised physical curses in their bodies. So, there's famine and disease. But keep in mind the root problem was disobedience. So, what do you think is the solution to the problem?"

Anna's hand flew up, and she answered at the same time. "Elimelech should repent, worship, and obey God!"

"That's exactly right, Anna. But that's not what he does. He looks at his situation: two sons in poor health and no way to feed them, and he decides in verse one that it's time to head to Moab, where the enemies of God live comfortably with enough to eat. He's dead by verse 3. His sons decide to break the law of God and marry Moabite women, and they're dead by verse 5. More disobedience did not solve the problem!"

Margaret Hunt, a 60-year-old widow who owned a local dog-grooming business, pursed her lips in the second row. "Why was going to Moab disobedience? In that situation, doesn't a good man do anything he can to provide for his family?"

"That's an excellent and important question, Margaret," Marie responded. She consulted her notes and asked, "Can you read Deuteronomy 23, verses 3-6 for us?"

Margaret read the verses about how God's people should relate to the Moabites, who refused to help them when they came out of Egypt and hired Balaam to curse them. Verse six ended with the instruction never to seek their peace or prosperity.

"Elimelech sought the prosperity of Moab in sinful violation of God's law. So, here's another question: If his choice was between dying in obedience or living in sin, what did God expect him to do?"

"He should die in obedience!" shouted Anna.

"And if our choice is the same, die in obedience or live in sin, what does God expect us to do?" Marie asked pointedly.

"We should die in obedience," June answered in a low voice.

"Much easier said than done, isn't it?" Marie agreed. "Women don't tend to think this way, do we? 'Die in obedience' sounds like the rallying cry of fighting men." She threw her arm up as if it held a sword to demonstrate. "But do women have a different Enemy than men have?"

The class of 15 women slowly shook their heads from side to side.

"That's right. Women have the same Enemy as men, and he does not treat us any differently. He hates us just as much as he hates men. That's why we need to be as prepared as men not only to die in obedience if it should come to that, but to live in obedience, too. I have nerd-girl bonus points for anyone who can think of a woman in Scripture who was prepared to die in obedience.

The women thought for a moment before Ava shouted out: "Esther! She said, 'If I perish, I perish.'"

"I knew you'd get it, girl!" Marie commended her friend and continued. "We need to know God's word as well as men, which means interpreting it carefully and with integrity. You can be sure that in Will's men's class down the hall, they're rightly dividing the word, and I intend to make sure we do as well."

Anna sat beside her husband in the worship service and appeared attentive as Pastor Jefferson preached his sermon. But her thoughts were back in the Senior Women's Sunday School classroom.

She had learned and been challenged in Marie Renniger's class and now felt convicted for her peevishness in being replaced. The fact was, when provoked to raise the bar of her lesson preparation, she'd given up instead of leveling up. Tearing down Marie would not change her own failing; she could see that now.

The lesson in Ruth had little to do with Anna's new self-awareness. Spending time in God's word and seeing His glory revealed in it had brought change. She recalled this too was a blessing promised in the

Bible.

And we all with unveiled face, beholding the glory of the Lord, are being transformed into the same image, from one degree of glory to another. For this comes from the Lord who is the Spirit. – 2 Corinthians 3:18

As Pastor Jefferson preached, Anna silently prayed, thanking God for His mercy to her, helping her let go of her petty desires for retaliation, and sparing her the embarrassment of putting them on display.

Chapter Twenty-Nine

"Are they giving the coffee away for free tonight?" Will grumbled as he parked his SUV across the street from Latte Da. He hoped he and Shelby would have the place nearly to themselves on a slow Sunday evening, and he criticized himself for not gathering information on the coffee shop's peak hours before asking for the date.

She'd requested to meet him instead of picking her up at her brother's house. At 7 p.m., Lovie and Chase wouldn't be in bed, and she thought it best to shield them from the uncertain outcome of a first date with their mailman. She also protected herself from possible prying questions, which children are notorious for. She had a daymare that Will would stand in their front hall, helping her with her winter coat, when Lovie would blurt out : "Are you going to marry my Aunt Shelby?"

Will walked into the busy coffee shop expecting to scout for any available table in the throng of customers. Instead, Shelby was already seated at a cozy, two-seat table between the frosty front window and an electric fireplace exuding faux flames and minimal heat. He smiled at the sight of her, and she waved him over.

Her face was still flushed pink from her four-block walk to the shop in the crisp November evening air, and she wore a jaunty, fern-green cashmere cap on her strawberry blonde hair. Impressed by a glimpse of this naturally attractive woman, Will noted the transformation of his jittery nervousness to alarming nausea as he walked toward her.

"You look lovely this evening, Shelby," is what he'd practiced saying as his opening line on the drive from his apartment to Main Street. "You beat me here!" is what came out as he took the empty seat across from her, removed his leather driving gloves, and set them on the table.

"Not how you planned it?" She asked with a casual laugh. "Should I have been fashionably late? I could go out and come back in a few," she offered.

"Idiot!" he chastised himself internally. He told himself to ignore the queasiness and get back on track. Still, he owed her a response to her question.

"No need," he tried to sound as casual as she did. "Would you like to try the coconut snowball coffee, or would you prefer something else?"

"The coconut snowball sounds delicious – almost like dessert!" she answered.

"I'll be right back with it," Will stood too quickly and regretted it. A rush of internal heat and a wave of nausea almost knocked him off his feet. He grabbed the back of his chair, took a stumbling step before regaining equilibrium, and then walked to the counter to place their order.

As he waited in line, he chided himself. *"She probably thinks I'm drunk. 'Would you like to try the coconut snowball coffee, or would you prefer something else?' I sounded like a waiter at a two-star restaurant. Man, this is not going well. There's no way I should put coffee in my stomach. I wonder if they have peppermint tea. Good, they have paper cups! She doesn't have to know what I'm drinking."*

He stepped up to the barista and placed his order. "I'd like one large coconut snowball coffee and a large peppermint tea."

"We don't have peppermint tea. We have chai tea, though. Would you like that?" asked the nose-pierced, pink-haired employee with a string of music notes tattooed down one side of her neck.

"Is that good for an upset stomach?" he asked.

The girl taking his order shrugged off her lack of knowledge on the subject.

"Okay, I'll try the chai tea."

"Skim or whole milk for the coconut snowball?"

He didn't know. Should he go back to ask Shelby which she wanted or wing it? He went with winging it.

"Skim," he answered with pretend confidence. Then he paid for his order and stepped to the side to wait for the prepared drinks. He turned to look at Shelby. She was watching something outside the window, which reflected her face to him as if she were looking in a mirror. He wondered what to say when he returned to their table and could not think of anything intelligent or witty. *"Lord, help a guy out,"* he prayed.

When his name was called, he returned their drinks to the table and set the coffee in front of Shelby before reclaiming his seat. "For you, madam," he said.

"Two-star waiter! You did two-star waiter again, you freak!" he scolded himself as he watched her take a careful sip.

She detected the skim milk immediately, and an ever-so-slight scowl stamped her face before she could erase it. *"He thinks I'm fat,"* she conjectured from the ingredient.

Will noted her initial expression and judged this date was already swirling above the drain. At a loss for words, he sipped his chai tea. *"Wow!"* he evaluated of his first experience with the beverage. *"They dumped a spice rack in this thing. Ugh-oh!"*

As a child, Will vomited after eating a cinnamon roll and determined he wouldn't eat cinnamon again. Over the years, he convinced himself and his family that he was allergic to it. Whether he was or wasn't, the fact that he'd consumed cinnamon rattled his precarious nerves and stomach. He felt he was going to wretch. Imminently.

Will pushed away from the table, bolted to the men's room, bent on reaching a stall before the inevitable happened, and almost made it. He careened through the bathroom door, crossing the threshold before his stomach released its contents. His momentum carried him through the regurgitated fountain, which plastered his unzipped jacket and the rugby shirt beneath it. What landed on the floor caused him to slip and land in the puddle on his backside.

He sat, feeling better but unsure what his next move should be. He was surveying his condition and the pollution he was sitting in when a stall door opened. A 30-something man with shaggy brown hair and a goatee emerged and looked at him pitifully.

"Dude!" he exclaimed, and without offering assistance, moved his man purse to the opposite side of his body and stepped gingerly around him, out of the restroom.

Will washed himself in the sink as best he could before completing a walk of shame through the coffee shop to where Shelby sat. The smell reached her seconds before he did.

"I need to go home," he confessed, picking up his gloves from the table.

Not knowing what else to do at the abrupt end of this record-setting brief date, Shelby reacted with careless laughter. She raised her cup of fat-free coconut snowball coffee in salute as Will walked through the coffee shop and out the front door.

Chapter Thirty

The sign on the door read: "OFFICE," but technically, there were two offices behind the door off the vestibule of Grace Fellowship Church. The smaller outer room had just enough space to hold three, four-drawer metal filing cabinets, a bulky copier machine, a utilitarian coat rack with some duct tape at its base, and the self-assembled desk and worn office chair Ava occupied during her working hours. In her small workspace, a large west-facing window was a luxury. Ava could watch the sun back-light the trees down Sycamore Street as the afternoon progressed.

The copier shared wall space with the door to the Pastor's inner office, which bore the name 'Jonathan Jefferson' written in white letters on a black plastic nameplate. Both rooms walls looked like muddy tan made dingier by years of accumulated scuff marks. Ava vowed to have them painted if she had to do it herself. Perhaps cheerful yellow, she thought.

Ava unbuttoned her brilliant blue wool coat and hung it on an arm of the coatrack before settling behind her desk at the start of her three-day work week. She was glad for the slower weeks between the holidays when church members occupied themselves with preparations for Christmas. That meant she could reasonably expect making headway on her project to remove deceased or inactive members from the church rolls. Or, as she jokingly referred to the project: "Siphoning Off The Slackers."

Ava's initial project assignment involved adding a light pencil line through the name of anyone listed in the handwritten membership ledger who would be over 100 years old. Next, she assigned Pastor Jefferson and his tiny group of deacons to go through the book and put a checkmark in front of every name they knew to be active. They would define 'active' generously – anyone who'd attended at least one service in the past 12 months – and they would have to rely on their collective recollections of seeing them in church. It wasn't foolproof, but it was a place to start.

Once the ledger markings were complete, Ava made a spreadsheet of all the names without a line or check mark. Two days before Thanksgiving, Ava and Pastor Jefferson met at the home of Norah Collins, who graciously agreed to identify from the list former members who had passed or moved away. At 89 years old, Norah wasn't the most senior member of the congregation, but she attended regularly, and her mind and memory were sharp. With her help, Ava could cross off 72 names from the list of inactive members. The church would send a letter to the 35 remaining people, inviting them back into fellowship and advising them of the church's intention to remove them from the membership roll if they declined.

Today, Ava's task was to compose the letter and address envelopes. When she'd finished a draft of the letter, she brought it to the Pastor for any recommendations he might have. Relieved that he approved it without changes, she printed the letters. On his way home, Pastor Jefferson dropped the stack of stuffed and stamped envelopes in the mailbox outside the post office.

Christine heard Will's heavy footsteps on her porch and waited until she saw him crossing Tamarack Street before she stepped outside to retrieve her mail from the discrete metal box mounted on her house. At the center hall table, she sorted through the small pile – four Christmas catalogs from online retailers and five end-of-the-year donation requests from charities who persistently wasted their printing and postage on her. She supposed the letter from Grace Fellowship Church would be of the latter ilk.

Christine read the letter and let it fall from her hand onto the floor. "What does this Jefferson think he's doing?" She seethed audibly at the signature lying on her hardwood floor. Her next move was to retrieve her phone from the butcher block kitchen counter. She touched a contact on the screen and tapped a foot while she waited for him to answer. Her call went to voicemail.

"Luther!" she tried and failed to hide the anxiety in her voice. "They're trying to remove me from membership at Grace Fellowship Church. I need you to stop them! You know what to do."

Luther Hall had semi-retired from his two-man law firm. He was handing it over to his son, Eric, who had an ambition and vision for expansion Luther had grown too weary to entertain.

The only thing he was very tired of was being Christine's, his sister's, legal water boy. She regularly requested that he write threatening letters to intimidate people into doing or stopping doing what she required. He'd told himself they were only letters – words on a paper – and that writing them didn't make him as hateful a person as she, the instigator.

He started doing her bidding when he was younger than Eric, now in his early 40s, and had the same ambition. His older sister was becoming a wealthy woman; without children, he would be her logical beneficiary. So, Luther kept his eye on the prize and did what she wanted, pro bono. Now he understood the price he'd paid in eroding self-respect. His minor act of rebellion against her was to let her calls go to voicemail even though they both knew he'd eventually comply.

CHAPTER THIRTY-ONE

All were finally present and accounted for at Thursday Meeting as Cal and June slipped into chairs ten minutes after the others. Cal had a late afternoon doctor's appointment, and June promised she'd take them to dinner at Roadhouse BBQ afterward since, even with little appetite, Cal could be tempted to eat barbecue. They wouldn't have been late, except Cal's doctor tinkered with his medications and prescribed a new one, which they had to pick up at the pharmacy so he would have a dose before his dinner.

"You both reek of smoked meat, and now I'm hungry again even though we've had dinner," Grant whined jealously.

Cal said nothing in reply but wore a silly grin.

"Have you started discussing Christmas?" June inquired. "Is everyone going to be here for it? We will."

"Marley's family has been invited to her college roommate's South Carolina beach house for Christmas week, so Marcus and I will be here," Ava answered.

"Grant and I are having a late Christmas with our little clan in Florida in mid-January, so we'll be home," said Marie.

"I've got nowhere to go," Elodie shrugged.

"Then you won't need to dress up!" Cal shouted, chuckling with amusement at his little joke.

June and Elodie both looked sideways at him, Elodie with a tiny frown in her expression.

"Okay, so we're all going to be here. Are we repeating Thanksgiving with the neighbors or having a quiet Christmas with just us?" Marie sought clarification.

"Won't Bobby be in Florida with his daughter's family?" Elodie reminded them by proposing a question.

"I believe da Norman's are going over da river to dere grandmudder's house," informed Marcus, adding holiday flair to his vague knowledge the neighbors would travel sometime around the Christmas holiday.

"I believe da Norman's are going over da river to dere grandmudder's house," Cal mimicked with a straight face.

Grant nearly spat out his teeth. "Cal! That was dead on, buddy!" he belly-laughed.

Marie couldn't help but smile, and the corners of Ava's crinkled eyes betrayed a reflex of amusement. Elodie's former frown reappeared and deepened. June elbowed her husband.

"That wasn't kind," she whispered.

Marcus took the mocking like a sport and rolled his eyes. It was Garage Cave behavior, which he didn't mind.

"Well, moving on," Marie tried to steer the discussion forward. "How about I write our names on slips of paper, and let's draw for a Christmas morning gift exchange? That way, we buy and receive one gift. Everyone good with that?"

Without waiting for the positive response she assumed was forthcoming, Marie got up and walked to the study across the hall to make the name slips. Behind her, she heard Cal's voice asking, "Everyone good wit dat?" repeating her words but maintaining his impersonation of Marcus.

"Stop!" June pleaded softly to him.

"Calcium, what's got into your feed?" Elodie wanted to know.

"My feet?" Cal bent over to inspect them. "There's nothing in my feet except feet," he giggled. He did not immediately upright himself, stuck in his folded-over position. "Help me," he breathed out through his giggles.

"I should leave him like dat," Marcus muttered as he turned to help Cal right himself.

"That's it, Elodie!" June exclaimed. "He just started a new medicine. It's made him loopy!"

"It's made him hysterical," Grant started laughing again. "His medicine is doing wonders for me!" he added.

"Get a grip, Grant!" Ava scolded him. "Let's just finish drawing names, and June, you can get your guy to bed."

Marie returned with folded slips of paper held in the palm of her right hand. "Okay, everyone, pick one and keep the name to yourself so it will be a surprise on Christmas morning who your gift came from. I'll take the one that's left."

"Should we have a theme for the gifts?" Ava asked. "Since we're all new to Kentucky, maybe we could have a Kentucky theme."

"I'm not in favor of a theme," Elodie grimaced. "I'd rather they were more specific to the person's needs."

"No theme, then," Ava agreed amiably.

Marie made her way around the room with her cupped hand outstretched.

"I've got yours, too," June whispered to her husband when it was her turn to pick a name.

"I want to see it," Cal whined, and June handed it to him.

"It says 'Grant,'" he told her in a loud stage whisper, ruining the surprise element for Grant.

June's cheeks flushed pink, and she looked around at her friends. "Sorry," she mouthed to Grant.

"Well, now that we've settled that, how 'bout we adjourn this meeting?" Ava was eager to put an end to June's embarrassment.

Heads bobbed in agreement as June helped her husband stand and steered him down the hall.

"A theme is a wonderful idea!" Cal shouted in June's ear.

"We're not doing the theme, dear," June corrected.

"I'm going to buy Grant a Kentucky thoroughbred racehorse he can keep in the Garage Cave," Cal began formulating an illogical plan with no attempt to moderate his volume.

The others exchanged amused looks except for Elodie, who wore an expression of concern.

"I'm going to give Grant a name for his horse, too," he continued. "Hoof Hearted! It'll be named Hoof Hearted. I read that somewhere. Didn't make it up myself," he yelled to June as she led him into their bedroom and closed the door.

CHAPTER THIRTY-TWO

Bobby made solo visits to his son at the Kentucky State Reformatory in LaGrange after his initial trip with Jonathan Jefferson in September. The new warden's effort to make visiting days equitable with a weekly rotation of which days were odd or even complicated things for Bobby. He'd turned 70 years old the day after Thanksgiving and found it challenging to keep up with the calendar kaleidoscope.

The only fact he was confident of was that his son, prisoner 043094, was allowed visitors on even days since his number ended in an even digit. He relied on DeShawn to track the rotating schedule and tell him at the end of a visit when he could come again. Bobby wrote the date down in a small notebook as soon as he returned to his car. It was one more thing on the pile of his life's circumstances that Bobby resented – the fact he was beholden to a maddening schedule of when he was able see his son.

Bobby trudged into the large visiting room and sat on a metal bench on one side of a knee-height Lucite table, mindful not to bash his shin on it as he had on his first visit. He'd yelped in pain and drawn the attention of alert guards.

"The table is clear so they can see what happens underneath. It's knee-high to make it difficult to pass anything under it," Jonathan explained to him, and Bobby remembered to be careful afterward.

"Hey, Dad!" DeShawn sat across the squatty table, wearing a khaki uniform and a replica of his father's smile on happier days.

"Hey, son! You look well," Bobby began, forcing a cheery tone.

"Ha, thanks. God is good to me."

"What?" Bobby's exasperation seeped from a crack he hadn't meant to reveal.

"God is good to me," his son repeated.

"I mean, I heard you. I don't know why you'd say that," Bobby retorted, bewildered.

DeShawn held up his left hand with fingers splayed and lowered them one by one as he recounted his blessings: "Jesus saved me. Get three squares a day. I get great books and time to read 'em. Health is good. I have people who love me. So, like I said, God is good to me."

Instinctively, Bobby leaned back to mirror in physical distance the relational distance he sensed with DeShawn. He caught himself before he toppled backward from the bench and muttered an expletive.

"Whoa there! You ok, Dad?"

Bobby sighed, and his shoulders sagged. "The truth? No." For a few seconds, he wondered how much more truth to share. He began hesitantly. "We used to like the same things, and now..." He left his thoughts unfinished.

"And now Jesus saved me, and I've gone further from you than these prison walls?" DeShawn filled the gap.

"Pretty much," Bobby admitted. "You're like quicksilver. Just when I thought I had you back, you squirted away from me again."

"Quicksilver, huh? Good analogy. I understand where your head is at now, and I completely get it. I'd feel the same way in your shoes. Dad, I'm so sorry my faith hits you like losing me again. What can I do to help you?"

Bobby's throat tightened at his son's acknowledgment of his feelings, and he would have choked up had the unexpected question had not thrown him off. Indeed, what could DeShawn do to help? Bobby couldn't ask him to give up his faith, but he could ask him to explain it.

"I don't understand how you give God so much credit for goodness when he's taken so much away from you. Don't you ever get mad at him?"

"God didn't rob the gas station and scare a man to death; I did that," DeShawn answered candidly. "Despite what I've done, God shows me His kindness every day." DeShawn raised his left hand again to remind his dad of the blessings he'd enumerated earlier. "Now, here's the stupid part: despite God showing me kindness every day, do I ever get mad at Him? Sure do!"

Bobby raised a curious eyebrow. He remembered Marcus' suggestion that DeShawn might have that in common with him.

"There was a man who came here for doing the same thing I did. He robbed a convenience store with an accomplice who ran from the store, was hit by a car, and killed. His charges were the same as mine: armed robbery and manslaughter. I got 25 years, and this dude got seven! Come and gone from here a long time ago. Don't think I didn't have words to say to God about that. It wasn't fair. And that was just the worst one. I've seen guys get 10, 12, and 15 years for almost the same thing. Made me jealous and mad at God every time. I'd have been out years ago if I had that time. Why'd I get 25?"

Bobby hadn't considered DeShawn's opportunity to compare charges and sentences with other convicts. It was unfair. "Aren't you still mad about it?" he asked.

"No. And I feel ashamed every time it happens. When things go down, and I don't understand what God is doing by allowing it, I go back to what I *do* know. I know God loves me; He's working all things out for my good – not my happiness, but my ultimate good. I also know God is just. Even if justice doesn't come on my timetable, He handles it on His. So, this is what I do, Dad. I confess to God I got my head up my butt about things I don't understand, and I've failed to trust Him for the things I understand. I tell Him when I'm standing on Heaven's balcony,

I'll look back and agree everything He did was the perfect thing to do, and by faith, I'll believe it now, too. And you know what happens next? The anger's gone, and I'm at peace."

After hesitating, Bobby began to smirk and shake his head from side to side.

"You think I'm ridiculous?" DeShawn asked with hurt stamped on his face.

"Not you. What's ridiculous is how you've found peace inside this prison, and I haven't known a day of peace in my so-called freedom outside. But I'm glad for you, son."

"My peace comes from knowing God. He's out there too," DeShawn nodded toward the door his father would exit through 30 minutes later.

"Yo, bro," Jonathan answered the phone at the parsonage after seeing the caller ID from the Kentucky State Reformatory.

"How's it goin', man?" inquired DeShawn's familiar voice.

"It's going. Did you tell him?" Jonathan was eager for an update.

"Negatory. He was asking questions about God. Thought we'd stay on that subject. He's visiting Claire's family in Florida for the holidays and will be back at the end of January."

"Okay. Your call. But you serve out in three months. You need to tell him when he gets home. What about the other thing?" Jonathan pressed.

"No," DeShawn answered. "Not yet."

CHAPTER THIRTY-THREE

Shelby heard the slot in the front door squeak open and close from her seat at the dining room table, an end of which served as her workspace. She waited a few minutes to retrieve the mail, wanting to be sure Will was down the street when she collected it. A single notecard lay on the braided entry rug. It was addressed to her, and she tore it open.

"Dear Shelby,

I write this to you from the brink of death by humiliation, hopeful I may claw my way from the edge. Please accept my sincere apology for the abrupt and revolting conclusion to our meeting at Latte Da. The combination of the first date since my divorce and a beautiful woman made me nervous. So nervous.

If you have a soft spot for geeky mailmen with weak stomachs who may reveal more redeeming characteristics with a bit of encouragement, I hope you'll let me know. I'd love and am asking for, a second chance.

Sincerely,

Will"

She studied the neat draftsman-style printing on the small envelope and inside the card with a picture of coffee beans on the front. She'd think about the request from the insecure guy who wrote that she was 'beautiful'.

***

"Colored or white lights?" Marie asked, standing with Ava, June, and

Elodie before racks of Christmas lights in Big Mart.

"I think white lights are elegant and will look nice with the house," Ava stated her preference.

"If we go with white lights on the boxwoods out front, they'll coordinate with white-light electric candles in each window. Wouldn't that be pretty? Shouldn't cost too much," June added.

"It won't cost us anything because we don't have to buy them. I have a box full of candle lights in the attic," Marie offered.

"The house is gonna be decked!" Elodie gushed. "But can I make one suggestion?"

"What's that?" June encouraged her.

"We passed some big red plastic bells in the other aisle. Could we hang 'em above the porch steps with some greenery if I bought two? Would give a dab of color and a focal point."

"Look at you with the decorating flair! That's a brilliant idea, El!" Ava remarked.

"I'm going to dash off to grab something I need across the store. Meet you all at the benches by the restrooms when I'm done," June informed her friends. It was an infrequent opportunity for her to be away from Cal, and she hoped to make the most of the occasion and purchase supplies to make her Secret Santa gift without the others on her heels.

She was on her way to the back of the store when she passed the women's clothing department and spotted a tunic in a darling Christmas print. It had brightly colored vintage ornaments on a black background with teal ribbon swirling throughout, and it called to her.

"Oh! I have to try that on. I'll just take a minute," she thought, making her way to the rack and picking out an extra-large size before hurrying to the dressing rooms.

She rushed into an empty room, dropping her purse and peeling off her coat and pink knit tunic top. She didn't want to make her friends wait for her, and she still had to get what she needed at the back of the store. June pulled the Christmas tunic off its hanger and over her head, tugging a bit to get it over her chest. It seemed to fit perfectly, and she admired the silky drape of the fabric in the mirror. She'd buy it.

Decision made, June lifted the tunic to pull over her head, but it wouldn't come back over her chest the way it had come on. Arms crossed above her face, holding the side edges of the garment, June tugged gently upward to no avail. The top was stuck, and when she realized it, she became panicked and claustrophobic. Tugging became more aggressive, and June began to sweat with effort and adrenaline. There was nothing else to do but yell for help.

She stopped tugging and cried, "Please, help me!" hoping someone in a nearby dressing room or an employee in the area would respond. She waited a few moments before crying out again. Still, no response. June let down her elbows to take a few deep breaths and try to calm. On a third plea, she added a bit more volume. No one came.

"I need help!" June eventually screamed without dignity or reservation.

Elodie, Ava, and Marie were walking by the shoe department when they heard the commotion and bolted toward the distressed voice.

"We can help! Unlock the door," Elodie instructed the woman, not realizing who it was.

June quit yelling and bent at the waist to lower her torso. She twisted the knob with one hand and opened the door.

"June? Is that you?" Marie asked the woman who wore familiar black leggings.

"Maybe," came a soft, sniffling answer.

"Put your arms down for a second," Marie instructed, entering the dressing room. She helped June with her arms and pulled the tunic back down as it was meant to be worn so she could assess the solution.

"Guess you'll be buyin' that and wearin' it outta here," Elodie commented, smirking.

June responded with a pouchy mouth. Her mascara was smudged under her eyes, and small blonde strands were pasted to her sweaty forehead.

"Hey! There's a side zipper!" Marie noted and reached to unzip it. She helped June lift the top easily over her head.

Once the tunic was off, June slumped, sat on the floor, and cried tears of embarrassment and relief. Marie sat next to her, and Ava and Elodie sat down just outside the open door of the dressing room.

"June, you poor thing!" Ava consoled, reaching inside to pat June's leg.

"It's okay now; you're okay. It's happened to all of us," Marie soothed.

"Still believe you have to buy it 'cause you sweated all in it. Luckily, it's cute on you," Elodie contributed, taking a pragmatic view of the situation.

June grabbed her pink tunic and pulled it on, wiping her face with the hem. "You really think it's cute?" she asked.

"Nothing is as cute as you, June," Ava chuckled. "Now, who will help us get off the floor?"

"Oh. We didn't think this through," Marie lamented.

Indeed. It took a minute and an ungraceful process for the four senior women to get to their feet again in the Big Mart.

CHAPTER THIRTY-FOUR

Christine guarded the petite desk, given pride of place in her home office. It was a burled walnut escritoire that had belonged to her mother, grandmother, and great-grandmother and sat in a corner of the north-facing room to display the craftsmanship of the pigeonholes, drawers inlaid with bits of oyster marquetry, and silver drawer pulls. She made it her habit to sit at the desk while the crew of three cleaning ladies went about their bi-monthly tasks ever since a thoughtless dimwit came perilously close to spraying the piece with canned polish. It was a two-hour commitment Christine usually endured by thumbing through gardening magazines and rose catalogs.

Her cell phone rang as she manned her post at the desk. She glanced at the caller ID, which read "Luther." It crossed her mind to let her brother leave a message, as it seemed she must always do when calling him, but she was bored with the magazine in her hand.

"Hello?" she answered as if she didn't know it was him.

"I can't make it work, Christine," he jumped right into his reason for calling.

"Explain yourself," she retorted.

"I can usually come up with a far-fetched yet slightly plausible reason for demanding what you want. Not this time. Churches have every right to regulate their membership; requiring periodic attendance is not unreasonable. I've got nothing to work with here that will make this happen." He answered with a hint of impatience.

"Don't tell me you've run out of creativity, brother."

"Speaking of creativity, do you have to be a one-trick pony, Sister? Are letters from my office the solution to every problem you encounter? How about making the church a generous offer to retai your membership?" Luther countered with a heavy sigh, evidencing growing irritation.

"Well, one costs me nothing, and the other costs me something," she matched his irritation. "Hang on a minute; the cleaning service is leaving."

Christine scribbled a check at the desk, handed it to Sylvia, the crew leader, and escorted them out the back door.

"I'm back," she spoke into her phone and paused before continuing. "Okay, Luther. It chafes me, but I'll try your suggestion," she conceded.

"Good. I know you need this, and it's your best chance," he softened. "It also wouldn't hurt if you threw up some Christmas lights on your house and showed you're part of the greater community. People will respond to that."

She pressed the end-call button on the phone, reclaimed her seat at the desk, and reached for a piece of monogrammed stationery. The ivory linen sheet with a swirling gold foil W at the top remained blank as Christine gathered her thoughts and determined the amount certain to garner a positive response from Grace Fellowship Church. Confident of success, she wrote out her proposition and prepared the check. Will would be along soon to collect it from her mailbox.

Ava knocked on Jonathan's office door and let herself in before he responded. He looked up from his sermon preparation to see her walking toward him, mouth agape and holding out a letter. She said nothing as she handed it to him but remained in place to watch her Pastor's reaction as he read the contents.

Pastor Jefferson,

I received your letter indicating my 60-year membership at Grace Fellowship Church will be terminated at year's end unless a monthly appearance is made. Having severe misgivings about the Christian nature of such a threat, I offer a counter-proposal.

Enclosed, you will find a check for $50,000 to retain my membership at GFC without further hazard of removal for the duration of my lifetime. Cashing the check will suffice as your favorable reply.

Sincerely,

Christine Williams

Jonathan let out a low whistle and sat back in his chair. Ava held up the check still in her hand.

"Well, that's a first!" he remarked at last.

"I thought Marcus and I had seen it all," Ava said incredulously. "What are you going to do?"

"Before I tell you, let me ask: What would Marcus do?"

Ava lowered herself onto one of the two straight-backed chairs in front of the Pastor's desk and thought briefly. "He'd say church membership is not a commodity for sale - at any price," she declared.

"Then he and I are on the same page. I have to tell the deacons about this. But I will also tell them we can't possibly accept Mrs. Williams' offer. Sound like a plan?"

"Sounds like a good plan," Ava encouraged. She stood and placed the check before him on the desk and turned to go.

"I just want to know one thing," she hesitated at the doorway.

"Why?" Jonathan guessed.

"Yeah. Her membership obviously means a great deal to her, but not enough to attend services. Could it just be to ensure her obituary says she was a church member? That used to be important to people 40 or 50 years ago, but not anymore. Besides, she could write a check for far less than that amount, and other churches would happily oblige. I just don't get it."

"I don't get it either." Jonathan was stumped. "But I've got a sermon to write and a group text to send to the deacons. I'll ask them to come a few minutes before Sunday service and confirm we're not selling memberships to Grace Fellowship Church."

Ava closed Jonathan's door and sat down at her own desk. "Thought I'd seen it all," she muttered, turning her attention to the remaining unopened mail.

CHAPTER THIRTY-FIVE

Grant opened the lid of the wet garbage cart with one hand and, hanging onto the knotted top of the trash bag, flung it backward in his other hand to get the momentum needed to heave it up, over, and into the cart. Marie had cleaned the refrigerator, and the bag was loaded with expired condiments and uneaten leftovers. It landed with a squishy thud on top of previously deposited bag, and Grant dropped the lid. He was eager to get back inside the house before the light rain soaked through his flannel shirt.

He turned toward the house and glimpsed someone sitting on the Norman's back porch steps, sheltered by the overhanging roof. The figure had elbows balanced on knees and head in their hands. *"Micah,"* Grant noted and headed inside his back door.

"How about a game of cards?" Marie suggested to her husband as he brushed droplets off his sleeves.

"Sure," Grant muttered.

"You said 'sure,' but you don't seem sure," Marie observed.

"I should do something first. I'll be back in a few minutes." Grant headed to the front closet to retrieve a coat and knit cap. As he came through the kitchen again, he said to Marie: "Micah's sitting on his back porch steps. I should check on him – doesn't look like all's well."

"Take your time, then," Marie encouraged.

Grant headed out the back door and out of his comfort zone. Given the choice between playing a quiet game of cards with the woman he loved and diving into the murky swamp of someone else's emotional upset, he'd take the former every time. Grant avoided drama. But he could not deny the gentle voice of the Spirit impressing him to talk to his neighbor, and he was not about to trade obedience for a poor night's sleep.

He walked across the driveway lit by the floodlight mounted on the garage and over to the back porch where Micah still sat, head in hands.

"Hey, man. I saw you sitting here when I took out the garbage. Want some company? If not, I have to play cards with my wife. I always lose, so it's not a bright prospect."

Micah looked up and smiled weakly. He moved over on the step, indicating Grant could sit. He said nothing.

Grant sat next to him. After a minute of feeling awkward and inadequate, he ventured: "So, how was your day today?"

"Am I a jerk?" Micah asked, ignoring Grant's question.

"Generally, no. Are you going to tell me something to challenge that opinion?"

Micah also ignored that question and asked another of his own: "You know Will is trying to date my sister?"

"He mentioned he'd asked her out. That's all I know. I don't get too invested in these things until we get a 'Save The Date' card in the mail."

"I shouldn't be too invested either, but here I am, wishing it wasn't happening," Micah confessed. "And the thing is, I have no idea why it bugs me. Shelby deserves to be appreciated by a man, and Will's not a bad guy. I'm just struggling with it. She's floating on a cloud around here, and I think she can tell I'm not on board – which makes me a selfish jerk."

"Lord, send Marcus over here!" Grant prayed with urgency. He felt over his head with Micah, but Marcus did not appear.

"If you're not sure why it bothers you, maybe it's not what's really bothering you," Grant heard himself say.

"Hmmm." Micah considered the suggestion, and the men sat in relative silence. Lovie was watching holiday programs inside the house, and the men could hear the faint strains of the theme song from Frosty The Snowman.

"I'll be glad when Christmas and New Year are over," Micah groaned.

"Me too! We're going to Florida in January, and I'm ready to see my grandkids and put my feet in some warm sand," Grant enthused. "But you probably have a different reason," he added more soberly.

"I just want to be done with the last of the firsts, you know?" Micah replied.

Grant didn't know what he meant and turned to Micah, wearing an expression that requested further elaboration.

"This year, we've been through the first Valentine's Day without Dahlia, the first Easter, anniversary, birthdays, family vacation, back-to-school, Halloween, and Thanksgiving. Christmas and New Year are the last of the firsts to get through. They've all been hard. But then comes the anniversary of the day she died. Do we commemorate that? Is there cake? I don't want to make a big grief-fueled holiday of it, that's for sure. And what comes after that? Do we start a fresh cycle of the seconds?"

"I'm sorry, man," Grant sympathized as he comprehended Micah's burden. He didn't have a clue how to reply past those simple words, so he blurted out what came to mind. "I'm sorry, too, that you got the third-stringer sitting here with you. Marcus and Cal seem to know what they're doing when they talk to people.

I'm not sure what to tell you, Micah. If I think about putting myself in your shoes, I'd cry like a baby, and I suppose you have. And after that, I guess I'd do what I thought best. Everyone's different, and I don't believe there are rules. You want cake? Have cake! You want to let the anniversary slide by quietly? Do that. This is your grief and your family, and you're in charge.

I want to tell you, though, from my perspective you've done a great job. Chase and Lovie seem to be doing well, and that's huge. I didn't know your wife, but I bet she'd be proud of how you've held your family together so well despite this horrific loss." Grant was out of thoughts and words.

Micah looked Grant in the eye and said, "Thank you. Hearing another man say that, especially you, means a lot."

Grant lay in bed, wondering what Micah meant by "especially you." He didn't have the nerve to ask Micah why he'd said it. But before he drifted off to sleep, Grant prayed:

Thank You, God, for the privilege of encouraging Micah. Thank You for making Your strength perfect in my weakness. Please help Micah survive these upcoming holidays and thrive in the New Year. He'll only thrive if You draw him to Yourself and give him repentance and faith. I ask these gifts for him in Jesus' name. Amen.

Chapter Thirty-Six

One by one, the houses and landscaping on Cedar Street were bedazzled with strings of holiday lights and evergreen wreaths with colorful bows. Marcus and Grant wrapped the boxwoods surrounding their porch with the new white lights and placed one of Marie's electric candles in each of the side and front-facing windows. Elodie insisted on hanging the red bells and a few small branches of white pine on the porch header herself. They were off center, but nobody commented on that.

Micah Norman outlined his home's eaves and porch railing with large, classic-colored bulbs while Chase and Lovie poked a half-dozen three-foot plastic candy canes into the ground on either side of the front walkway. Shelby covered the front door with a life-sized mylar portrait of Santa, neatly cutting out the mail slot and doorknob. Their holiday decor left no doubt children lived in the house.

This year, even Bobby McBride, who always visited his daughter's family in Florida for Christmas and skipped decorating altogether, made a tiny effort. He tossed a Grinch welcome mat on his front porch, which actually couldn't be seen from the sidewalk.

What shocked them all was when a decorating company with a lift truck came to install dangling icicle lighting along the roofline of Christine Williams' house. They also hung natural green wreaths with red plaid bows on each front window. Bobby, who'd lived kitty-corner from her for 40 years and knew for a fact she'd never decorated her home in

December, declared hell officially frozen over.

The Downtown Committee commissioned new light pole banners that read: "Festive Faircourt" in cherry-red letters on a snow-white background bordered in lime green. These banners appeared intermittently all over town, but they were concentrated down the four business blocks of Main Street, where each black light pole had a planter box at its base and was connected by long strings of patio lights near its top. Each planter was filled with red twig dogwood branches, short-needled green boughs, and painted white pinecones. Additionally, business owners coordinated to have the corners of every street-level window sprayed with flocking to mimic frost.

Two enormous boxwood wreaths with red velvet bows hung side by side on the white front doors at Grace Fellowship Church. But the decoration that drew every eye was the elegant, life-sized nativity scene displayed in the left side yard only 20 feet from the sidewalk. Covered by a rough-hewn lean-to and illuminated with three floodlights, the set included Mary, Joseph, and baby Jesus in a manger, one golden-winged angel, a donkey, three shepherds, and six sheep in various positions. Jonathan and Kesha Jefferson had just finished repainting all the figures in the church basement while trying to keep their energetic boys at a distance with snacks and a children's holiday movie in another room.

The result was worth their effort. Grace Fellowship's nativity scene rivaled all others in town, including the one displayed by the grand Catholic church, Saint Anthony of Padua, whose life-sized scene was ill-maintained and shabby.

The plan was to meet outside the friend's house at 6:30, after everyone had dinner, and then walk together to the downtown tree-lighting event. All the shops would be open late that Saturday evening, and Latte Da was providing free spiced cider and hot chocolate courtesy of the Downtown Committee, which spent the small remains of their annual budget on it. At 8 p.m., Santa would arrive on a Faircourt fire engine and throw the switch to illuminate a 22-foot blue spruce set up in front of the courthouse.

The friends filed out of their house and down the porch steps, waving goodbye to Cal, who would "hold down the fort," as he claimed. Bobby greeted them as he approached: "Sure is a good night for walking about – clear and crisp!" Rover was at his heels for the moment but would abandon him before the next block. He wasn't a following cat.

Lovie darted from her house, pulling a cap over wild blond tresses, her pink nylon coat unzipped and flapping as she ran to greet June, who hadn't seen her in several days. Shelby and Chase stepped onto their porch, and Micah followed, closing the door behind them.

Marie stared at Christine Williams' house adorned with bright LED icicles while they waited for the rest of the Norman family to reach the sidewalk. She wondered what they could do to affirm and reinforce her unexpected participation in the neighborhood Christmas decorating. Ava noticed her friend's steady gaze across the street.

"Deep thoughts?" she asked Marie.

Before she could answer, Micah announced cheerfully: "Okay, all here. Let's go!"

"Wait!" Marie exclaimed. "I was wondering...I had an idea...before we go downtown, let's sing a Christmas carol across the street."

"Directly across the street?" Elodie wanted clarification.

"Yes. Let's reward her for her effort at participating in the neighborhood Christmas decorations. Clearly, they're for our enjoyment more than hers since she doesn't see them inside her house." Marie made her case.

The others exchanged glances all around to gauge mutual agreement. Ava understood the potential for influence on their neighbor would likely be in small gestures. She threw her support in first. "Let's do it!" She gave Marcus a light elbow nudge when no one else was forthcoming.

"Okay, we can do dat," he was persuaded. He grabbed Grant's arm and crossed the road as an example to the others, who cautiously complied and followed.

"Well, pick one I know," Bobby grumbled as he went along.

"Handle's Messiah it is!" Grant teased.

"We know *Deck The Halls*," Chase spoke for the Normans.

"That's a great opener! Let's sing that one and *Silent Night,* and then we'll be on our way," Marie was pleased to wrangle two songs from her reluctant choir.

Elodie shot her a look over the rim of her glasses but took her place as the group formed two lines at the bottom of Christine Williams' front porch.

June hummed their pitch, and they all broke out into Deck The Halls, a muted version.

"Louder!" Marie chirped at them.

Obediently, everyone raised their volume and sang it through. As the last fa la la la la faded, no one was sure Christine had heard them. She never appeared at the door. Undeterred, Marie prodded June to start them on *Silent Night*. They sang reverently through the old carol. June, Grant, and Shelby carried the melody, and Ava and Elodie sang beautiful harmony. They sounded pretty decent until they got to the first "heavenly peace" when four voices cracked, and someone hit a clunker on the high note slide.

When they finished the song, they shuffled down Christine Williams' walkway and began their trek downtown for the tree-lighting festivities and free goodies.

"I saw her in an upstairs window. She saw us. She heard us!" Ava informed the group.

"Does your wife realize she can't sing?" Chase, acting the imp, whispered to Grant.

"She knows, but that doesn't stop her. Sings from her heart, not her mouth," he replied.

Chapter Thirty-Seven

"**S**ilas!" Chase spotted his friend half a block away and shouted his name in greeting.

Shelby froze. If Silas were here at the Christmas tree lighting event, his dad would be, too. She allowed the rest of the walking party to pass her, positioning herself at the back of the pack to give herself time to collect her thoughts before their inevitable meeting. She'd only received Will's note yesterday afternoon and hadn't come to any conclusion about the requested second chance. Instead, Shelby spent the time feeling sorry for herself that Dahlia wasn't there to talk it over with. She'd always trusted her best friend to warn her about the weirdos and jerks after losing confidence in her instincts to spot them. She grieved for Dahlia anew. But ready or not, decision time was upon her.

Shelby gave herself the once-over in a boutique shop window. Mascara and lip balm were all the embellishments she'd applied for the family outing, and they would have to do. She was glad she'd worn her ivory hat and mitten set with her fitted black pea coat, which looked smarter than her everyday army green parka.

"Will, Sam, Silas," Marcus nodded as he greeted each family member.

"Dad, can Silas and I take Chase and walk by ourselves? We'll meet up at the Christmas tree at eight o'clock. I'm old enough to watch out for them and make sure they behave." Sam made his plea.

"I'm not Chase's father, but I'll let you and your brother test your wings. Remember, this is a test," Will responded.

"Can I go, Dad?" Chase petitioned Micah, who instinctively looked for support from Shelby. She'd been right next to him but wasn't there now.

"Okay, I guess. This is also a test for you!" he responded, following Will's lead.

The boys hurried off toward the bakery, Flour & Flake, where kids could frost their own Christmas cookie for 25 cents. Will, who'd spotted Shelby, made his way toward her. He did not know how their reunion would play out, but he was eager to put himself out of his misery one way or another. The week since their disastrous date had been filled with self-recriminations and mental flagellation. He recognized those thoughts came only because he still had tenuous hope of a relationship with Shelby. Whether she dashed that hope or encouraged it, at least the uncertainty would be eliminated, and he counted on that bringing relief.

As he neared, she made eye contact and gave him a warm smile, and it told Will what he needed to know. He returned her smile wholeheartedly.

"I hear there's free hot chocolate at Latte Da," Shelby kiddingly suggested and laughed.

"I hear there's a 'Wanted' poster with my face on it in their window for the crime of destroying their men's room. I'm afraid I can never go there again as long as I live," he answered playfully.

"That's okay. It would only be a real problem if you got banned from Maco's Tacos. Do you think we can avoid a biohazard incident there?"

"I limit myself to spilling my guts at one business establishment per calendar year. So, as long as we go before New Year's, we'll be golden. Were you asking me for a date?"

Shelby couldn't help but chuckle. This guy was quick and witty.

"My grandmother says women who ask men for a date are 'brazen.' She's the last human being on Earth still using the word 'brazen'."

"I'm sure I misinterpreted what you said," Will corrected himself.

"What I meant was, would you go out for tacos with me next Friday after work?"

"I would," Shelby answered, touched by Will's sweet concern to uphold her reputation in Grandmother's estimation.

They walked several steps behind Shelby's family and neighbor friends. They continued a relaxed conversation about the shops they passed, their mutual affinity for Faircourt, and a shared commitment to support its local businesses. Their conversation didn't get too personal, didn't delve into deep convictions or painful histories, just kept it light and friendly. And fun.

As he listened to Shelby share her opinion about the vintage silver tree and color wheel in the window of The Copy Shoppe, Will reveled in happiness and in happiness's first cousin: relief. They'd addressed their awkward situation head-on, laughed at themselves, and moved past it. He believed he'd also navigated past 'two-star waiter' comments and demonstrated to Shelby that he had a personality underneath his initial nerves. His confidence found a footing. He was glad for the second chance she gave him and realized it showed on his face when he caught his reflection in the window. *"So, that's my happy face,"* he thought. *"I'd almost forgotten."*

"...between whimsical and garish," Shelby continued. "It's not the aesthetic but the nostalgia that draws me to it. It represents a time when life was less hurried and more respectful – when people didn't expect to be on a first-name basis the minute they met someone."

"Our parent's generation let that go. I wonder why," Will mused. "I agree; it's a shame, Miss Norman."

"This is a red-letter day! Nobody has ever called me 'Miss Norman' in my entire life, I think.

"Sounds pretty retro/hip. Do you like it?"

"I do, actually," Shelby grinned.

"Then 'Miss Norman' it will be."

After strolling both sides of the four-block business district, it was time to meet the boys at the Christmas tree. Will spotted them, walking on the curb.

"See, Dad; no one's had their teeth bashed out in a gang fight or gotten wasted. Did we pass the test?" Sam asked with a bit of sass.

"Prove it!" Will matched his son's saucy attitude. "You can walk straight, but let's see those teeth!"

Sam, Silas, and Chase dutifully produced wide-faced grins.

"What do you think, Miss Norman?" Will sought her input.

"Looks like they aced that test," she answered with a wink directed at her nephew, Chase.

Down the street on the previous block, the fire engine delivering Santa to the tree lighting blew its horn, and Will put his arm around Shelby protectively, who, at that distance, was not in the least bit of danger.

Lovie, approaching with Micah and her neighbors, saw the mailman's move toward her aunt and taunted: "Oooooooo!"

Unembarrassed by the seven-year-old's mocking, Shelby leaned into Will's side. Since childhood, she hadn't felt protected by a man for too long and appreciated his consideration. Will kept his arm around her throughout the lighting ceremony.

No one in the Cedar Street group recognized the man in the red suit making a big production of flipping a switch, though they knew his name: Luther Hall. He'd played Santa for the Faircourt Christmas Committee for the past 15 years. He considered it his way of giving back to the community even though the back of the fire truck he rode on displayed a sign advertising his legal services. Despite what he told himself and others, Luther's motive wasn't purely altruistic.

Once Santa flipped the switch and ooohs and ahhhs abated, the friends and neighbors began a brisk walk home in the chilly evening air.

"What's that swishing noise?" Marie asked her walking partner, Elodie.

"Oh, probably my bread wrappers!" she answered.

"Your what?"

"My boots have a little wear, and I didn't want wet feet. Didn't you ever hear of wearin' bread bags over your socks to keep your feet dry? Been doin' it since I was a kid. Everybody did it back in the day!" Elodie explained to her friend.

"Well, you could stop doing that now that bread costs nearly the same as a cheap pair of rubber boots at Big Mart," Marie suggested.

"Nope. Not giving up my bread bags for winter walks. Brings me back to my childhood like few things can anymore," Elodie insisted, grinning.

Marie laughed and teased: "I don't know how far you plan on taking your childhood regression, but don't start wearing diapers just yet!"

Elodie smiled again, wrapper tops poking from her boots and swishing as she walked. "Too late," she whispered under her breath too softly for Marie to hear.

Chapter Thirty-Eight

"Mornin', Caledonia. Good to see you up and at 'em!" Elodie greeted her breakfast partner, who was waiting for the coffee to finish brewing.

"Caledonia? Don't even know what that one is," Cal confessed, chuckling.

"It was what Scotland was called before it was called Scotland."

"Okay, then. Not even 7:00 a.m., and I've already learned something today."

Elodie opened the pantry cupboard and frowned. No more oatmeal left. Then she perused the contents of the fridge and freezer.

"If I made French toast and sausage, would you eat some?" she asked.

"With my ears shaking! Wow. A cooked breakfast on a Thursday and learnin'. This is shaping up to be a great day."

"Well, go sit down and get outta my way," Elodie instructed.

"Yes, mam!" Cal poured his coffee and obediently went to the breakfast table.

"You got your actual Secret Santa gift for Grant all figured out?" she made conversation as she pulled ingredients from the fridge.

"As a matter of fact, I do. Ought to be arriving next week," he answered confidently.

"I'm jealous. Time's gettin' short, and I still don't even have an idea for my person, let alone done with it. Well, I take part of that back. Every idea I have blows the bank account," she lamented.

"Too bad I'm not your person; otherwise, I'd say 'go ahead and blow the bank account,'" Grant laughed as he strode into the kitchen.

Elodie brushed off his comment. "You want French toast and sausage, too?" she asked.

"That's a dumb question," Grant answered, giving her a side hug. He opened the dishwasher, pulled glasses out of the rack, and put them in the cabinet above.

"Well, you need to get outta my hair and give me some space. Go sit with Caledonia over there."

"What's Caledonia?" Grant asked Cal as he took a seat beside him.

"Scotland before it was Scotland. Everyone knows that!" Cal answered smugly, winking at Elodie.

"How 'bout you, Grant? You got your Secret Santa gift in the bag?" Elodie asked.

"No. I have the opposite problem; all my ideas are too inexpensive. I don't want to look like a cheapskate."

Elodie looked over the top of her glasses at Grant. "It's never bothered you before," she cracked a sly grin.

"Yup. Grant's tighter than two coats of paint," Cal piled on, and Elodie burst out laughing.

"What's so funny?" Ava asked as she strolled into the kitchen with Marie at her side.

"We were discussin' Grant's frugality to his face," Elodie replied.

"Oh, yeah! Grant's got deep pockets and short arms," Ava readily agreed and then froze. She looked at Marie and mouthed, "I'm sorry."

"No offense taken," Marie soothed. But with hands at her sides, she waggled her left one at Grant to flash the generous diamond ring, silently assuring him she appreciated his money management skills. It helped calm his defensive posture and take his friend's teasing in stride.

"But we were also discussin' progress, or lack of it, on our Secret Santa gifts. You girls got yours figured out?" Elodie moved the conversation into safer territory.

"I do," Ava answered.

"I'm all set," Marie affirmed.

"I smell sausage!" Marcus yelled, emerging from the study and heading toward the kitchen.

"Looks like I'm cookin' for everyone. You girls included?"

Ava and Marie nodded their confirmation, and Elodie dumped the remaining sausage links from the package into the skillet.

"Good morning, Beautiful," Marcus gave his wife a peck on her cheek.

"'Beautiful' isn't cookin' your breakfast. I am!" Elodie chided him.

Marcus was approaching to get a mug for his coffee and offered her a fist bump, which she accepted with a smile.

"Does anybody have anyting pressing for Tursday Meeting? Do you tink we can skip it tonight?" he asked.

Glances were exchanged, and nobody objected. Cal agreed for himself and June, who was having her devotional time at the piano. The sweet notes of *Jesus Paid It All* drifted into the kitchen.

"Looks like you're free to abandon us," Grant noted dramatically before adding, "on the condition you tell us what you'd prefer to be doing."

"It's not my preference, but I need inspiration for da Secret Santa assignment. Tought it would be helpful to see what da mall has to offer. Christmas is less den two weeks away."

Ava put her hands on her hips and shouted an accusation. "Who are you? And what have you done with Marcus?"

Marcus raised his eyebrows, speechless.

"The real Marcus Van Zant has never, in his lifetime shopped for a Christmas present before December 23rd. So, where did you hide his body? He'll want a Christian burial," Ava feigned seriousness.

Elodie put her spatula down and stared thoughtfully at Ava as she continued her good-natured rant. "I hope you might shop for me while you're at the mall tonight. What a delightful change it would be not to get what's left in the stores after everyone else has picked through the merchandise!"

"Ah, truth spoken in jest," Grant observed, grateful to have the spotlight on one's perceived shortcomings shifted to someone else.

"I'd go with him if I were you, Ava," Marie advised. "I gave up leaving Grant's presents to chance long ago."

"It's true. She buys what she wants and hands it to me, saying I bought this for her and should wrap it. Actually, I have no qualms with that," Grant admitted.

"And I'm never disappointed. Not since that year you tried to give me a certificate to be fitted for golf clubs and a package of lessons. I prefer things I want instead of things you want for me." Marie firmly stated this and then kissed her husband's bald head gently.

"Live and learn, guys," Grant laughed.

CHAPTER THIRTY-NINE

ovie popped a chunk of sugar cookie dough in her mouth behind
June's back. They had planned to bake cookies together since the
Faircourt tree-lighting gathering, and this Saturday afternoon was perfect. The first snowfall of the year covered the town with a baby blanket
of white powder, and holiday music floated to the kitchen from the
living room where Rennigers and the Van Zants were watching White
Christmas.

"Are you excited about the snow, Lovie?" June asked

"I wuv da snow! I hope there's enough to swed on later," she answered
as clearly as she could manage.

"Got a mouthful of dough, do you, girl?" June stated rather than
asked with a tiny chuckle.

Lovie looked up at her dolefully, through long eyelashes, and gave her
a guilty smile.

June picked up the corner of the apron she'd tied around Lovie's body
and wiped away a bit of dough that missed her mouth. "There's no
harm. Just remember, we're making cookies for many people – all your
household and this one. I can tell you, Mr. Renniger, Mr. Van Zant, and
Mr. Sherman can eat their weight in Christmas cookies, so we must crank
them out."

"What about Mr. McBride? Will we make some to give to him?" Lovie
asked, concerned for the neighbor she thought was lonely.

"Mr. McBride is away visiting his granddaughters and their parents in Florida. He won't be back until the end of January. But I'll tell you what: You can make a special cookie just for him, and we'll put it in the freezer until he comes home. How's that?"

Lovie sifted through the collection of Christmas cookie cutters on the counter and selected a large house-shaped one. "I'll make him a house and frost it yellow like his real house!" she exclaimed. Then she furrowed her brow.

"What's the matter, dear?" June noted the change in her expression.

"If I wanted to make a house cookie for you, I don't know how to decorate it to look like stone," she lamented.

June, always looking for an opportunity to share the love of Jesus with her young neighbor, saw her chance. "Hmm. You're right; that's a hard one. But since this house isn't my forever home, why don't you make it look like what you think my heavenly home might resemble?"

"There are houses in heaven? That's weird. I thought there were just clouds up there," Lovie answered.

June reminded herself not to go down the rabbit hole of eschatology with the second-grader. There is no need to distinguish between the current Heaven and Earth and the new ones. *"Keep it simple,"* she thought, *"and get to the reason for Christmas."* She glanced at the timer set for monitoring the batch of cookies in the oven and saw there were still five minutes before she needed to take them out.

"Jesus told his friends that He was going to prepare a place for them with many dwellings, and He promised He would return one day to gather all His friends still on Earth. Are you His friend, Lovie?"

"I don't know," she answered honestly.

"Would you like to be?" June asked directly.

"I don't know," Lovie repeated, afraid of disappointing her neighbor.

June scrambled to find her footing. *"Maybe she doesn't know. Surely the Holy Spirit must work in her heart to give her repentance and faith,* and if this is not His timing, all my prodding will be for nothing," she reasoned.

She watched the little girl with a blonde ponytail, wrapped in an adult-sized apron covered in pink cupcakes, walk to the kitchen table and investigate the old Tupperware bowl filled with food coloring, plastic bottles of candy decorations, and small tubs of sprinkles. She was so sweet, mischievously fun, and forthright, and, June realized, spiritually lifeless. June forced back tears, eager to breach the rims of her eyes. *Have hope!*" she admonished her own heart.

Now, June needed to talk about Christmas if only to revel in her delight in the outrageous wonder that God would come to Earth as a tiny baby, bringing the hope of salvation for all who would believe. So, she pivoted.

"It's good to say you don't know when you don't," June reassured her. "Too many people pretend to have answers to things they're unsure of, which can cause a lot of trouble. Always say what you mean, Lovie," and, after a pause, continued. "Now, I mean to tell you everything I like best about Christmas, and then you can tell me what you like best, okay?"

"Can I go first?" Lovie negotiated.

"The floor is all yours!" June agreed.

Lovie looked at the floor in confusion. "I don't want it. Do you mean for me to mop it?" she asked, unfamiliar with the old-timey idiom.

"Sorry. That was grandma-speak. It means you can talk, and I'll listen."

"You have to use the grandma-speak with other grandmas if you want me to understand what you're saying," Lovie explained as if June were also seven years old. And then she giggled as she recalled, "Sometimes Daddy doesn't understand what Chase is saying when he teenager-speaks."

"I'll try to keep it in mind," June tried to hide her amusement as she sat at the table next to Lovie. "Now, back to what you like best about

Christmas."

"Okay. I like presents best, of course! And making cookies and eating cookies. And I like Daddy is home for lots of days and that I don't have to see Joey John at school for two whole weeks because I don't like him. He spit at me on the playground. He missed, but I spit back and got caught. Then I had to sit alone in our empty classroom even though Addy and Lena saw him spit first and told the teacher. She didn't care." Lovie gulped some air and began again. "Oh, and another thing I like is I told Aunt Shelby I couldn't remember what Momma looked like, and she got me a framed picture of Momma and me for my nightstand. I love that picture! Momma's so pretty. Now, I'm done. It's your turn!"

Lovie had a way of knocking the breath right out of June. It was impossible to come at her with an agenda or even its spiritualized cousin: intentionality. For all the good June longed to pour into this precious girl she adored, Lovie would measure and accept the doses on her terms. In her seven-year-old life, there had been injustice and heartache, and Lovie was growing a hard little shell to protect herself. She took control where she could. "Now, I'm done. It's your turn," she'd said. *Checkmate,*" is what June heard. *"The best you have isn't bigger than my pain."* And though Lovie wasn't mature enough to express herself that transparently, June saw it clearly.

"I like presents, too," June began. "And the very best present was when God came to Earth as a baby, lived sinlessly, and died on the cross for my sins so that I could have the assurance of a heavenly home with Him. No one will ever be mean to me in that home, and no one I love will die again."

Then June looked Lovie square in the eye and explained as if she were also 65 years old.

"Life isn't like that now, is it? For some reason, we expect it to be even though this world is full of sin. Our hope for lasting joy and security is found only in Christ and His promises. It can never be placed in this life and the things that won't last."

She wasn't sure if what she'd said would stick with Lovie or even if she understood it. The first batch of cookies was ready to come out of the oven, and as June rose to get her oven mitts, Lovie threw her arms around June's waist and hugged her. Indeed, Lovie did not understand all that June said. But she loved how she said it – like she was a significant person who deserved a significant answer. Lovie saw that clearly.

Christine Williams added two more logs to the fire she'd started in her oversized living room fireplace to warm up the elegant house prone to drafts. She returned to the couch, facing the picture window to watch the powdery snow fall. She covered her legs with a faux-fur blanket but could not relax. Anxiety squeezed her heart. For the third time that day, she reached for her smartphone and pulled up her banking app. Grace Fellowship Church still had not cashed her check.

Chapter Forty

Latte Da had few customers at 6 PM on a Monday, although the surrounding shops on Main Street enjoyed steady traffic. It was crunch time for gift finding, and Marie had driven Elodie the few blocks downtown after dinner. Elodie said she had direction for her Secret Santa gift and was confident she would find what she was looking for in one of the shops. To keep the "secret" in Secret Santa, El suggested Marie park herself in the coffee shop until her mission was complete. She'd meet her there later.

Marie sat in a stuffed chair close to the front window to people-watch as she sipped a hazelnut latte. She recognized Shelby Norman as soon as she came into view, even though she was enveloped in an army green parka, and waved to her through the window when she got closer. Shelby waved back and entered the coffee shop.

"You here by yourself?" she asked Marie, brushing snowflakes from her uncovered hair.

"I brought Elodie downtown to go shopping, and I'm waiting alone for her unless you join me. Will you?"

"Sure. I'll be right back," Shelby answered and walked to the counter to place an order, which was produced quickly.

"That was fast," Marie remarked as Shelby set down her drink and removed her coat.

"Well..." Shelby waved an arm at the empty tables and missing patrons.

"They don't have much to do at the moment." She arranged herself in a comfy chair next to Marie.

"What did you get? I don't frequent coffee shops often and never know what to order. I just defaulted to their flavor of the day, which is hazelnut," Marie made small talk.

"I got a special called Coconut Snowball. I tried it before, and it's pretty good."

"You come here often, then?"

"No. Actually, just once, with Will," Shelby volunteered a tidbit of personal information.

"Ahh, Will," Marie added a playful sultriness to her voice.

Shelby giggled. "We were here not more than ten minutes before he vomited in the men's room and went home. I've been on speed dates that lasted longer."

"Get out! My first date with Grant was at a movie theater, and he bugged out before the introductory credits concluded. I didn't know why until he sent an apology note a few days later. He said he'd gotten a migraine and feared he would throw up on me. That's funny that Will did the same thing to you," Marie laughed.

"Seriously? I had no idea this was a thing – right down to sending an apology note. Will did that, too."

"It's either a man thing, or you and I are extraordinarily terrifying women," Marie was regaining her composure.

"I'm not terrifying," Shelby assured her.

"No. But you are intimidating. Not to me, of course, because we're birds of a feather. But, you are, girl."

"Noooo," Shelby was disbelieving.

"You're very pretty and on the quiet side. Men can't handle that combination. They assume still waters run deep, and they're intimidated if they can't figure out what's going on underneath the pretty. I, on the other hand, have other qualities that people find intimidating, but we'll save that discussion for another day."

Shelby took a long sip of her coffee and considered the plausibility of her neighbor's assertion. Finally she said: "I can't help either of those things, nor do I think I would if I could."

"Good! Just be yourself," Marie agreed.

"But..." Shelby was unsure of how to say what she felt.

Marie helped her. "But you want him to like you."

"Yes. Unfortunately, I come with some baggage in my past."

"Sin! You come with sin in your past. So does Will. So did I. So does everyone. You're not special like that," Marie cut to the chase. She was a bottom-line girl, but she could see Shelby had tensed her jaw in reaction to her words. So she softened them.

"I was married before I was married to Grant Renniger. For three years until he walked out and said he didn't love me – never loved me. I thought either he was the world's greatest actor or I was the world's stupidest girl because I had believed he loved me. It seemed more probable that I must be stupid, so that's what I told myself."

Marie noticed Shelby relaxed her jaw and moved forward, engaged in her words. "And then, of course, I was damaged goods as a divorcee. I'm still the only one of my close friends who is divorced. It used to bother me when I was your age, but now I realize everybody is damaged goods because of sin, and they know it deep down. We don't all sin the same, but God is holy, and His standard is perfection, so it only takes one sin to deserve eternal separation from Him. The fact is, I deserved separation from God way before I was divorced."

Shelby's face brightened. "You're right, I messed up way before..." She left that sentence unfinished but continued. "I never imagined that realization could be a comforting thing!"

"Girl, whatever sin in your past has you thinking that you're marked or damaged because of it, let it draw you to Jesus in repentance so you can receive the forgiveness that will free you from the weight of shame you carry."

"Marie, I'd give anything to be free of it," Shelby confessed.

"Do you mean that? And what if you had to give up *everything* instead of giving up *anything*?" Marie challenged her.

"Does it cost everything?" Shelby asked with wide eyes.

"It may."

Shelby sat back in her chair and let out a deep sigh. "What do I have if I don't have forgiveness? What is my life without freedom from shame and peace with God?" she asked quietly.

"You can have that forgiveness and freedom right now. You don't have to live without it another minute if you're ready to tell God you're sorry for every sin against Him, big and small, and that you're trusting in Jesus' life, death, and resurrection to save you from condemnation."

"Here?!" Shelby was startled by the suggestion of imminent availability.

"Right here on the holy ground of Latte Da," Marie smiled, scooched to the edge of her seat, and offered her hand for Shelby to take. "All you have to do is ask. He's never refused a request."

And through a simple and sincere prayer of repentance and faith, God saved Shelby Norman in the coffee shop.

CHAPTER FORTY-ONE

"God saved Aunt Shelby," Chase whispered to Marcus, seated beside him at Grace Fellowship Church's Christmas Eve service.

"I heard dat," Marcus whispered back. He patted the boy's knee and looked down the row, grateful Shelby had invited Micah and Lovie to attend church with her and Chase.

"Aunt Shelby bribed Dad and Lovie to come tonight with a meatloaf dinner," Chase confided.

"She make good meatloaf?" Marcus was interested.

Chase nodded his head up and down vigorously.

"Shhh," Ava gave her husband a gentle nudge.

He turned to her with an apologetic grimace.

After the opening prayer, Pastor Jefferson instructed the congregation to stand before the worship leader, who led them in singing a few carols. June accompanied on the piano. She'd gotten the call requesting her to fill in for the regular church pianist, Beth-Ann Sharp, who accidentally flipped a pot of boiling water and scalded her hands that afternoon. June gave Lovie a little wave from her bench on the platform.

Standing in the row directly in front of Grant and Marie were little old Bill and Martha Torres, both into their ninth decade, holding hands as was their custom in church.

"I hope we're that cute at their age," Marie murmured to Grant.

"We should start practicing now." Grant took his wife's hand and gently squeezed it as June played the opening chords of *God Rest Ye Merry Gentlemen*.

Down the row from the Rennigers, Elodie tapped Cal on his arm.

"So glad you felt up to coming. It wouldn't have been the same without you here, Cavalry," she whispered, forgetting she hadn't even known Cal last Christmas besides an introductory video chat meeting.

"Me too," he answered, smiling back at his friend.

Sitting at the far end of the pew, Shelby stole a glance at Will and his boys sitting across the aisle, and she smiled when she saw he was looking at her.

"Merry Christmas," she mouthed to him.

"Merry Christmas," he returned her greeting with a full smile that raised his eyebrows.

A few days prior, Shelby had told him of her confession of faith in Christ. Naturally, Will was delighted, both for her sake and his own. But he kicked himself for assuming her spiritual condition because she'd been attending church with Chase. He had intended to ask her about it when they'd met at Latte Da, but that was derailed. So, when Shelby told him on her front porch about her serendipitous encounter with Marie at the coffee shop and what had taken place, he rejoiced with her. But he also made a mental note never to get the cart before the horse again.

When the congregation finished singing *God Rest Ye Merry Gentlemen*, June began playing a few introductory bars of *Away In A Manger*. From the back of the sanctuary, a careless latecomer let the heavy security door close loudly behind her. As she marched the length of the center aisle, all could see a mature blonde woman wearing a tan cashmere overcoat with a mink fur collar, matching mink hat, brown calfskin gloves on her hands, and a designer purse on her arm. She sat in the front row, even though everyone else was standing.

"I don't believe my eyes! It's Christine Williams!" Marie said excitedly to Ava beside her.

"I don't think she's here due to a spiritual awakening. She had to come or lose her membership next week. That's why she made such an entrance – so we couldn't miss her." Ava tried to curb her friend's enthusiasm. The only one in the household she'd told about Christine's attempt to buy her membership was Marcus, since Jonathan had asked what he would do in that situation. Ava wanted her husband to confirm her prediction, and he did.

June was so shocked to recognize the elegant visitor that she briefly lost her place in the song and stumbled on the piano keys. From then on, she kept her eyes on the sheet music before her and played through *O Come All Ye Faithful* and *Silent Night* without a hiccup.

After the carols, Pastor Jefferson preached a brief sermon on Matthew 1:23:

Behold, the virgin shall conceive and bear a son, and they shall call his name Immanuel.

He explained the meaning of Immanuel and the implications and applications of God being with us. When his sermon concluded, ushers distributed small taper candles with drip catchers to each adult in attendance, and these passed a flame amongst themselves until they were all lit. Then, the overhead lights were dimmed, and the congregation sang *Go Tell It On The Mountain* by candlelight.

Pastor Jefferson stood in the foyer to greet his congregation and wish them a Merry Christmas as they exited the church and headed home. Christine Williams made a beeline for him.

"My name is Christine Williams, and you may not remove my name from the membership rolls because I'm here!" she was emphatic.

"Welcome, Ms. Williams, we're so glad you came!" Jonathan was cheery.

"I did not care for your sermon," she was abrupt.

"That's okay," Jonathan replied.

"Nor did I care for your piano player, who might take a lesson here or there," she barked.

"Alright. That's okay," Jonathan nodded.

"And those vanilla-scented tapers should have been unscented," Christine reprimanded.

"Maybe so, but that's okay," Jonathan agreed.

"Why are you repeating 'that's okay' like a poorly educated parrot? Are you dim, young man?" she demanded to know.

"It's all okay because we're here to worship God, Ms. Williams, not you. I hope next time you're with us, you'll have a much better experience for having a clearer expectation of who we're trying to please." Jonathan was unflappable under the torrent of her disapproval.

"Really!" was all Christine Williams could manage to sputter as she walked away. She'd been put in her place and knew it.

CHAPTER FORTY-TWO

Elodie was singing in the kitchen at 7:00 a.m. She woke up with an earworm of the last carol sung at the church service yesterday evening and had *Go Tell It On The Mountain* on repeat. As she sang, she slid a large pan of frozen, pre-made cinnamon rolls into the heated oven for Christmas morning breakfast.

June joined in the next verse, and Elodie, who had her back to the hallway and hadn't seen her emerge from her bedroom, was startled.

"Girl! You about gave me the widow-maker!" she exclaimed as she closed the oven door and stood upright. She braced herself against the island and touched her heart to emphasize her claim. "Not used to seeing you this early, either."

"Oh, I'm sorry for the fright, Elodie. But it's Christmas morning! Merry Christmas!" June apologized and giggled. "Cal's awake and will be right along. And as soon as the smell of those cinnamon rolls hits the vents, the Rennigers and Van Zants will be down here in a jiffy."

And she was right. Before the rolls were out of the oven, Marcus made drip coffees for everyone except Grant, who was already sipping his tea with honey.

"The rolls are ready to come out, but they still have to cool a bit. Elodie, do you mind if we set them outside on the porch so they'll cool faster?" June pleaded.

"No problem. I guess someone's in a hurry for cinnamon rolls,"

Elodie answered gamely.

"Someone's in a hurry for Secret Santa gift opening," Cal tattled on his wife.

"I've been so excited about this first Christmas in Faircourt with all of you. It's just been Cal and me for all these years, and there's not much we can do to surprise one another. So I can't wait to see all my friend's surprises when we open our Secret Santa gifts," June confessed.

"Awww," rang the chorus from Ava, Marie, and Elodie while the guys looked at one another and wordlessly agreed to let the women's response suffice.

"I'm all for speeding up the process to dive into those rolls," Grant offered to carry the pan to the porch with outstretched hands. Elodie shoved oven mitts on them and let him take them away.

"While we're waiting, why don't we all get our gifts and put them under the tree so we'll be ready to open them after we eat," Marie suggested.

"Let's do dat," Marcus agreed.

Ten minutes later, they extricated gifts from hiding places and put them under the lit tree in the living room, and they consumed still-warm cinnamon rolls with pleasure in the dining room.

Dabbing his mouth after eating his second roll, Grant announced: "June, I believe the moment you've been waiting for has arrived!"

She didn't need to hear it twice. June abandoned her coffee and half-eaten second roll for a seat in the living room, and the others followed her lead.

"We should remember that it's Jesus' birthday, not ours, before we open gifts. Grant, would you mind reading us the Christmas story from the Scriptures?" June requested.

Happy to oblige, Grant reached for his cell phone in his back pocket and pulled up the Bible app. He read the familiar Luke chapter 2 passage solemnly.

"Never ceases to amaze me that God sent His Son in such humble circumstances," Ava commented when Grant had finished.

"He has given us much better than Jesus had," Cal agreed, looking at their surroundings.

"So many wonderful gifts, not including the ones under the tree!" Marie added.

After a pause to reflect on God's kindness to all of them, June rose to retrieve her gift and presented it to Marie.

"All this time, I thought Elodie had me! I was a little put out when she asked me to drive her to town to buy it." Marie laughed as she opened the beautifully wrapped package. "Aprons! Three of them, and they're beautiful prints!" Marie gushed.

"I remember you said when we baked pies at Bobby's house that regular aprons got soaked when you cleaned. So, I made you water-resistant ones that wouldn't," June explained.

"How thoughtful! Thank you!" Marie got up and hugged her.

"Me next!" Elodie shouted, already out of her chair. She handed a box to Marcus.

"Uh-oh. What could dis be?" Marcus wondered aloud. He opened the lid and saw a wad of tissue paper. He lifted it and was surprised to see the loudest, gaudiest silk bow tie he'd ever seen. Marcus held it aloft for all to gaze upon, and Cal gasped in astonishment.

"I didn't know what to get you until your wife said you'd want a Christian burial. Then it came to me! You need a bright tie to be buried in so the angels will see you comin'."

"No doubt dis will do!" Marcus answered. "I like it!" he added, noting the quality.

"There's more in the box," Elodie prompted.

Marcus dug through more tissue paper and found two bags of imported Ethiopian coffee beans. "I like dese, too!" he said, clutching them to his chest and breathing in the delightful scent.

Sitting on the floor next to the tree, Ava moved a massive box to June's feet.

"For me?" she squealed, tearing the elegant foil wrapping. Inside, she found a smaller wrapped box and laughed. "This keeps the surprises coming!" Inside that box was another.

"Last one," Ava chuckled.

June pulled out three CDs of Sovereign Grace music, which would all be new to her sacred music collection.

"Grant said you commented on the music in his car when he took you joy-riding before your birthday party last summer," Ava explained.

"This is that? I'll love it then. So edifying! Thank you! The gift thrilled June.

"You lucky girl! I was left with your name," Marie joked as she handed Elodie a package that looked as if it had been professionally wrapped.

"Oh, am I now?" Elodie asked, accepting the package. Once opened, she lifted a lilac-colored chenille robe from the box. "This is gorgeous!" she shouted, holding it against her body. "Thank you, Marie!"

"Now you can retire the one with the tattered cuffs," Marie suggested.

"Oh, that's not happenin'. My momma bought me that one!"

"I didn't know that. Well, you can return this one then."

"Nope. Keepin' it, too. No law sayin' a woman can't have more than one purple robe. This one will be for showin' off," Elodie said with a grin.

"I guess da men are left," Marcus said, bringing Cal a large gift bag emblazoned with the face of Saint Nicholas.

Cal lifted the bag by its handle, and the bottom fell open, depositing a pile of folded fleece on the floor. Cal bent to pick it up.

"Whoa, this baby has some heft to it!" he remarked with surprise.

"It's a weighted blanket. I researched, and da internet says it helps wit restless legs at night. A little bird told me about dat problem," he added with a sly grin. "I hope it helps you."

"Your internet research was a waste of time. I could have told you it helps. Should have asked me." Elodie muttered.

"I'll make a note of dat for future reference: Ask Elodie before asking da internet," Marcus teased.

"If it helps me, it will be a godsend. I appreciate it, Marcus," Cal thanked him.

"If it helps him, my shins will appreciate it!" June added.

Grant rose from his seat, retrieved his gift from under the tree, and handed Ava a box that looked like a 5-year-old had wrapped it.

"Keep your expectations low," he whispered to her.

"Wrap this yourself?" she taunted him. "Next year, you could ask Lovie for help."

Ava set to undoing Grant's sub-par packaging efforts and produced a thermal lunch bag from the box. The outer material had tiny pink roses with green leaves on a Robin's egg-blue background. Her initials were monogrammed in white thread at the top. Also pulled from the box was a matching carafe for hot or cold drinks.

"This is beautiful, and I can use it for work. Tell me Marie didn't help you pick this out," Ava challenged.

"He tried to enlist my help, but I refused on the grounds he would have to reveal the name he drew, and that was against house rules," Marie confessed.

"She left me high and dry," Grant sulked.

"You didn't need her, Grant. You did good on your own, and I wouldn't mind if you were my Secret Santa every year!"

Grant brightened at Ava's encouragement. "I'm glad you like it."

"Okay, Cal. What'd you get, Grant?" Marcus demanded.

Cal grinned. "Ava, can you reach that last bag and give it to Grant?" he requested.

Ava obliged and handed Grant the red bag with a knotted green ribbon.

"Doesn't look like you got dat horse!" Marcus chuckled.

Grant pulled two boxes out of the bag. "Golf balls! I need these. Thanks, man!"

"Take a closer look," Cal instructed.

Grant opened one box and saw the balls were customized with a picture of a thoroughbred racehorse and, underneath, the words: Hoof Hearted.

"Oh, but I did get that horse!" Grant roared. "Two dozen of them!" And he passed them around so the others could inspect them and laugh.

"This has been so much fun; let's do it again next year!" June suggested.

"Fine by me, and God be willin'," Elodie spoke for everyone.

CHAPTER FORTY-THREE

"You're not serious!" Elodie laughed but placed her hands on her hips, indicating she didn't honestly think it was funny.

"Yes, I am serious. If we take all the Christmas decorations down today, we have the rest of the week to clean and reorganize the house so it's in good shape for New Year's Day. We should start the New Year in shipshape! It's what I've always done," Marie declared.

"But, it's only the day after Christmas. I've always left my decorations up past New Year's Day and, most of the time, past Martin Luther King Jr. Day, too!" After a brief pause, she asked: "What do Ava and June say about it?" hoping to enlist their support.

"Ava says she doesn't care one way or the other," Ava answered from her seat at the breakfast table. "And you won't know what June says until after she gets up and has her piano devotions."

"Is June aware, Marie, that you like to rip the Baby Jesus from his manger the day after we celebrate His birth?" Elodie was not giving up.

"Aware and complicit. She helped me take down my decorations and pack them away last year on December 26th. And if memory serves me correctly, June took down the nativity set by herself and committed the 'ripping' of Baby Jesus from his little bed," Marie retorted.

Elodie's shoulders sagged as she adjusted to the prospect of being prematurely de-Christmased. "Well, I can listen to the holiday music station until New Year's Day, or do you have a law against that, too?"

Marie chuckled at Elodie's melodramatic pout. "No law against it. Clutter the air with the Ghost of Christmas Past if you feel you can't move on with your life," she needled her friend.

The matter was settled. Marie asked Ava to enlist the help of her husband in bringing down the wreath and ornament storage boxes from the attic – when she'd finished her coffee, naturally. Grant would be tasked with removing the lights from the outside bushes and Elodie's bells from the porch header. To appease Elodie, Marie intended to ask June if she would play Christmas carols on the piano when she'd finished her devotions there. Cal, if he was up to it, could "supervise" the entire operation.

While Grant was about his task outside, he noticed the silver compact car parked in front of Bobby McBride's. It wouldn't have caught his attention if someone wasn't sitting in the driver's seat just staring at Bobby's house. Grant tried to be inconspicuous as he strained to get a better look at the occupant without attracting reciprocal attention.

He pulled a string of lights off a bush and turned toward the vehicle, pretending to concentrate on winding the rope around his forearm while taking stealthy glances at the driver. It was most definitely a woman with long black hair. *"Hispanic?"* he wondered. Setting the coil of lights on the ground, he pulled another string from the bushes and kept his eye on the woman casing his neighbor's house. But as he wound these lights around his arm, the woman started her car and turned right onto Tamarack Street. Then she parked in Bobby's driveway and stared at his house from the back side. With the vehicle's rear end facing Grant, he noted the license plate number. *"Guess I'm the Neighborhood Watch now,"* he thought.

"Are you okay with tuna sandwiches and chips for lunch, Dear?" Marie asked, poking her head out the front door. Christmas carols from June's piano flowed from the open door to the front yard.

"Marie, come here!" Grant beckoned in a low voice.

"I don't have shoes on," she answered him.

"Come here anyway, please," he said insistently, cocking his head and raising his eyebrows at her to communicate urgency.

Marie walked onto the porch in stocking feet, closing the door on the wafting carols. As Grant was about to point out the silver vehicle in Bobby's driveway, it turned onto Cedar Street and sped away.

"See that car? It was casing Bobby's house! A woman was – just looking over his house – front and back!" he relayed. "I got the license plate number. Do you think I should call the police?"

"Was she doing anything besides looking? That's not illegal," Marie reminded him before continuing. "Maybe she just stopped to text someone. It could be completely innocent like that."

"I don't think so," Grant's suspicions were not easily placated. "Maybe I should call Bobby in Florida and give him a heads-up."

"For what purpose? There's nothing he can do from Florida but worry. Here's my suggestion: Why don't you, my darling amateur sleuth, keep an eye on Bobby's house for him? If she comes creeping back with a crowbar and breaks in, then you can call the police."

"Perhaps you're right. And I will keep an eye on Bobby's house for him." Grant picked at another string of lights on the bush before him. "Hey, can I have a sandwich with leftover Christmas ham instead of tuna? Dijon mustard, not mayonnaise."

"Your wish is my command, my lord," she agreed and blew him a playful kiss.

As Marie turned to go back inside the house, a flatbed truck with a scissor lift pulled up in front of Christine Williams' house across the street. On the driver's side door was the emblem of the same company that had hung the icicle lights and wreaths on her house a few weeks ago.

"Would you look at that! Christine Williams wants her Christmas decorations taken down the day after Christmas, just like I do. It may be the first and only thing we'll ever agree on!" Marie marveled.

"We did see her at church on Christmas Eve," Grant recalled, challenging her assumption.

"Ava says she made an appearance so she wouldn't lose her membership next week."

"Since when is Ava the seer of hearts and motives?"

"Fair enough. But being in church doesn't make Christine Williams a Christian any more than standing in the Garage Cave makes me a Buick."

"Point taken," Grant agreed. He returned to completing his task and anticipating a good ham sandwich.

For a minute, Marie watched the men across the street expertly maneuver the scissor lift from the flatbed to prepare for removing the decorations on Christine's house. *"She can't be all that bad if she likes her house in shipshape for the New Year,"* Marie smiled and entered the house.

CHAPTER FORTY-FOUR

Micah planned to take Lovie and Chase to visit their grandparents, Dahlia's mom and dad, for a day after Christmas, so Shelby was fine with Will picking her up at home for their second attempt date. This time, they were going on a lunch date. And this time, it would not be in Faircourt, where any witnesses to misadventure would be locals. Maco's Tacos was out. Will was taking Shelby to Dos Loros in LaGrange, a safe distance of 14 miles away.

She was standing on the front porch when Will pulled up to the Norman house, and as soon as she saw Will, Shelby hurried down the porch steps and into his vehicle.

"Good afternoon, Miss Norman," Will greeted her with a wide smile.

"Good, good. All set. Let's go!" Shelby instructed.

Will laughed, put the vehicle in drive, and pulled away from the house down Cedar Street. "Either you're in a hurry to get this party started, or there was a change in Micah's plans, and the kiddos are home," he speculated.

Shelby relaxed as they turned onto Maple Street. "Neither, but both are good guesses. I was watching the workers across the street taking the lights off Christine Williams' house when I spotted her in an upstairs room looking back at me just before you arrived. It freaked me out a little, I guess. I've heard that you never want that woman setting her sights on you."

"I can testify to that! When I got my Postal Service job four years ago and started this route, I committed the sin of short-cutting across her grass instead of keeping to the sidewalk. She sent a certified letter on her brother's legal stationery informing me that straying from community easements was trespassing on private property. And trespassing on private property is a Class A misdemeanor punishable by a fine of $500 and a year in jail."

"No!" Shelby gasped in disbelief.

"Sure did. I keep to the sidewalks now and think of it as a metaphor for staying on the straight and narrow," he laughed.

"That's taking lemons and making lemonade," Shelby observed. "What a commendable attitude."

"Thank you. But in the interest of full disclosure and reasonable expectations, I don't always have a commendable attitude. I try to get there, but sometimes it takes a minute. Or a month."

"Same," Shelby confessed.

"So, tell me about yourself. Besides where you live, your brother's family, and that you go to Grace Fellowship and like to knit, I don't know much about you." Will was eager to learn.

"How do you know about the knitting?" Shelby asked in genuine surprise.

"Well, I deliver your magazines."

"Duh!" Shelby chided herself. "So, you just discovered something about me – I can overcomplicate and miss the obvious."

"Not the end of the world unless you had career aspirations of becoming a super sleuth," Will dismissed her self-consciousness.

They continued their getting-to-know-you banter until they reached their destination on LaGrange's Main Street, notable for the active train tracks running down the center.

Dos Loros was already popular despite being open for only six months. In contrast to the sign above the entrance, which featured a vibrant male parrot on either side of the gold lettering, the décor was a subdued palette of neutrals against a backdrop of ashy black. No sombreros. No heavy wooden furniture. It featured Spanish graffiti spray-painted in colorful but muted tones on dull black walls, contrasting with ornate ivory-painted bistro chairs around aluminum-legged tables covered with black tablecloths, above which hung oversized vintage lightbulbs in clear glass pendants.

"This is nice. Not your typical décor for a Mexican restaurant," Shelby said in approval after they had been seated and ordered.

"Pastor Jefferson recommended this place to me. Said he and Kesha had been here and loved it."

Shelby winced. "Is Pastor Jefferson aware you are taking me here?" she asked nervously.

"He does not. He just mentioned it was an excellent Mexican restaurant. Why? Is my asking you out for lunch supposed to be a secret?" Will was perplexed.

"No. Well...Perhaps we should keep things on a need-to-know basis."

"Okay. No problem." He paused while the waiter placed their sodas and a basket of chips with queso on the table. "But, I'd like to understand your reason instead of making one up in my head – which I will most certainly do because I'm insecure like that."

Shelby gave him a sympathetic smile of understanding. "Will, you acknowledged earlier that you don't know much about me, which is true. You'll discover I have some baggage: hurts and sins in my past. I want to minimize the potential embarrassment of people learning we've broken off before we ever started should you decide my stuff is a bit much for you."

Will took a chip from the bowl, swiped it in the queso, and popped it in his mouth, giving him a moment to think about his response. Shelby waited, eyes averted, studying something invisible in her lap.

At last, he answered. "Of all the explanations I could have made up about why you'd want to keep a relationship with me on the down-low, your fear of my bailing on you would never have crossed my mind. Not ever, so I'm glad I asked. Shelby, look at me," he prodded.

She looked up and met Will's eyes. He continued. "The fact is, we don't know a lot about each other, but we're starting that journey. Here are two things you should know about me: I also have hurts, history, and sin. Who knows? Maybe my stuff will be too much for you. Two, there are no sinless people on this planet, and I'm not expecting one to show up until Jesus returns. When the time is right, the best we can do is shine a light on our sin because our Enemy works in darkness. When we acknowledge our sin, it takes away his power to shame us. After we acknowledge it, the next step is to encourage one another to walk in the power of the Holy Spirit to avoid repeating it."

Shelby relaxed her tense shoulders. "I get what you mean about Satan shaming us when we hide our sin in a dark corner. Will, what would you say if I told you there's not a single one of the Ten Commandments I haven't broken?"

"I'd say that doesn't make you as unique as you think it does. And I'd remind you of what the Apostle Paul says in Romans 8:1:

There is therefore now no condemnation to those who are in Christ Jesus.

Chapter Forty-Five

Marie whipped up a pot of Stuffed Pepper Soup and a basket of heat-and-serve rolls to spare Elodie, June, and Ava from making dinner. It was the least she could do after cracking the whip on them all week to get the house ready for the New Year. After they'd eaten, she convinced the lot of them, plus Grant and Marcus, that with teamwork, they could flip all the upstairs mattresses before it was time for Thursday Meeting.

"I quit Marie's chain gang," Ava moaned as she splayed herself on Elodie's mattress, the final flip of the evening.

"Can we just have Thursday Meeting right here instead of walking all the way downstairs? Everyone's here who's going to be here," Grant requested, sinking to the floor and resting his tired back against a lilac-colored wall.

The only one missing was Cal, who had gone to bed after eating half a bowl of soup.

"Sounds good to me," replied Marcus. He dropped to the floor and rested against a side of Elodie's vanity with the enormous round beveled mirror.

Marie found a space for herself next to Grant on the floor, and June and Elodie joined Ava, sitting upright against the headboard on the bed.

"Whoever's running this meeting better get after it before I fall asleep right here," June announced.

Marie looked to Marcus, his head tipped back and eyes shut. She knew he wasn't asleep, but he wasn't leaping into action either. When she looked at her husband, Grant was already shaking his head no.

So, Marie began. "First of all, I want to say how thankful I am for your help cleaning floors, baseboards, and hall paneling. Also, for the carpet shampooing and light fixture cleaning. The house looks and smells spic and span!"

"Don't forget da basement clean-up of all da cobwebs and waterproofing of dat back wall. I tink I'll smell dat stuff in my dreams for a week," Marcus reminded her, still with his eyes closed.

"Yes, Marcus. I appreciate that monumental accomplishment, too. You and Grant did a great job. You all cleaned this place like it was a crime scene. Thank you!"

"Are we done?" June asked meekly.

"My back is done!" Elodie groaned.

"We're all done!" came a chorus from Ava, Grant, and Marcus.

"For now," Marie chuckled in semi-agreement. "Now, onto future business. This might not be a good time to ask since everyone's exhausted, but what do we want to do for New Year's Eve tomorrow? Anything?"

"Probably after a good night's sleep, we'll be refreshed and ready to ring in a New Year, I'd guess," offered June.

"If we're going to play games – and we should – maybe instead of a heavy dinner, we could make a large veggie tray with dip and snack on that all evening," suggested Marie.

"A large veggie tray?" Marcus opened his eyes and sat upright. "Are we ringing in a New Year of gloom and deprivation?"

Grant chuckled and extended his arm to give his friend a symbolic fist-bump of solidarity, which would suffice for an actual fist-bump since getting up was out of the question for the time being.

"And fruit?" Marie believed this was a real concession.

"Yes, and carbohydrates made of white flour and sugar," Elodie suggested.

"Now we're getting somewhere! And chocolate," June was emboldened.

"And summer sausage, beer cheese, and man crackers – not the girly kind!" Grant demanded.

"Dat's a party!" Marcus shouted.

"Okay, okay, okay," Marie relented. "I get the picture. One artery-clogging, sugar-spiking charcuterie board coming up!"

"How does everyone feel about sharing New Year's resolutions tomorrow night? Is everyone making one? Is anyone making one?" Ava inquired.

"I hadn't thought about it, but it's good to be intentional about living and to have goals," Marie reflected.

"I resolve to have a resolution by tomorrow night," June chuckled.

"I'll meditate on it," Elodie was noncommittal.

"I agree with you, Baby Doll, about being intentional, but my track record at keeping resolutions is dismal," Grant confessed.

"Dat makes two of us," Marcus commiserated. "But I don't tink dat means we don't keep trying."

"Hmm," is all Grant answered in response.

"Any other business to discuss? Does anyone have plans we all should know about?" Marie asked.

"We're going to Florida in two weeks. Be gone a week." Grant reminded everyone.

"Take me with you!" Elodie pleaded.

"I'm sure David and Daniel would love to see you. It's been a while, hasn't it?" Marie responded.

"Last time I saw your boys was Daniel's weddin' to Andie. That three or four years ago?"

"Four years in March," Grant answered. I remember because Marie and I called it Daniel's 'March Madness.'"

"It was hard because we loved his first wife, Ruby, so much," Marie lamented.

"That divorce was hard for everyone," Elodie agreed.

"Is it wrong to hope a marriage might not work out?" Ava asked out of the blue. She explained to all the faces looking at her, "Marley told me last week that Marit is having trouble getting pregnant, and it's causing tension with Robbie."

"Dat so?" Marcus' comment let them know this was news to him, too.

Ava turned to him and said, "I guess I kept my counsel about it until I got a better attitude. It hasn't happened yet, but the question slipped out because I've been thinking about it a lot. I want to blame Robbie for the estrangement from Marit, so it's difficult to care if he left her. I know it would hurt Marit, but I don't care about that either. I should, but I don't. That's why I didn't say anything."

Marcus laid his head back on the vanity and closed his eyes again. "I should care too, but I don't. Whether or not we care makes no difference to her and only hurts us," he said and sighed heavily.

Ava looked at Marie, surprised at what had just passed her husband's lips. They both saw – everyone saw - a glimpse of the father-hurt Marcus worked to contain over the past year. And in his voice, they heard a weariness that was deeper than his physical tiredness.

CHAPTER FORTY-SIX

"Don't you eat all the beer cheese, Callisthenics!" Elodie warned as she handed him a napkin to swipe the dab that clung to his whiskers.

"But it's so good! Is there more in the fridge?" Cal asked hopefully.

There was, but Elodie didn't want him to know that. Instead, she prodded him to take his turn at the Monopoly game they were playing with June and Ava at one end of the dining room table. The four of them had colluded earlier in the day to occupy themselves with a long-lasting four-person board game, leaving Grant and Marcus to suffer playing cards with Marie. Grant and Marcus, they reasoned, were strong, healthy men who stood the best chance of not being wholly aggravated by Marie's competitive streak, now in full bloom at the other end of the dining table.

"How long till dey drop da ball?" Marcus asked, raking the fingers of his cardless hand through the white goatee that appeared and disappeared on his chin as his mood dictated.

"The night is young, my friend! We've still got two hours," Marie answered, consulting her cell phone screen and missing Marcus' impatient eye-roll.

Grant took his turn drawing a card, beamed, and proclaimed: "Gin!" He laid his cards down for inspection and noticed his wife's frown. "You can't win every time, Baby Doll," he soothed and began collecting the cards.

Marcus seized the moment. "How about we take a break to share our resolutions before da New Year arrives?" he suggested. He considered how he might extend the conversation so the proposed break would become permanent and he wouldn't have to resume the card game.

"Okay. Potty break first, then let's reconvene in the living room on more comfortable chairs," Ava agreed and amended the suggestion.

By dumb luck, Marcus extended the 'potty break' to forty minutes. He stood by the living room window, waiting for the women to return, and commented to Cal and Grant about a passing car driving slowly down the street. This elicited a barrage of questions from Grant about the color and make of the vehicle and the gender of the driver – none of which Marcus could identify. Grant then relayed his experience of seeing a woman lurking around Bobby's house the day after Christmas. Seeing an opportunity, Marcus convinced Grant he'd been derelict in watching over their neighbor's house since that troublesome incident. He volunteered to go with him and ensure there'd been no forced entry, playing to Grant's paranoia about someone casing the house while Bobby was away.

"By da time we get our coats on, walk over to da house and mosey around, walk back and put our coats away, it'll chew up anoder twenty minutes," Marcus figured.

"Has Bobby's house been converted into a meth lab in his absence?" Marie teased when the guys finally arrived back in their living room.

"Not yet," Grant answered defensively. "If you were Bobby, wouldn't you like to know your neighbors kept an eye out on your property while you were away?"

"Of course, dear." Marie yawned and patted the couch for him to join her on it.

An unconscious chain reaction of yawns spread around the room before Marcus initiated their discussion of resolutions.

"So, I'll begin," he said, getting everyone's attention. "I am resolving to be more tankful to God for who He's made me and what He's given me. I struggle wit bot of dem when I compare myself to oders. I cannot figure out how to measure my progress, but I tink my heart will know."

Cal's critique was out of his mouth before he could stop it: "It doesn't do any good to tell someone not to compare themselves to others because I tell myself that all the time with no success. But I'm surprised to hear you say you struggle with confidence and gratitude because you're among the few people I compare myself to. I admire you, Marcus."

Marcus felt his throat tightening with emotion and decided he could not draw out a conversation on the subject of himself. He smiled at Cal and said, "Tank you, broder."

Sitting to Marcus' left, Grant went next. "I have got to be more intentional about sharing my faith with the guys I work with at Grassy Creek. And when I say 'more' intentional, I mean 'any' intentional. I've failed to share the gospel with anyone, and it bothers me. I ask myself, 'Has God been good to you, and is He worthy?' and the answer is 'Yes.' Then, I ask myself, 'So, are you a lily-livered coward?' The answer must be 'yes,' too. So, with fear and trepidation, I'm looking forward to golf season starting again in March. Pray for me."

"I will pray for you, Grant," June spoke up. "I'll pray that God will give you the courage of a lion and the wisdom to understand when to unleash it."

"I couldn't have said it better, June!" Marcus responded and slapped Grant on his leg.

"I guess I'll just keep this going in a circle," Marie said, fiddling with the gold chain bracelet on her left wrist. "Like Marcus, I can't measure my resolution, but I think my conscience will be convicted. There's too much I/Me/Mine in my life. I see it, and so do all of you. It's one thing to diagnose a problem but another to cure it. Of course, I can't sanctify myself, but I can raise my awareness and call out to Jesus. He's my only hope of salvation and more Christlikeness.

"That's pretty much what I was gonna say. If I didn't know better, I'd say you copied off my paper," Elodie whined. "I've felt convicted that I need to treat certain people better than I have. Just been too caught up with myself to be concerned that I haven't represented Christ well. So, same for me, Marie. I need less of me and more of Christ."

Nobody wondered who the "certain people" were that she referred to. She'd had a terrible start with Bobby McBride and only recently started speaking to him like a human being.

"Okay, my turn then," June piped up. "I can measure my resolution because it's either do it or don't. I intend to get involved with the children's ministry at Grace Fellowship. I love children, as you've all seen. I've had a little pity party since Shelby moved in next door, and I don't have Lovie all to myself. But now, pity party's over, and I've decided to channel my gifts and desires to minister to other children."

Cal picked up his wife's hand and squeezed it gently. "You've always had a way with them," he complimented her and grew somber. "None of us knows how many days we have left or if this New Year's Eve is our last. I probably think about it more than most, though. I resolve to focus on finishing well. My health isn't strong, but my determination is. So this year, I want to do all I can to serve the Lord and not waste time worrying about what I can't do. And I want you all to know that I pray for you daily. I can do that."

A chorus of murmured 'thank yous' replied.

"And last but not least," Ava began. "I just want to say 'good riddance' to this past year! No doubt, it was the most painful of my life. Thank you, all of you, for your kindness and understanding. I have no idea how I would have managed without all of your support. You were truly God's provision for my needs.

I was having difficulty summarizing what my resolution for this upcoming year will be. But as I listened to you, it seemed to be an amalgamation of everything you've said. I want to be more focused, thankful for what I have, and willing to share God's goodness and gospel with others. I've spent over a year nursing my hurts, and it's time to remember others struggle with hurts, too. Focusing on the girls I don't have is unhealthy because, as Scripture says, hope deferred makes the heart sick. I don't want to be heart-sick anymore, so I'm putting away my hope - tucking it away in my old cedar chest, so to speak. I'm not abandoning it, but I don't want to look at it daily. It's time to face the future with resolute perseverance and finish well."

"Good for you, girl!" Marie encouraged her friend through drowsy eyes.

"I'm right beside you, Ava," Marcus added his support.

"It's gotta be close to midnight, right?" Elodie wondered.

"Well, fifteen more minutes. We could turn the television on," suggested June, yawning.

Marcus got up and turned on the station broadcasting the activities in Times Square, but within 5 minutes, everyone had nodded off in their seats. Despite their best intentions, nobody was awake to ring in the New Year when it finally arrived.

Chapter Forty-Seven

"Happy New Year, Mom!" Grant greeted his mother when she answered the phone. "How was your Christmas with Gerard and Amy?"

"Oh, you know your brother. He didn't let the dust settle on us. There were a ton of church activities and things to do with their grandchildren, and, as Senior Pastor, he's expected to attend them all. I'm glad he brought me home yesterday before their watch-night service. I don't stay up late anymore, nope. As a matter of fact, I don't wake up early like I used to either," she said from her bed, unconsciously smoothing wrinkles from the flannel sheets that still enveloped her at 9:05 AM.

"Apparently, I don't either, even when I try to do it. I fell asleep in a chair before the ball dropped last night. None of us here made it. But I'm still an early riser. I wake up before 6 AM whether or not I want to," Grant confessed before turning his concern back to his mother. "Mom, let me ask you – was it too much for you at Gerard's? Do you want me to talk to him?"

"Honey, I'm feeling my years," she sighed. "But I'd still rather wear out than rust out. I can tell your brother when I need to skip an event and lay low for a bit."

"Oh! No doubt you're able, Mom. The question is, are you willing to do it?" Grant prodded.

Louisa Renniger side-stepped his question and responded: "There'll be no need. Your brother is retiring from First Baptist at the end of May. So, he won't have all the holiday obligations next Christmas. Of course, I'm sure he'll still be the evangelism dynamo he is today. I don't see that slowing down, do you?"

"No," Grant answered peevishly.

"That's probably where he'll invest his freed-up time. He told me about a ministry a lay member of his congregation started. They set up a canopy outside the local courthouse and asked people going in if they'd like prayer before meeting the judge. After they pray, it gives them the opportunity to ask if they're ready to meet their ultimate Judge and present the gospel of God's grace to them. Gerard thinks he'd like to join them when he retires."

"That's great," Grant responded, sounding irritated.

"What's wrong, honey?" G-Lu read her firstborn's tone.

"Do you know I've shared the gospel with exactly one person in my entire life? One person, Mom! What kind of Christian does that make me? A sorry excuse for one!" Grant complained about himself.

"Is that your brother's fault?" his mother asked pointedly.

Grant was unprepared for but not surprised by her directness. He hesitated before answering. "No. I guess I made it sound as if I resented the gifts God had given him. I don't resent them. I'm glad there are people in Christ's Church who have the obvious gift of evangelism because they make up for slackers like me," Grant said with a forced chuckle. "But I will admit, I am jealous of that gift, and it's my resolution to be more faithful in sharing the gospel this year."

"Why?" G-Lu questioned.

"Why am I resolving to share the gospel?" Grant puckered his face at the phone in his hand.

"Why are you jealous of that gift?" his mother clarified.

"I would prefer to answer 'why am I resolving to share the gospel,' if you want the truth," Grant answered.

"I'm sure you would! But it's not what I want to know," G-Lu smiled into her phone.

"Why am I jealous of that gift?" Grant restated the question, buying himself precious seconds to think of an answer. "Well, two things come to mind. One, it's a measurable gift. I've always been a numbers guy, Mom. If people respond – or even if they don't respond – you can still measure how many times you've shared the gospel. Ministries always report how many people have heard the gospel or come to Christ through their efforts. If I'm being frank, the second reason I'm jealous is that evangelism is a critical gift. The Church doesn't grow without evangelists; they also benefit from seeing the fruit of their gifts in heaven. The Church still gets by if the encouragers or givers don't do their jobs." He concluded with a drawn breath.

"What I hear you saying is that you want to be seen," G-Lu distilled his response to a concentrated sentiment.

"No!" Grant objected. "I didn't say that!"

"Didn't you?" his mother was unfazed by his vehement denial.

"I said I want to measure...I want..." he stammered. "I want...a gift critical to the Church." He stopped speaking, and G-Lu refused to step into the void. After several uncomfortable seconds, Grant acknowledged what his mother saw. "I guess I want to be seen," he admitted, ashamed.

"Now, we're getting somewhere. Grant, honey, everyone wants to be seen. Even I, at almost 95 years of age, want to be seen. I make myself difficult to ignore, don't I?" she laughed at herself before continuing. "And those who prefer to be behind the scenes still want to be acknowledged for their place there. It's human nature. We need to be valued, seen, if you will. I'm sorry if you don't feel valued, Grant."

Grant stopped her there. "It's unfair to those around me, including you, to say I'm not valued. Of course, I know you value me – and Marie, our boys, and our friends. I am blessed with people who love me and value me."

"But you want more?" G-Lu guessed.

"Oh, now you're meddling!" Grant took a good-natured poke at his mother before turning serious again. "So, that's where my human nature betrays my sinful nature, is it? When I reveal my discontent with what God's already given me?"

"You're a smart man, Grant. God gifts His Church to fulfill His purposes, not ours. So, we need to be content with our gifts and employ them to the best of our ability and beyond our ability with His help. We can trust God is good and that our faithfulness with whatever gifts He's given us will be rewarded as He sees best. And without our sinful nature dragging us down, we won't waste time jealously comparing ourselves in our heavenly home. Perhaps we might practice that right now," she encouraged. "But with all that said, honey, I can appreciate a sanctified desire to share the gospel. I'm going to pray God gives you purified motives, opportunities, and then the delight of sharing His offer of salvation with others."

"Thanks, Mom. God has used you to help refine my motives," Grant acknowledged with genuine gratitude.

"Ha! That's my gift!" G-Lu exclaimed. "But rarely am I thanked for it!"

Chapter Forty-Eight

Shelby sat gingerly on the wobbly memorial bench at the end of the grave plot for John Henry Holmes, Sr., conveniently situated across from the one she intended to visit: Dahlia Leigh Norman.

"Good grief! It feels like there's nothing between me and the concrete. If I'd known my tush would freeze on this bench, I'd have layered up," Shelby laughed nervously, addressing the headstone.

It was her first visit to her best friend since she was laid to rest exactly one year ago. Micah hadn't mentioned any plans to visit the grave himself or take the children there, so she waited until he left for work, and the kids caught the school bus before driving to Faircourt Memorial Cemetery. It shocked her to see the ground over her friend's grave already flattened and covered with dormant grass. In her memory, it was still a mound of brown earth blanketed with funeral flower arrangements. *Had an entire year really passed?* she wondered.

"So, I'm dating again," she began, hoping to keep the one-way conversation light. "Now, don't have a fit; I'm seeing Will, our mailman. It's only been two dates, and the first one shouldn't count, but he's a good guy. And not hard to look at, either," she chuckled and brushed back the hair that light winds blew into her face.

That was all the material she had for light conversation. Her emotional gear shifted effortlessly to genuine conversation like they used to share.

"I miss you, Dally. I miss skipping workouts at the gym to get tacos instead. I miss inheriting all your wrong shade of lipstick purchases. I miss going with you and the kids to the park and having more fun than they did. So many things, Dal...You took all the fun with you. Since the day you died, it's like someone replaced all the lightbulbs with 25 -watt ones. Everything got dim.

You'd be so proud of Chase and Lovie, though. Of course, it bewildered them – the shock of it. There were outbursts and attitude. But they're doing so much better. We talk about you – remember you. Miss you.

Micah - well, he's a little slower but coming along. I heard him crying in his room after we all went to bed. It's less frequent now, but I heard it two weeks ago. Dally, I'm such a coward! He needs someone to talk to, but I don't go to him because I don't want either of us to be embarrassed. What good would it do him if I cried along with him? Is that what I should do?

But just so you know, I've heard him laugh, too, and that's getting more frequent since Chase discovered he can make his dad laugh with tales from his school day. Can you believe it's his last year of middle school? Anyway, Chase always has a story for Micah. He works to come up with something every day just so his dad will laugh. He's developing such a tender heart – a softie like his momma.

And your little Lovie-belle follows me around the house like I keep chocolates or cookies in my pockets. She's attached herself to me, for sure. I hope you don't mind. But she shares her affections with Miss June next door, too.

Miss June is one of the people who moved into the Scott's house. There's a whole horde of senior citizens who bought it. Well, when I say 'horde,' I mean three couples and a single woman – all long-time friends. I know you and Micah were hoping a family with young children would buy it, but what you got are young-at-hearts instead. They're all sweet in their own way, and they've been so kind to our family. They're the reason

Chase and I...

Well, I should tell you about that. Both Chase and I have become Christians. Chase was first. The people next door invited him to church and explained the gospel. Chase asked me to church, and then Marie explained the gospel to me – but at Latte Da, not in church. Dally, it makes sense to me now! And the lightbulbs have started getting brighter for me. It's amazing; there's a calm inside of me that wasn't there before. The babies...I'm forgiven...and for everything else, too."

Shelby stopped speaking, alarmed at the realization. And then, bitter tears flowed down her cheeks, and sobs escaped her chest. She fled from the bench to the frozen grass covering Dahlia's grave and knelt on hands and knees.

"Dahlia! Where are you?" she yelled to the lifeless body below. "Did anyone tell you that Jesus died for our sins? Did you believe? Dally, I'm so sorry! I would have told you about Jesus, but I wasn't alive myself. I was as dead as you are now – only you're not completely gone! You're alive somewhere. Oh, Dal, where are you?" Shelby repeated her question, dreading the answer. Fixed on all fours and disregarding the January cold, she sobbed and grieved a long while for her precious friend as if she'd lost her anew that day.

Spent emotionally and exhausted physically, Shelby crawled back to the bench and pulled herself up onto it.

"Jesus, I don't know what to say or even if what I want to say is allowed. But her life ended so suddenly; she didn't see it coming and didn't have a chance to repent or believe. I don't think so, anyway. We always said we'd be little old ladies together, that there would be years ahead to make other choices and reinvent ourselves. But You...You had the final say. You gave me life and Dahlia, death. It should have been the other way around. She didn't kill her children; she gave birth to them – loved them. So, why? I'm not the one who should be here. Why am I above ground and Dahlia below?" Shelby prayed and expected an answer. She needed an answer.

She didn't receive the audible voice from heaven she wished for. Instead, she recalled the words from Psalm 139 that June had shared with her weeks ago in her kitchen: *"[God] writes in a book all the days He has planned for us before we're even born."*

And in her heart, she understood it was her answer. The Scripture confronted her with God's sovereignty over His creation without further explanation. Period. End.

Shelby stood and returned to her car, looking like she'd fought a battle. Her blue jeans were stained and soaked below the knees from kneeling in melting frost; her eyes were red-rimmed and puffy; and her hair was wind-tousled. Indeed, she had battled. And although she didn't feel like a winner, neither did her Enemy.

CHAPTER FORTY-NINE

Marcus and Grant would have canceled Garage Cave night if they'd only thought of themselves. The Garage Cave was still going to be chilly even with the space heater set on high. The pantry was light on man-food snacks since the New Year's Eve binge. And they'd also need to round up substitutes for Cal and Bobby.

Micah and Will were the most obvious candidates, but Grant had reservations about pairing them up since Micah expressed discomfort about Will dating his sister. However, Marcus, always ready to wade into emotional waters, thought it the ideal scenario for the two men to address the issue since they'd have older men there for support and counsel.

"We don't want dem coming to blows over dis," Marcus cautioned.

"If I'd never told Marcus about my conversation with Micah, I wouldn't have to be any part of this," Grant chastised himself before relenting. "Well then, how 'bout we host men's game night in the basement instead of the Garage Cave? We can move the space heater down there, and it's bound to be warmer," Grant suggested.

"Dat's fine. I'll tell Micah and Will dey have to bring da snacks," Marcus agreed.

"If you haven't figured out the way into Shelby's heart, you've found the direct route to mine," Grant gushed as he took the bag of honey-mustard pretzel pieces from Will's hand. He figured he could play the bull-in-the-china-shop, charging into conversational territory ripe with potential for drama, as long as Marcus was there to pick up the pieces.

"Well, I remember the ruckus this stuff caused the first time I was invited to men's game night, and figured I'd bring the people what they want," Will laughed and took his place at the card table.

"It's showing just dat kind of consideration dat makes a good man," Marcus acknowledged, equally pleased. "But you have stiff competition for da title of 'snack king.' Micah brought a plate of homemade chocolate chip cookies - wit walnuts and still warm."

"I concede the title!" Will said, bowing in feigned obeisance toward Micah.

"Shelby made them," Micah admitted with apparent reservation.

Will reached for a cookie and took a healthy bite. "Delicious!" he mumbled with his mouth full.

"He'd say that if they tasted like charcoal briquettes, which they do not," Grant needled. "I'm sure because I'm about to eat my fourth!"

"Pace yourself, Grant," Marcus rebuked.

"You're right," Grant conceded. Instead, he opened the pretzel pieces bag, dumped the contents in a plastic bowl, and plunged his hand in to retrieve a fistful. He clutched them to his chest so he wouldn't drop any.

Micah chuckled at Grant and turned his attention to Marcus. "What's the game tonight?"

Marcus flipped a box of cards onto the table. "Rook!" he exclaimed. "Since it's a game for partners, I'll spare you both and take Grant." His claim would leave Will and Micah as partners.

"Don't let him fool you. He wants me because he knows I'll do the math," Grant defended himself while chewing.

Marcus dealt the cards, and the men made their bids. Will won the bid for his team; in short order, they won the first round. Micah matched his strategy and success in the second round. And the third.

"Okay, you guys. Settle down," Marcus admonished.

"They're on a roll!" Grant complained.

Will and Micah's team did not settle down. They continued to win bids and rounds until the game was a total wipeout.

"So dat was a lot of no fun," Marcus grumbled.

"Look at my head! Is there blood? I feel like I've been beaten about the head!" Grant stood and lamented with dramatic flair.

"I could go upstairs and ask Marie for some gauze," Micah taunted.

"Ha! We make a good team!" Will nodded at his partner.

"I bet that's what you say to my sister," Micah shot back with the kind of laugh that stayed in his throat and conveyed he was not amused.

Sensing it was time to panic, Grant looked at Marcus, who was studying Will.

"Not yet," Will met the challenge graciously. "It's too soon to know."

"Here's what I know," Micah pounced. "My family has just been through the kind of year that nightmares are made of. I lost my wife. My kids lost their mother. And Shelby lost her best and only real friend. There are no spaces within the walls of my house for more loss or pain. We're packed full. So, I swear, if you bring an ounce of it to Shelby, a pound of it will be returned to you."

Grant's eyes widened, his palms became clammy, and he thought he could feel his blood pressure elevating. This was even less fun than being beaten. To make matters worse, Marcus continued to study Will. He didn't jump into the fray.

Will drew a deep breath and let it out slowly as he sat back in his chair. He caught Marcus' eye before he answered Micah. "I'd love to be able to tell you that won't happen, Micah, because I'm not keen on hurting Shelby or being hurt myself. I haven't attempted to date anyone until four years after my wife divorced me for the sole purpose of avoiding pain. But if it's a guarantee you're looking for, I haven't got one. I'm a sinful man, and the older I get, that fact becomes more clear, not less. When I think I have a grip on myself, pride, jealousy, and selfishness rear their ugly heads and remind me I'm not the man I want to be. Frankly, it's humiliating, but I've learned the value of dropping any pretense I'm better than I am. And I'm encouraging Shelby to do the same. As we get to know one another as sinners reliant on the grace of God to make us both more Christlike – because that's both of our desires – then we'll forgive when we inevitably hurt one another. Or, she may decide I'm not what she wants. But she's going to know there's some brokenness under all this eye candy," Will finished, trying to lighten the heaviness of his confession.

Leaning forward in his chair across the table, Micah looked Will in the eye and responded: "So, your strategy is to under-promise and over-deliver?" He would not make this easy.

"Is that what it sounded like to you?" Will asked with genuine curiosity.

"That's what it sounded like to everyone!" Micah attempted to draw Marcus and Grant to his side.

"Not to me," Marcus spoke up with gentleness. Grant shook his head from side to side.

Micah's expression turned pained. He had assumed the older men would understand his concern and back him up. Their reaction caught him off guard.

Marcus stepped in. "What would you say if you were in Will's shoes? Would you say what da broder wanted to hear, or would you tell him da truth he didn't want to hear?"

Micah sat back in his chair as he appeared to consider the question. After a prolonged pause, it became clear he wouldn't answer at all.

Marcus turned his chair toward Micah. "Of course, you want to protect your family. Dat's what a good man does. But you shouldn't protect dem from da possibility of happiness and love. Shelby tinks she may find dat wit ugly old Will here. Let her enjoy da possibility. And if it ends in hurt, remember: a bruising is not da same as a stab wound. All hurt is not equal, and you don't need to fear it all. Eye-candy! Sheesh!" He paused and added with a full-faced smile, "And dere may come a day when you, too, will be ready for happiness and love again."

Micah swallowed hard and tried to stop the tears that welled up. It was as if Marcus had pressed a release valve when he'd said not all hurt needed to be feared. Instead of the hurt he feared for Shelby, his own pain sprang to his eyes and spilled over. He was used to it happening since he had lost Dahlia. But he preferred it to happen in the privacy of his own bedroom rather than in the view of other men.

Will understood it well, having shed plenty of tears in the year he'd lost his wife to divorce. "That's just liquid fear pushed out of hiding," he acknowledged.

Micah gave him a grateful half-smile, and Marcus gathered up the cards and gave Will a nod, an understated gesture of respect for how he'd handled himself.

Grant took the last two cookies off the plate and stuffed them in his mouth to soothe his frayed nerves.

Chapter Fifty

Marcus hit the radio button in his van to turn it off after the weather report. "Looks like you're getting out of town just in time," he remarked to the Rennigers as he pulled into a spot at the Louisville airport's departing flights unloading zone. "Eight to twelve inches of snow falling tonight will give me a workout tomorrow.

"You might recruit Chase to help you shovel," Grant suggested. "My brother and I used to go around our neighborhood after a decent snow-fall and make good money as kids. I bet he and Silas could make a killing at the homes of senior citizens around the church neighborhood if they wanted to."

"We'll think of you shoveling while we're swimming in the pool with the grandkids," Marie needled, opening the van door and stepping onto the sidewalk.

"Tanks for dat. And while you're swimming, you can also be tinking of who else will pick you up from the airport when you return," he sarcastically threatened from his driver's seat.

"We appreciate you, buddy," Grant said, pulling their bags from the back of the van. "Take good care of everyone back at the house and don't let the place burn down while we're gone. We'll see you next Saturday!"

"And please thank Ava again for teaching the ladies' Sunday School class for me these next two weeks. I know it's in excellent hands," Marie added.

"Have a good trip," Marcus shouted over his shoulder before Grant shut the door.

"Good morning, Grammy! Good morning, Papa!" 15-year-old Georgia greeted her grandparents as she entered the kitchen in red-plaid flannel pajama pants and a white, sleeveless crop top.

Technically, the kitchen was just a corner of the open-concept home the Renniger tribe rented in Naples, Florida, for their belated family Christmas. Boasting four bedrooms, three bathrooms, and a screened pool, Marie thought the private home she located on the internet would be more comfortable than the hotels they'd used for previous gatherings.

"Well, good morning, my Chipper Skipper!" Marie returned the greeting. "Is Little Grant awake yet? I have pancakes and bacon hot and ready."

Georgia laughed. "Make sure you call him 'Little Grant' to his face. He thinks he's a man since he turned 17. But don't get your hopes up that you'll see him before noon, Grammy. He sleeps in on Sunday mornings. Saturday mornings, too. Really, any day we don't have school."

"What about church on Sunday? Do you all go to a later service?" Grant wanted to know.

Georgia sat beside her grandfather at the kitchen island and answered: "We're pretty much Christers, Papa. We go to church at Christmas and Easter." She noted the frown on Grant's face and added defensively: "Uncle David and Aunt Liza, too! Do I smell coffee?"

"You drink coffee?" he asked her, disbelieving of that and the fact she was showing her bare midriff.

"Yeah. For at least two years now," Georgia answered blithely. "Andie and I always get lattes at the coffee shop."

Andie became Grant and Georgia's stepmother a few years prior, less than two years after their parent's divorce. Grant and Marie met their son Daniel's significantly younger bride for the first time at their rehearsal dinner. This would be only their second meeting since the wedding, and Marie hoped this week together would help them get to know Andie and make headway in building a warm relationship as they'd enjoyed with Daniel's first wife, Ruby, whom they missed dearly.

Grant shot Marie a look that communicated his dismay at their unchurched 15-year-old granddaughter, who had been consuming caffeine stimulants since she was thirteen. Marie set a plate of pancakes with bacon in front of Georgia. While her granddaughter dug into her breakfast, Marie returned her husband's concern with a shrug.

"I smell bacon!" Daniel announced, inhaling as he entered the open common space from the bedroom wing. His twin brother, David, and sister-in-law, Liza, followed behind.

"We hit the grocery store before we arrived yesterday afternoon. Got everything I need for my two days of cooking," Marie informed them.

She'd worked out with her daughters-in-law that each would be responsible for two days of cooking duty so she wouldn't have to do it all. Marie accepted Liza would make the vegetarian, gluten-free, dairy-free meals she'd started eating since her cancer scare last summer – information she withheld from Grant to keep him from fretting about it for weeks before their vacation.

"I'll go to the store tomorrow for my ingredients," Liza volunteered.

"We'll be ordering takeout for our meals. Andie doesn't cook," Daniel informed them.

"What do you mean, she 'doesn't cook'?" Grant looked at his wife, hoping for a sign from her that he'd misheard.

"She never learned, and she's not interested in it," Daniel said matter-of-factly.

"But she doesn't have a job! How can a woman who doesn't work say she doesn't cook either? Your mother had a job and cooked for you boys and me," Grant was perplexed.

"Grant!" Marie scolded as she wondered where Andie was, hoping it wasn't in earshot of what her husband had just said. "The younger generation does things their own way. If it works for them, they're fine," she tried to diffuse the tension she saw gripping Daniel's jawline. "By the way, where is your sweet little wife, Daniel?"

"She's a late sleeper. Do you have any opinions about that, Dad?" he challenged Grant.

Grant held his hands up in surrender. "I do not," he said. *I do not have any that you'd like to hear,"* is what he wanted to say.

"I have an opinion! Anyone want to hear it?" Liza exclaimed cheerfully.

"I do, Aunt Liza!" Georgia jumped in, eager to help distract her dad from being defensive and angry.

"I noticed the swimming pool has a heater. I think we should go swimming after breakfast. Hey, whose phone is buzzing?" Liza asked.

Marie looked at her phone on the large dining table, still on silent mode but lit up and vibrating against the wood. "That would be mine," she answered as she walked across the room to retrieve it.

"Hello, Ava girl! Miss me already?" She answered after noting the name on the caller ID. "Oh, no!" she exclaimed after listening a moment. Her reaction got everyone's attention. "Oh, that's awful! I'm sorry! Of course, whatever you need."

"What?" Grant interrupted.

Marie held up an index finger as a silent appeal for patience to wait for her answer.

"It's no problem at all. We'll be praying for you and that it's all resolved quickly," she spoke into the phone and then hung up.

"Remember the snow Faircourt was supposed to get last night? Well, they got ice instead – about 3/4" covering everything. It's pulled down tree limbs and power lines all over town, including on Cedar Street. Ava said it'll take days to restore power. Our house still has power by a miracle of God's hand, but the Normans don't. She asked if they could use our bedroom and the guest room to house them while we're away, and you heard me say, 'Of course.'" Marie relayed the situation to her curious audience.

"Marcus was right. We escaped the storm in the nick of time," Grant replied. *"And landed ourselves in the eye of another one,"* he mused.

Chapter Fifty-One

No one in the Norman family knew precisely when the power went out during the night. They only knew the temperature in their old drafty house was now a chilly 56 degrees. Chase and Lovie hastily packed a few warm outfits, clean underwear, and pajamas into shopping bags as instructed. Micah and Shelby, already packed, were gathering things from the fridge and freezer that were too dear to leave to spoil. Chief among these ingredients were two bags of frozen shrimp, a large pork roast, and a warehouse-store-sized box of pizza rolls that staved off teenage Chase's hunger pangs between meals. They'd bring these as well as a gallon of milk, two boxes of cereal, an unopened loaf of bread, and their lunchmeat supply to their next-door neighbors, who generously offered to put them up until their electricity was restored.

The family, after gathering the children and groceries, put on winter coats and carefully walked across several yards of icy terrain to their neighbor's porch. They noted and lamented the large limb of the old magnolia that lay broken on the lawn, leaving a gaping hole in the symmetry of the former beauty.

"Welcome to your temporary home!" Ava greeted the little family and ushered them into the center hall of 306 Cedar Street. "Take your coats off, and I'll show you the bedrooms you'll be using. You can put your clothes up there."

"I want to stay with Miss June!" Lovie said brightly.

Sitting at the piano in the living room, June heard the request and giggled.

"I'm afraid Mr. Sherman has already claimed that for himself. But you can stay with Aunt Shelby in a pretty pink guest room upstairs," Ava offered.

"Okay! I've never been in your upstairs," Lovie agreed.

Marcus and Elodie took the grocery bags to the kitchen, and the Normans followed Ava up the paneled staircase. Micah and Chase were ushered into the Renniger's comfortable bedroom, and Shelby and Lovie across the hall in the opposite front bedroom.

"We were just about to have a small home service in the living room since church is canceled. Drop your things, and you can join us," Ava invited their guests with more instruction than invitation in her tone.

"Come on, Dad!" Chase encouraged his hesitant father and, without waiting for a response, turned and headed down the staircase with Shelby and Lovie close behind him.

Two extra chairs from the dining room were brought into the living room for the children. However, they requested to sit on the floor as they had when they'd been part of Thursday Meeting last summer, and the request was granted. Chase sat at his aunt's feet and wiggled an index finger at her, indicating he wanted her to bend down to hear a secret.

"We got Dad and Lovie to church two months in a row!" he whispered.

Shelby gave him a thumbs up and a conspiratorial smile and, from the corner of her eye, spotted her brother trudging glumly down the stairs. She patted the empty seat on the couch next to her, and Micah obliged her direction.

June played a few bars of Amazing Grace on the piano to introduce the familiar hymn. Micah listened as the others, except for Lovie, who was unfamiliar, sang four verses. He felt self-conscious and out of place. The idea of having church in your home when the building intended for that purpose was closed by an act of God seemed strange to him. Fanatical, even. But he reminded himself that sitting through his neighbors' religious ritual was a small price to pay for the hospitality he appreciated.

When the singing ended, Marcus began teaching from the Bible. He didn't stand in front of them with formality but led from the upholstered rocking recliner, his open Bible resting in his lap. He introduced his text with a question: "If God wanted to get your attention, what would He have to do?"

Lovie, unfamiliar with the concept of a rhetorical question, raised her hand and shouted her answer simultaneously. "He should turn the clouds into letters to spell out a giant message in the sky!"

"That'd even get my attention," Micah thought, amused by his daughter's response.

"Yeah, dat would get a lot of people's attention! But, dere might be confusion about who da message was for. And if God put your name in dere, it wouldn't be private, would it?" Marcus reasoned. "Today, we're going to look at a different way God sometimes uses to get our attention. I'm going to read Psalm 13:

How long, O Lord? Will you forget me forever? How long will you hide your face from me?

How long must I take counsel in my soul and have sorrow in my heart all the day?

How long shall my enemy be exalted over me?

Consider and answer me, O Lord my God; light up my eyes, lest I sleep the sleep of death,

lest my enemy say, "I have prevailed over him," lest my foes rejoice because I am shaken.

But I have trusted in your steadfast love; my heart shall rejoice in your salvation.

I will sing to the Lord, because he has dealt bountifully with me.

Marcus explained how this Psalm, written by David, came after some great personal triumphs in his youth but before he was King of Israel – at a long, low point sandwiched in between. He pointed out how David felt then: like God was hiding, sorrowful all day long, and lifeless. Marcus wondered aloud if anyone could relate to such a low time.

Micah related, and suspected Marcus picked this text specifically for him.

As he continued to teach, Marcus noted how David's pain drew him to God in prayer and pointed out that that's precisely where God has our attention – when there's nothing to do but wait for Him to act on our behalf. And then Marcus encouraged the tiny congregation with some benefits of being in the place of waiting. He told them that their patience in waiting for God to act could be an offering of faith and love to Him and that Scripture promises in Isaiah 64:4 that God, indeed, acts for those who wait for Him. As his third point, Marcus highlighted how they could find delight in recalling how God had come through for them in the past, especially as it related to their salvation and how that made a world of difference for David. He concluded by explaining that salvation is obtained through faith in Jesus Christ as the Son of God, who died for our sins and rose to life in victory over the grave.

To end the service, Marcus prayed they would all honor God in their waiting seasons, confident that He was acting on their behalf behind the scenes and delighting in His history of doing so. The entire service lasted less than 30 minutes.

The ladies filed into the kitchen to prepare the day's main meal, and Micah excused himself from the men to go back upstairs to the Renniger bedroom. He closed the door, slumped in one of the matching cream-colored leather recliners at the end of the bed, and pondered a new thought: *"Could God be trying to get my attention?"*

CHAPTER FIFTY-TWO

"Bobby! What are you doing here?" Ava's voice rang through the entrance hall, catching the attention of Elodie, who was making pie crusts in the kitchen. "We weren't expecting you back until the end of the month!"

"I heard about the ice storm and thought I'd better hightail it home to ensure no water pipes had burst in the house. I should have left a key with Marcus before I left. Won't make that mistake again!" he answered.

"Come in, come in!" Ava offered. Bobby stepped inside the house as Elodie sauntered down the center hall, wiping floured hands on the apron she wore over a bright purple sweater dress.

"Your house is okay, then?" Elodie asked, inserting herself into the conversation.

"It's chilly but dry," Bobby answered.

"Have you had lunch? We just finished, but I could fix you a ham and cheese sandwich," Elodie offered as if making Bobby McBride a sandwich was part of her routine.

Bobby looked at Ava to gauge whether it might be a trap. Ava shrugged and disappeared behind the pocket doors of the living room, joining Marcus, Micah, and Chase, who were binge-watching old episodes of Petticoat Junction.

"Okay. I wouldn't mind that at all. Doesn't make sense to buy groceries till the power comes back," he replied and followed Elodie down the center hall. He observed her gait was off.

"Is your back still giving you trouble, Elodie?" he asked, concerned.

"It's on my last nerve! Ice packs, heating pads, and pain relievers are not curing this ailment. I'll probably have to take myself to a doctor," she lamented as they entered the kitchen.

June was sitting at the kitchen table with Lovie and Shelby, engrossed in coloring a mandala poster with colored pencils.

"Look what the cat dragged in!" June teased when she laid eyes on Bobby. "You've been missed," she added more thoughtfully.

"Hello, ladies," Bobby acknowledged June and Shelby. "And Little Miss," he nodded to Lovie.

"Do you want to color with us? We've got lots of pencils," Lovie invited.

"Miss Elodie is going to make me a sandwich. So, I'm going to sit over here at the counter and eat it. Don't want to get crumbs or anything on your pretty picture," he excused himself.

"That's a good idea," Lovie accepted his explanation and resumed collaborating on the intricate design with her aunt and neighbor.

Bobby pulled a stool from under the island countertop overhang and sat down, trying desperately to ensure his astonishment over Elodie's spontaneous offer wasn't apparent on his face. He watched her prepare the sandwich, slicing it diagonally and adding ridged potato chips to the plate.

"Glad your house wasn't damaged," she said sincerely, sliding the plate in front of Bobby. "It's funny – neighbors on both sides of our house without power, yet we kept ours."

"The way the power lines run, Christine Williams should have kept power, too, if you all had it," he explained, taking a bite.

"She did. We saw lights on at her house," Elodie recalled. "They're sayin' power should be restored later this afternoon. It's a shame you had to shorten your visit to your daughter's family."

"Honestly, I was ready to come home. With two teenage girls in the house, that family runs around from activity to activity with their hair on fire. 'Cept for Christmas Day and New Year's Day, I didn't see much of them," Bobby admitted. "Besides, I felt bad leaving DeShawn over the holidays. He'll be surprised to have a visitor again this weekend."

"I hear we have more company," Cal chirped, walking into the kitchen.

"Yeah, I'm back. Good to see you, Old Timer. How are you doing?" Bobby stood up to shake Cal's hand.

"I'm better than I deserve. Good to see you, too. I guess you're taking the risk that El might poison you," Cal laughed, noticing the partially eaten sandwich where Bobby had been seated.

Elodie scrunched up her face and furrowed her eyebrows at his comment.

"If it's poisoned, I'll die a happy man! Miss Elodie fixes a mean ham sandwich," Bobby defended her.

"She does a lot of mean things, that's for sure," Cal blurted and laughed at his own joke. "But we love her anyway," he added quickly.

"I'm gonna show you what mean is when I finish these chicken pot pies I'm makin' for supper and give you peanut butter and jelly, Calcium!" Elodie threatened and turned her attention back to her pie crusts.

"Oh, you've made her mad now," Bobby laughed at Cal.

Cal walked around the island and gave Elodie a side hug. "Nobody made this woman mad – she was born that way! And I can say that because I'm her favorite around here. Isn't that right, El?" he looked up at her and playfully batted his eyelashes.

"You're not right in the head. Go on now and stop botherin' me." She tried to scold Cal but couldn't contain the smile that forced its way onto her face. She couldn't deny he had become her favorite, but she didn't think he needed to put it out there the way he did.

Lovie looked up from her coloring. "I'm your favorite around here, aren't I, Miss June?"

"Indeed, you are, my sweet little Lovie – right behind Mr. Sherman," June corrected without looking up at her husband, who was feeling chipper, and for that, she was glad.

"Aw, that's not fair! He's two people's favorite," Lovie complained.

"There's still room in my fan club. I'll even let you be President," Cal offered his young neighbor as consolation.

"Not going to happen," Lovie retorted dryly as she resumed coloring.

"Lovie! Be kind," Shelby rebuked her niece with a whisper.

"I made you a Christmas cookie, Mr. McBride!" Lovie remembered.

"That's right, she did. Been waitin' in the freezer till you got back," Elodie said as she retrieved it for Bobby.

"Would you look at that! Looks just like my house," Bobby said, inspecting it. "This will make a good snack for me tonight. Thank you, Little Miss."

"You're welcome," she answered politely to satisfy her aunt. And then, with an air of mischievousness to retaliate for being called out, she looked at Aunt Shelby and declared: "Your favorite is Will now."

Shelby reddened. "What do you know about that?" she asked, startled.

"Nobody tells me anything, but I hear things. The word's out there."

The word was now out to Bobby, who'd missed the progress in Will's dating aspirations while he was away. But it wasn't news to any of the others present, who all tried to hide their amusement at the child's bluntness.

"Hey! There's your back porch light on, Bobby! Your electricity must be back. Probably yours too, Shelby," Elodie announced from her vantage point at the kitchen window.

"Aww, do we have to go home now? I like it here, except for the church part we had to sit through. That was boring," Lovie declared.

And just like that, the child's bluntness made them sad.

Chapter Fifty-Three

By Thursday mid-morning, residents cleared fallen limbs from their yards and heard the sound of chainsaws all over Faircourt. A troupe of enterprising high-school senior boys offered to cut and cart away logs in their fathers' pickup trucks for free, split them at the home of Rusty Akin, whose daddy owned a log splitter, and sold the cordwood at houses with working, smoking chimneys. Free removal was too good a price for homeowners, including the residents of 306 Cedar Street, to ask if the boys were insured, which they weren't. The teens cut up and removed the large magnolia limb from the yard without incident.

Grace Fellowship called in professionals to remove several large limbs that had fallen on the church property, mainly in the cemetery. Unfortunately, the heavy branches knocked a few headstones off their bases, and one was cracked in half. Pastor Jefferson would call a monument company in Louisville to come out and reset the headstones, but the cracked one would require notification to the deceased's family. It was an old stone, and he didn't recognize the name engraved on it, but Pastor Jefferson thought Ava might dig into the church records and track the family down when the office reopened next week.

Shelby heard the mail fall through the slot in the door and rushed to catch Will. She hurried from her workstation at the dining table, scooped up the mail on the floor, and opened the door as Will stepped off the porch stairs onto the sidewalk.

"It's my favorite mailman!" she gushed, wishing she'd put some forethought into her greeting and been more clever.

"What a coincidence. Mine too!" he teased, delighted she'd made an effort to catch him. They hadn't spoken since before the ice storm, nor had they had a chance to since the Normans had been staying with their neighbors. "Glad to be back under your own roof, I'll bet," he ventured.

"I am. I have more privacy, especially with Micah back at work and the children back at school. The neighbors were gracious, but I missed my alone time. I learned something that concerns you, though."

Will raised an eyebrow in curious interest.

"I learned that word has leaked onto the mean streets of Faircourt that you and I are dating," she informed him.

"Really?" he tried to sound nonchalant. In reality, Will was pleased. He'd agreed to go along with her request to keep their status on the down low to spare her anxiety, but it wasn't his nature to keep secrets. If their relationship were already common knowledge, he wouldn't have to.

"Yup. We've been outed by a seven-year-old girl who keeps her ear to the ground and hears things," Shelby laughed.

"I guess nothing gets by Lovie. She's a bright one. So, what's our strategy now that our cover's been blown?"

"We'll have to mull that over."

"Would you be interested in mulling it over omelets at the diner on Saturday morning?"

"Make it waffles, and I would be!"

"Meet you there at 8 am?"

"No, you can pick me up here," she beamed at him.

Will grinned back at Shelby, then turned to continue his route. He headed down the walkway, and when he turned onto the sidewalk, he waved back to her, pleased to see she was still watching him. Very pleased.

"I appreciate your help, Elodie," June said as the two women finished stripping the Renniger's bed and replacing the sheets used by their storm guests with clean ones.

"Oh, you're welcome. I know they'll appreciate it when they get home," Elodie answered.

"What's this?" June stepped on a piece of paper and picked it up. "How sweet. It's a thank-you note to Grant and Marie from Chase. We must have blown it off the nightstand, flapping the sheets. What a thoughtful boy!" June placed it carefully on the nightstand where the Rennigers would see it.

"Remember how surly he was when we first met him?" Elodie reminisced. "That boy was a candidate-in-the-makin' for reform school."

"I remember," June said, sitting on the corner of the bed. "Poor Lovie took the brunt of it." June winced as she recalled the little girl's tears and bruises.

Elodie sat next to June on the bed. "He sure took to Marcus, though. Marcus won him over."

"Not just Marcus, but you, too! You invested your whole summer with both of them, and I think it did a world of good, especially for Chase," June corrected.

"Do you really?"

"No doubt about it. Between his mother's passing and his Aunt Shelby moving away unexpectedly, he needed a strong, stable woman in his life. You were that for him at a critical time. And while we're on the subject, I want to thank you for being a good friend to my Cal." June placed her pale pink hand on Elodie's creamed coffee brown one.

"I don't know what it is. He reminds me of my little brother, who passed at 16," Elodie was thoughtful. "But your husband's the wrong age, the wrong size, and the wrong personality."

"The wrong color!" June interjected

"That, too," Elodie chuckled, then grew serious again. "I guess it has to do with him being sickly and all those feelin's I had for my brother come back and land on Cal."

"You called him 'Cal'!" June exclaimed, interrupting.

"Yeah, but if you tell it, I will deny it," Elodie smiled.

"Your secret's safe," June assured her and patted her hand. "Anyway, thank you for being a sister to him and me. I know you don't have anyone lying their head on a pillow next to you at night, and you probably don't hear this much, but you are loved, Elodie. I love you."

"See what you've done? Now you've gotten hateful...sayin' things like that and gettin' me all choked...might as well have put your hands around my neck and strangled me!" Elodie bolted up, grinning.

"You probably haven't been hugged in a while either. Brace yourself, girl!" June stood up.

Elodie let out a tiny shout of distress and ran from the room, exaggerating the known fact she wasn't a hugger.

June ran after her, yelling, "Braaace yourseeelf!"

Chapter Fifty-Four

Bobby's initial task to visit DeShawn involved determining whether today, Saturday, was an odd or even day. Seated at his kitchen dinette, elbows on the table, head in his hands, he poured over the December calendar, trying to work forward from his last visit with his son. It frustrated him that this task was so difficult. Of late, every numerical problem grew difficult for him.

After several attempts, he gave up and pushed the calendar to the table's far side. He figured he had a 50/50 chance of it being a visiting day for even-numbered prisoners, and LaGrange wasn't that far away. He'd give it a shot and drive over there.

Bobby was ecstatic to see the familiar faces of the families of even-numbered inmates as they got out of their cars. His shot paid off and he high-tailed it across the lot, down the walkway, and took a place in line for screening – a big Bobby McBride grin plastered the width of his face. He'd missed DeShawn while in Florida and was happy it worked out that he could see him today. He tried to imagine how surprised his son would be to be called from his cell to the visiting room because he had a visitor. It wasn't hard to guess. DeShawn's face would brighten like his father's now. Of course, Bobby would have to wait a little while for him to reach the visiting room since DeShawn had not anticipated a visit, but that was nothing.

As he waited his turn to be let in, Bobby noticed a slim young woman with brown eyes and wavy black hair past her shoulders, wearing blue jeans and a cream-colored jacket, leaving the room. They made brief eye contact, and he thought: *That was a quick visit. She probably argued with whomever she visited. Too bad.*

A guard let Bobby into the visiting room in no time, where DeShawn already sat at a table. He approached him and sat on the opposite side of the Lucite table, careful not to bang his shin again.

"Hey there, boy! Are you surprised? I came back early because of the ice storm and figured I'd take a chance this was an even visiting day – and I was lucky. Sure is good to see you. Surprised you, right?" Bobby exuded.

"You sure did surprise me, Dad," DeShawn breathed heavily before remembering to smile. "How are Claire and her family?"

The question curbed Bobby's exuberance. The brother and sister had no contact during DeShawn's incarceration, and Claire didn't share her father's joy that he had reestablished a relationship.

She told her father: "Dad, I grieved him with you and Mom when he went away and cut us off all those years ago. Then, I healed, and I have no need or use for him back in my life. It's fine if you want him, but he's a stranger to me and mine. I'm good where it is."

"Son, she's just not used to hearing your name again and how things have changed. Give her time. Maybe she'll be ready when you're released in a few years. But she's good. Happy. Her husband and daughters are all good, too." It was all Bobby could offer to explain why Claire hadn't at least written her brother.

"So, Dad, about that," DeShawn began, setting aside the issue with his sister. "I won't be getting out in a few years." He watched his father's expression become confused. "I'll be getting out in eight weeks."

"What? What! Are you serious? How?" Bobby was floored. He studied his son's face and knew he wasn't joking.

"I'll serve out in eight weeks. They take time off...well, I won't explain all the details. I will complete all the time required in eight weeks. On March 10th, I'll be out of here."

"Your birthday! How 'bout that? On your birthday. I don't believe it! I mean, I believe it, but...I just can't believe it," Bobby stammered, running his hand over his short white hair.

DeShawn laughed and gave his father a minute for the news to sink in.

"Oh, boy! I've got work to do!" Bobby's thoughts raced. "It's just been me in the house for so long, and I've kind of let things go. Nothing's been done with your old room, and it's just not proper for the grown man you are now. And the upstairs bathroom could use some work if we share it. And a car! You'll need a car. That's no problem. I can pick one out of the lot for you. Of course, you'll have a job at the lot. I was considering selling the business because Auntie and I are about done with working. But now I can buy her out, and it'll be there for you. And your stove... that's waiting for you, too." Bobby was figuring it all out on the fly.

Suddenly, all the dreams he had for his son were reignited. DeShawn would soon be a free man, and Bobby's impulse was to recreate the security and support he had given him when he was 18. The only scenario he could imagine was bringing his boy back home. It was all he wanted.

"Whoa, Dad! You planned my whole life for me in thirty seconds." He tried to make it sound more like a feat of strength than an intrusion by adding a laugh to his comment.

"I just wanted to tell you that you don't have to be concerned about anything, son. I'll help you with anything you need." Bobby relaxed his shoulders, which had been tense with excitement.

"And I appreciate that, Dad. I really do. I've seen so many guys serve out and have no one to help them on the outside and no home to go to. A lot end up right back here," DeShawn explained.

"You'll never have to worry about that. And you're never coming back here, either," Bobby added as a statement of fact.

"You got that right. I've been living for the Lord inside these walls, and I'll live for Him outside them, too." DeShawn looked his father in the eye. "You know that, Dad, right?"

In his excitement at the unexpected news and how his mind had taken off with him, Bobby had forgotten. But he answered slowly, "I know."

"And Dad, all the things you want to do for me are great, but I can't." DeShawn watched his father's shoulders sink even lower as he said the words. He felt bad. He understood his father was unprepared. But he had to finish telling all his news. "Dad, I have a wife."

Chapter Fifty-Five

"Come in," Marie responded to the soft knocking on her bedroom door.

Ava walked in and sat on the bed where Marie unpacked her suitcase. She expected Grant and Marie to be chatty at dinner, sharing about their time away in Florida with their kids and grandkids and updating their friends on family news. Instead, the couple who returned late that afternoon seemed subdued, almost glum. When Grant donned his winter coat and knit cap and headed out for his evening constitutional, Ava seized the opportunity to chat with Marie alone.

"So, while we were encased in ice, you must have enjoyed the sunshine. Looks like you got a little color," Ava observed as her friend took laundered and folded clothing from the case and put them away in her bureau.

"Does it? Good. Pasty white is not a good look for me," Marie responded as she kept moving.

"Did you have a good time?" Ava got right to the heart of it.

Marie stopped and leaned her hip against the bureau for balance and support. "Unfortunately, no. A miserable time was had by all. If you want the truth, I wish I could erase the entire week from everyone's memory."

"Oh, I'm so sorry, Marie. Sit down and tell me what happened." She motioned to the chairs at the foot of the bed and sat in one of them.

Marie lowered herself into the other.

"It was supposed to be a wonderful week of family time together – Christmas presents, relaxation, David and Daniel brother-bonding, good conversation and food, beach walks with Liza, games with Little Grant and Georgia, and connecting with Andie. That was my plan. Instead, we aggravated one another like eight ferrets in a five-gallon bucket. In fact, Daniel, Andie, and the kids left a day early. It was not good, though there was peace in the house after they left. But by then, David and Liza were worn out from trying to tamp down all the eruptions of temper and pettiness. It'll be more relaxing for them when they both return to their jobs tomorrow," Marie confessed.

"Liza's back at work? Her cancer is gone, then?"

"Seems to be. Her latest scan showed no issues, though she's sticking with the food modifications she adopted during therapies – she now eats vegan food. No gluten either. She looks great and says she feels great. She's been back at work since around Thanksgiving."

"Did Grant do okay with adapting to the meals Liza made? Ava's mind was buzzing with questions.

Marie gave her a deadpan stare for a moment. "Are you kidding? You know how inflexible he is regarding what he'll eat. The first night, she made these delicious vegetable/lentil nori wraps, and Grant wouldn't even try a bite. He claimed he wasn't hungry and played the victim simultaneously. He was so childish I wanted to spank him and send him to his room. But he beat me to it and sent himself to our room. No one saw him for the rest of the night which was fine by me. I didn't miss his pouting. And it probably did him good to miss a meal. Although, for Liza's second night to cook, he ate an entire box of granola bars we'd brought and didn't even come to the dinner table."

"So, he ate vegan and gluten-free anyway!" Ava noted and laughed.

"Ha! Didn't even think of that. Yes, he did," Marie chuckled.

"But it sounds like Daniel and Andie were the major sources of conflict?" Ava guessed.

"Not without Grant's help. Are there concerns about Andie's parenting style – or rather, lack of it? Yes. She thinks she's Little Grant and Georgia's BFF instead of their stepmother. She gives them no structure and no discipline. Anything goes. Of course, she has no structure or discipline herself. And apparently, nobody is going to church except on holidays – including our Daniel and David. But for the love of peace, Grant could not keep his mouth shut about it, as if continuously harping on it would change their minds. Plus, even when he didn't run his mouth, his facial expressions made clear pronouncements even his grandchildren understood.

Ava, Daniel has no complaints about his wife, so why should Grant? I can see why Daniel was upset with his father. From what I observed, Daniel is trying hard to make this marriage work, and he supports Andie. Grant forced him to be defensive, and Daniel didn't appreciate it, which is understandable," Marie explained her perspective of the situation.

"What about Andie, with her new father-in-law's appraisals swirling around her?" Tell me she was oblivious."

"I'd tell you that if it weren't a sin to lie. It'll suffice to say she used the phrase 'crabby old man' in reference to her father-in-law more than once. It's what she'll call him from here on out. And I may join her!"

"No, you won't," Ava admonished, though she had nothing to add. "Well, at least Andie's not mad at you, is she?"

"I'm tainted by association. While waiting for our flight at the airport this afternoon, I noticed she'd defriended me on social media. So, there's that."

"Mercy!" Ava let out with a sigh. "And Little Grant and Georgia? Was that okay?"

"Typical teenagers. They got twitchy if their phones were out of their hands for longer than ten minutes. They texted their friends back home more than they spoke to us or even their Aunt Liza and Uncle David.

It was hard to get them engaged with us. I bought a new board game with great online reviews from young people while we were there and could not even bribe them to play it. You won't be surprised to hear their grandfather had something to say to them about their lack of respect. Of course, that went over like prune pudding."

"Such a hard age – teenagers. They think they know it all and have no idea of all they don't know," Ava said sympathetically. "So, what's your plan to straighten out all the dented relationships?"

Marie sat forward in her chair to answer. "Here's my question, Ava: Why do I have to straighten out the dents Grant makes?" It was a rhetorical question because Marie continued without missing a beat. "Why can't that man take responsibility for fixing his own messes? It shouldn't be my job. It was supposed to be a wonderful vacation with our adult children and grandchildren, and Grant is responsible for ruining it for everyone. I will not clean this up for him. If I do, it'll teach him nothing. He's figured out how to treat friends like family. He'd better get a clue about how to treat family like friends!"

Marie stood up, walked around to the bed where her empty suitcase lay, and zipped it closed like it was never to be opened again. Ava understood she was signaling her clear position, and the conversation ended. She reminded herself Marie hadn't asked for any advice, so she kept quiet. Still seated in her chair, she watched Marie stomp the suitcase out of the room, presumably on its way to the attic. And she heard Marie mutter as she walked out of the room: "He can unpack his own suitcase, too!"

That night, Marie slept in the guestroom.

Chapter Fifty-Six

Whether Marie's "headache" was real or feigned, Ava wasn't sure. But on Sunday morning, she didn't go to church. The plan was that Ava would teach the Senior Ladies Sunday School class that day, since the Rennigers were returning from their vacation the previous day, and Marie would not have time to prepare a lesson.

Because the class was cancelled the previous Sunday due to the storm, Ava emailed her prepared notes on Ruth 2 to each class member for private study. Today, they were working through chapter three – which nearly ignited World War Three. Ava asked Wilma Ray to read the final five verses of the chapter, which she happily obliged to do. It all blew up over verse 15.

And he said, "Bring the garment you are wearing and hold it out." So she held it, and he measured out six measures of barley and put it on her. Then she went into the city.

Only Wilma read the verse from her beloved New King James Version, which says, "he measured out six ephahs of barley" instead of "measures." After she finished reading, June had a question.

"Wait! In the lesson notes on chapter two that you emailed us last week, it said an ephah of barley weighed between 35 and 40 pounds, didn't it, Ava?"

Ava consulted her notes and confirmed June's recollection.

"That would mean Boaz put at least 210 pounds on Ruth's back, and she schlepped that load back to Naomi's house in the city. That's impossible!" June objected.

"Hmm. You're right. Six ephahs of barley would require the strength of Samson," Ava agreed. "Good eye for detail, June! But the problem doesn't exist with the English Standard Version. It says 'measures' instead of 'ephahs,' and measures can be anything."

"Does your ESV italicize the word 'measures'?" Anna Cramer wanted to know.

"It doesn't," June answered for the teacher.

"Well, it should. My King James Version also uses the word 'measures,' but it's italicized to let the reader know the word isn't in the original Hebrew text and was added." The former class teacher, Anna, tried to be helpful and not smug.

"My New King James Version has 'ephahs' in italics!" Wilma defended her preferred version.

"Then the NKJV just flat out got the translation wrong, and the KJV got it the most right," Elodie chuckled, unconcerned with what her tone projected.

Wilma's face reddened, and Ava sensed she had an emotional response ready to erupt.

"And that concludes our lesson for today! Come back next week when you'll hear Marie ask: 'So, what's everyone's favorite translation of the Scriptures?'" The class responded with strained, nervous laughter.

June, who felt terrible she'd brought up the issue, jumped to Ava's rescue and offered to close in prayer. She thanked God for His Word and asked that He would help the ladies in the class love Him with all of their minds as well as their hearts, souls, and strength. She also prayed for unity to honor Him.

Ava walked out of the classroom with an arm entwined through one of June's.

"Thank you for your prayer after class. It was just what we needed,"

Ava said in appreciation.

"It was the least I could do. If I had thought one step ahead, I could have seen it would lead to a translation debate. They're almost as passionate as the Halloween debates," June laughed.

"I know you were just thinking out loud. But I should pinch Elodie for throwing gas on Wilma's fire."

"If you really want to torture her, hug her instead," June laughed.

"Ha! You're not wrong," Ava laughed along.

"Hey, Ava! Would you come here for a minute? I have to ask you something before I forget about it," Pastor Jefferson beckoned her toward the office entrance.

"Save me a seat in the sanctuary," she requested before letting go of June's arm and heading toward her boss. "What's up?" she asked.

"We have a broken headstone in the cemetery and need to notify the family. They'll be the ones to decide whether to replace it or repair it. But it's an older stone – from the 1970s. Can you research our records and see what you can find for family leads?"

"Can do!" Ava assured him. "What's the name on the stone?"

"Clarkson Dean Williams," he recited.

Ava wrote the name on an old bulletin she pulled from her Bible. "I'll get right to it on Tuesday."

Inside the sanctuary, Ava found her place between Marcus and June.

"How was class?" her husband asked as the prelude started, and everyone stood up.

"I'm glad Marie's back on deck next week. We started down the translation-debate road," Ava whispered back to Marcus.

"I'm sorry for dat," he said apologetically but with an amused expression.

Marcus was a veteran of passionate debates about which translation of the Bible was most accurate, most understandable, or even most likable. When he pastored, he was often asked his opinion on the subject, only to discover he was expected to validate the questioner's settled opinion. Eventually, he encouraged those who sought his opinion to learn Hebrew and Greek.

"Do you see what I see?" June leaned over to ask Ava.

"You mean Christine Williams in the front row? Can't miss her in that mink hat," Ava answered.

"No. Over there," June nodded toward Will and Shelby, standing two rows ahead and to the right.

They were holding hands.

Chapter Fifty-Seven

"I'm sure winter will be back, but I loved this Spring-like day," Cal commented as he and Marcus tended to the supper dishes and kitchen cleanup.

"It sure has perked you up, Broder, and I'm happy for dat. Dis must be da 'January Thaw' I read about. But you're right, dere's still two more months of winter to go," Marcus agreed.

Cal opened the kitchen window to let the balmy breeze blow in before wiping down the island counter. Then he looked around to see if anyone else was near before confiding to Marcus at low volume: "The warm day sure felt good, but I've started a new treatment. Immunotherapy, they call it, and I think it's helping. Won't know until I get some tests, but I'm more energetic."

Marcus stopped loading the dishwasher. Having picked up on the confidential nature of the information from Cal's tone, he responded in a near-whisper: "Dat's wonderful news. Why haven't you shared about your new treatment in Tursday Meeting? Are you going to tonight?"

"No! If I gave an update every time something changed with me, Thursday Meeting would turn into the Calvert Sherman Health Report. I don't want that. Of course, June knows everything, but things are so up and down with me that I want to keep this one quiet, especially from Elodie. If I tell it, she might quit fixing me treats."

Marcus threw back his head and laughed. "Ok, den, your secret is safe wit me. And Cal, tank you for sharing dat.”

"I figured if anyone in this house knew how to keep a secret, you did. So, are we ready for Thursday Meeting?" Cal asked, draping the dishrag over the faucet to dry.

"Is Grant back from his walk yet?"

"Yup. Heard him flying up the stairs to the bathroom just a few minutes ago."

As soon as they were all seated in the living room, Ava took charge of Thursday Meeting. She had news to share that she'd been holding in for two days, just waiting for this moment.

"The mystery of mysteries has been solved!" she announced, grabbing everyone's attention.

"You learned why the chicken crossed the road?" Elodie asked, trying to act serious.

Ava rolled her eyes and answered, "The other mystery of mysteries, Goofball. I know why Christine Williams is so determined to keep her membership at Grace Fellowship Church, even if it means having to attend services. Her late husband is buried in our cemetery, and according to GFC bylaws, you must be a member to be buried there. She needs her membership because she wants to be buried next to her husband!"

"Wooow," June breathed out slowly.

"Did she tell you that?" Marie asked.

"I mean, I haven't asked her, but it's the only thing that makes sense. Her husband's headstone broke in the ice storm, and I had to look up his family. His name was Clarkson Dean Williams. He died December 1, 1978, and he was married to Christine Williams of 307 Cedar Street at the time," Ava explained.

"Aww, she's been without him for a long time – close to 50 years," June sympathized.

"Does Grace Fellowship allow that? Can you be a member just so you can be buried in the cemetery?" Grant asked.

"That's our Grant – always applying his rules to everyone else's life," Marie let the words fly impulsively, carelessly.

"I just asked a question!" he defended himself.

"It's a good question, Grant," Marcus intervened. "What do you tink?"

But Grant, aware his wife could not contain her still-simmering resentment, shut down and refused to answer. He was not about to invite more of Marie's public criticism and feared anything he said would fuel her fire.

Cal, feeling sorry for Grant, jumped in for him. "Well, when people become members, there are requirements. They need to profess Christ as their Savior and have to be baptized. I guess there are no further requirements after that unless you persist in sin and refuse to repent. Then you get booted, dismembered, or whatever you call it."

"Dismembered! That's what I'm calling it from now on," snickered Elodie.

"After being in church ministry for 35 years with Marcus, I can say there were many times I wished there were some requirements for growth throughout membership. It was so frustrating dealing with Christians content to stay baby Christians forever," Ava confessed.

"I'm on board with that! We should have grades in church. You can't move on to third grade until you meet the requirements of second grade. And everybody wears a badge showin' what grade they're in," Elodie was thinking it through and animated.

June laughed out loud in response, though she didn't mean to. "I'm sorry I laughed, Elodie," she apologized. "But a picture flashed in my head of a classroom of middle school students taking a test, and everyone passing around notes and looking at each other's papers. They were all cheating."

Elodie was undeterred. "Work with me, people. See the vision: You move to the next grade by demonstratin' proficiency. For instance, everyone in third grade knows their books of the Bible in order. In the fourth grade, you might have to recite the Romans Road verses and use 'em to lead someone to Jesus. And you don't get to stay in one grade forever. You'd age out, just like you do in public school. We're not gonna pass people along in the grades. We're gonna dismember 'em. And before anyone says that's legalistic, think of it as 'structured accountability.' That's a good idea you're onto, Ava."

Elodie's vision of her wish for 'requirements for growth' horrified Ava who recognized its potential to become a yoke of slavery. "I don't want any credit for that scheme! We'd have to take the word 'Grace' off the church name," she was quick to respond.

"So, Elodie, what grade would you assign to each of us?" Marcus asked with a mischievous grin.

"Um, well, I haven't worked it all out," Elodie stammered. "How 'bout we get back to Christine Williams bein' buried next to her husband?"

"Now dat's a good idea. Very simply, it's not our call to make. It's up to da leadership of Grace Fellowship Church. Dey've said da requirement to maintain membership is monthly attendance unless you're incapacitated. So dat's it. But we can pray dat God draws Christine Williams to Himself trough our services, right?" Marcus brought the matter to a conclusion.

Grant and Marie got up and walked wordlessly up the stairs to their bedroom at the end of the meeting. The others exchanged silent glances of compassion for them. They'd all been through tough patches in their relationships.

Chapter Fifty-Eight

They held Garage Cave night in the basement again because, despite the mild weather, no one wanted to risk Cal catching a chill or worse. He was feeling better and demanded to be reinstated as a regular attendee. Grant turned on the space heater at 6:30 to ensure a comfortable temperature.

"I'm coming back with a bang, guys! I got the wife to make us a banana cream pie for our snack," Cal greeted the guys as he descended the basement stairs, pie in one hand, the other sliding along the handrail.

"I saw her making that this afternoon and hoped a piece would make its way to me one way or another," Grant was giddy with anticipation.

Cal was pleased to see Grant happy, even if it was only over pie. He wasn't privy to whatever he and Marie were fussing over since they returned from Florida, nor did he care to be. But he had sympathy for his friend.

"I would slap my own mama for good banana cream pie!" Bobby gleefully confessed.

"Dat's a pretty low threshold for slapping one's mother," Marcus observed with seriousness. Grant and Cal jumped on his train of thought, knowing Marcus was being deliberately dense.

"How long have you had these violent impulses, Bobby?" Grant queried somberly.

"We're obligated to report threats of elder abuse," Cal affirmed.

"Guys! Guys! It's just a figure of speech," Bobby interpreted. "Besides, my mama has long since passed."

"Oh," Marcus replied. Then he looked at Cal and Grant, and the three of them broke up laughing.

"Okay, you got me," Bobby held his hands up in surrender. "A guy goes away for a month, and his baloney detector gets a little rusty. I'll get it in working order again. Now, let's carve up that pie! We can make four pieces out of it, can't we?"

"That seems like reasonable portions," Grant agreed. "And I am serious about that," he added, so there was no misunderstanding.

Marcus scooped out massive pieces onto four Styrofoam plates, and the men sat back in their chairs and set upon the pie with plastic forks.

"This is delicious, Cal. Tell June I'm awarding her a PhD in pie-ology," Bobby mumbled with his mouth full.

Marcus and Grant uttered incoherent noises and nodded their agreement.

Bobby looked around and didn't spot any cards or dominoes. "What's the game tonight, fellas?" he asked.

"Ugh, I forgot to bring something down," Marcus replied, setting his pie plate on the table. "I'll be right back."

"No! No! Sit! We do more jawing than actual playing anyway," Bobby commanded.

"Let's say tonight's game is "Who Can Leave The Cleanest Plate?" Grant suggested.

"That's perfect," Cal agreed.

Marcus picked up his plate and resumed eating with a new goal.

"So, how was your visit with your family in Florida? Hope it went better than mine." Grant let the small admission of his misery out without elaboration.

"I'm sorry for you, Grant. To tell you the truth, my visit was just okay. The granddaughters are at that age where their friends influence their lives more than they want Granddad to. I didn't see a lot of them or their parents, who run them all over town. I spent a lot of time watching Rover chase lizards. But what you really should ask me is about my first visit back with DeShawn," Bobby replied.

"Okay then, how was your visit with DeShawn?" Cal asked, taking a breather from shoveling pie into his mouth.

"He's getting released from prison on his birthday, March 10th. That's just seven weeks from now," Bobby answered matter-of-factly.

"What?" Marcus almost choked. He set his plate on his lap to give his neighbor his attention.

"And that's not all. Told me he's married to boot! Been married for five years."

"If he's married, tell him to stay where he is," Grant grumbled.

Unused to Grant's recent negativity, Bobby looked to Marcus for an appropriate response.

"Grant, we'll fix you as soon as we hear Bobby out. Gotta wait your turn, buddy," Marcus directed. "What's DeShawn's plan?" he asked, returning his attention to Bobby.

"He wants to work part-time and attend seminary part-time starting this summer. His wife works – her name is Mariana – she's a nurse. She lives with her mother and takes care of her. Two brothers. That's about all I know. Oh, and she's a good Christian girl, DeShawn says."

"I bet that was a lot of information for you to get in one visit. I wonder why he didn't tell you all this earlier," Cal was curious.

"Asked him that. He said he wanted some time with me – just the two of us getting reacquainted before he brought his wife into the picture. He wanted to understand who I am and wanted me to know who he is. I'm not sure I believe that's the real reason. He used to tell me what he thought I wanted to hear when he was in high school. But who knows? My baloney-meter is rusty, right?"

"I don't know your son, but I know a few tings," Marcus began. "He's not da same person he was at 18. None of us are. So, give him da benefit of da doubt. If I were in his place, I'd want to figure out who my father was so I could tell my wife wit some certainty dat he was safe. Because you're not da same person you were back den either."

Bobby smiled, relieved. "When you say it that way, it makes sense." He picked up the pie he'd neglected and took a big bite. He chewed a moment, letting DeShawn's situation marinate in a mind newly freed of suspicion and upset. "I have a daughter-in-law!" he remarked aloud.

"I have two, but only one acts like an adult. Wish we could pick them. Why did that stop being a thing?" Grant complained.

"Okay, Grant. It's your turn. What happened in Florida dat has you and Marie in a snit wit each oder?" Marcus asked, shifting his focus.

"I don't want to talk about it," Grant sniffed and changed the subject. "I've been meaning to tell you something, Bobby. The day after Christmas, I spotted a woman in a small silver car sitting outside your house and looking it over real good – front and back. She had long dark hair. That was all I could make out since she was a good distance away from me. Got her license plate number though. Do you want it?"

"Long dark hair, huh? You should have gotten her phone number for me instead," Bobby laughed. "But thanks for keeping an eye on the place for me. I appreciate that."

CHAPTER FIFTY-NINE

Grant wanted to talk through his problem, but the person able to provide the best input, Marie, was unwilling. It made him even more anxious because it was not like her. Though they only employed it about once per year, Grant was used to their pattern of conflict to resolution: get irritated, dwell on it and get angry, spout off your grievance, give each other an hour or two – three at the most – of space, talk about it until every point has been expressed and discussed, mutually apologize, and finally, make-up "magic." It had been a workable system for 40 years. But for reasons unknown to Grant, Marie was maintaining the space phase. It had lasted over a week now.

It was late Sunday afternoon, and he was alone in their bedroom, hoping a Jets versus Giants football game he had no interest in would distract his worried thoughts. When his cell phone rang, he was relieved to see his mother's name on the caller ID.

"Mom! Where've you been? I've been trying to reach you for hours," Grant answered quickly.

"I went to lunch with Deaf Donald after the church service here. We got to talking and lost track of time. I forgot to turn my ringer on after church. Sorry about that. I hope you didn't worry I was dead in a ditch, as I worry about you when you don't answer my calls right away. Anyway, what's the matter that you're keen to talk to me?"

Grant grabbed the television remote, hit the mute button, and took a deep breath. "Mom, am I a horrible person?"

"You have moments. Is that it?" she asked unemotionally.

"Moooom," Grant whined into the phone.

G-Lu softened. "That's my short answer. If you want my long answer, I'll need some context to work with. Have you been accused of being horrible by someone you live with?"

"By Marie. Well, not in those exact words, but the sentiment is the same."

"I'm surprised. I could imagine any of your friends saying something like that to you, but I figured Marie had you sorted out. What got under her skin?"

"Our visit with the kids and grands in Florida didn't go as she imagined. She blames me."

"Are you to blame?"

"Yes, some. I'll take my share, but I'm not entirely to blame," Grant admitted.

"I'm just going to take a wild stab in the dark here. Was it anything to do with you telling people what they should or shouldn't be doing?" G-Lu wasn't guessing. She knew her son.

Grant felt rising frustration and understood it wouldn't go well for him with his mother if he let it show. But he wished she would omit the sarcasm from her comments when he was hurting.

"It had everything to do with maintaining my role as a godly father and grandfather both in example and expectation. Yes, I said some things and gave some direction to my family that were not well received. But what am I supposed to do? Am I just supposed to be a nodding lump who sits in a chair and watches whatever unfolds before me? Are my values and opinions worthless now?"

"You make a fair point, son. As parents and grandparents, we're not eager to let go of our influence in our family. When our children were young, their only values were those we taught. As teens, they did what we told them or faced the consequences. But as adults, they get to make their own choices and face more severe repercussions if they make the wrong choices. I was proud of you and Marie for not bailing your boys out of consequences of their dumb decisions in their young adulthood. They learned some hard lessons that stuck with them. But now it's their turn to parent - Daniel's anyway.

I know you want to give guidance, and your intentions are good. The questions you have to answer for yourself are: Do you value imparting guidance more than peace in your family? And, are they hearing what you say if they're so put off by it?"

Grant sighed. "It seems like giving up."

"But is it? You said it yourself earlier: you want to influence by example and expectation. Perhaps they don't have to be equal components. Maybe you lean heavier on your example. You don't have to verbalize your expectations. We're all aware of what you expect. We're not dumb," G-Lu added bluntly.

"You've given me something to ponder," Grant responded.

"I know you will. You're very fair-minded, Grant. I've always thought that about you when you weren't being horrible," she laughed.

Grant answered with a faint chuckle before adding, "She's really unhappy with me, Mom. It's been over a week, and she won't talk about it. She's not giving me the silent treatment or sleeping in the guest room like she did the night we got home, but it's pretty frosty all the same."

"Are you going anywhere?"

"Not even if there was anywhere to go," he answered determinedly.

"Okay, then. She's got a bee in her bonnet. 'Big mad,' as Elodie would say. She's still a godly woman, and the Holy Spirit can do what you can't. Pray for her. Love her. That's what your father used to do when I'd go off my rocker."

"Off your rocker, huh?" Grant smiled.

"A time or two," G-Lu, hearing the smile in her son's voice, smiled back in hers.

"Thanks for the chat, Mom."

"Any time. Have a good evening as best you can."

"Hey, Mom!" Grant tried to catch her before she hung up.

"What?"

"Your lunch with Deaf Donald wasn't like a date, right?"

"And what if it were?" she answered coyly.

"Then I hope you enjoyed yourself. You have a good evening, too." Grant put the phone down and shook his head at the thought of his 94-year-old mother on a date. And then the horrifying thought occurred: *"Oh, good grief! I hope she doesn't kiss on a first date."*

Chapter Sixty

"**G**et lost, Lovie!" Chase snapped at his sister when she wandered into his room.

"Your door was open," Lovie pleaded, justifying her entrance.

"Well, get your face out of here and close it," her brother ordered.

Lovie turned around, left Chase's bedroom, and closed the door hard.

"Can't get away with that at my house," Silas noted as he sat cross-legged on the floor in front of thousands of tiny blocks he and Chase were trying to form into a Chinese-walled castle.

"Away with what?" Chase asked defensively, though he had a good idea of what.

"Crabbing at your sister. Being mean. My dad calls it 'corrupt communication.' If he hears it – and he always hears everything in his small apartment – then you get a lecture on kindness that lasts an eternity and makes you wish he'd poke red-hot needles under your eyelids instead. It's just too much trouble to risk it," Silas explained.

"Glad we have a bigger house," Chase answered smugly.

Silas hesitated, wondering if he should risk speaking his mind and offending Chase since they'd just started getting together outside of school and church after Chase dumped him for his basketball friends. He took the chance to see if they were indeed friends.

"Maybe living in a smaller place helps you be a better Christian," Silas ventured, keeping his eyes on the building instructions he held and pretending partial focus on the conversation.

"I am a better Christian! Well, not better than you, but better than I used to be. Used to be, I would have shoved Lovie out the door."

"That's good, then. Progress. But don't be happy where you're at. Level up," Silas encouraged, emboldened by Chase's response to being challenged.

"Leveling up is hard," Chase sighed, set down the blocks in his hands, and rolled onto his back to examine the ceiling. "Is there a hack for it?"

Silas set down the building instructions and thought. "I'm trying to think of how my dad would answer that. We can't make ourselves better Christians. I've tried, and it doesn't work. But the more time I spend trying to know God better, the more it helps."

"Oh," Chase muttered and sat upright again. "It must be nice to have a dad that you can talk about stuff like this with."

"Yeah, I guess it is. It must be nice for you to be on the basketball team," Silas answered, wanting to say something positive about his friend's situation.

"I thought so too at first. But I wanted to quit after Trevor cussed me out at that game. I told my dad I would quit, but he wouldn't let me. He said I had to finish the season because I'd committed to my teammates. I don't know what commitment he was talking about, but I had to stick with it. I'm glad the season's almost over. Basketball's okay, but I don't love it," Chase admitted.

"It was all over school the next day that Lovie hit Trevor in the head with her shoe," Silas laughed. "I wouldn't mind having a little sister like that."

"I guess she's all right, but if you want her, she's all yours," Chase offered.

Silas' countenance brightened. "Hey, if my dad married your Aunt Shelby, what would that make you and Lovie to me? Some kind of family, right?"

Chase figured out loud: "If Aunt Shelby gets married, her husband is then my uncle. Your aunt and uncle's children are your cousins. You'd be my cousin!"

"That would have been cool," Silas speculated. "Probably not going to happen, though," he said, picking out yellow roof blocks from the pile in front of them.

Chase looked at him squarely. "Doesn't he like my Aunt Shelby?"

"He doesn't talk about her. I did see them holding hands in church today when they didn't think I could see. But he's going to Nashville for a job interview this week. I heard him on his phone – like I said, his apartment is small. Anyway, Sam and I aren't surprised. He told us a while back that Mr. Van Zant said he should look for a way to use his education in ministry, and he was going to send out his resume. He doesn't want to be a mailman forever. And Nashville's only three hours away from my mom's house. Sam looked it up."

Silas may not have been surprised, but Chase was.

Chase had a difficult time falling asleep that night. Over and over he flipped from stomach to back positions under the quilt his Grandma made for him, but his restlessness had little to do with a lack of physical comfort.

He'd observed his aunt at the dinner table that evening, trying to detect any hint of sadness over the possible departure of the mailman. But when Lovie mentioned needing to purchase Valentine's cards for her classmates, Aunt Shelby volunteered that she and Will had planned a date for Valentine's Day. And she did so with a goofy grin on her face, Chase observed.

He also remembered Silas said his dad didn't talk about Aunt Shelby to him and his brother. On the other hand, Aunt Shelby couldn't contain herself from mentioning Will at least once in every conversation. Chase wondered if his aunt might be in love with someone about to break her heart and weighed his options about what to do.

He could say nothing and keep what he knew to himself. However, he recalled blurting out to Ms. Elodie his secret knowledge that Christine Williams was rich at last summer's lemonade stand. Chase questioned his ability to keep a secret with more personal impact.

He imagined he might confront his mailman directly about his intentions. But Chase knew he wouldn't see Will again until next Sunday unless he pretended to be sick and stayed home from school. Even then, Aunt Shelby would still work in the house on a weekday. On top of that, Chase wasn't sure exactly when the interview in Nashville was to take place or what day to stay home.

Another option was to tell his dad what he'd learned and leave it up to him to tell his sister that Will would dump her for a new job. This would be his preferred option if it didn't make him feel guilty for adding one more responsibility to his father's burdened shoulders while he walked away unencumbered.

Chase decided he should ask God to show him what to do. And as he prayed, he fell asleep.

Chapter Sixty-One

"I've never been in this church before. It's a beautiful old building," Bobby complimented his son's best friend, Pastor Jonathan Jefferson, as Jonathan let him through the vestibule of Grace Fellowship Church and back to his office study.

"She's got a few wrinkles here and there, but she's holding up pretty good for her age," Jonathan replied as he opened the door to Ava's anterior reception office.

"Was that comment about me? I don't know if I should be glad or mad," Ava smiled and looked up from her computer screen. "Hello, Bobby!" she greeted her neighbor.

"That comment was regarding our building, but if it makes you glad, it can suffice for both," Jonathan chuckled. "Right this way," he ushered Bobby into his office and closed the door.

Bobby sat at the small, six-seat conference table in a corner of the office and looked around the room. One office wall was lined with floor-to-ceiling bookcases crammed so full they obscured any organization that may have existed. Stacks of books were placed in front of rows of books pushed to the back of bowing brown-painted shelves. An L-shaped oak desk sat about three feet in front of the bookshelves with a computer and keyboard on the short side and a printer on a corner of the main table area. The chair behind the desk was modern, breathable black mesh. The mid-century oval conference table set with orange fabric chairs on casters, where he sat, was well worn. Against a backdrop of powder blue walls, it would have been dreary if not for two enormous south-facing windows that flooded the room with natural light, which turned otherwise dingy mismatched furnishings into a quirky, eclectic collection.

Jonathan sat at the conference table beside Bobby and turned his chair to face him.

Bobby got right to the purpose of the meeting he'd requested. "You knew he was married." He said it with just a hint of a question in his tone.

"I married them," Jonathan admitted forthrightly before adding, "He asked me not to tell you."

"I'm not here to blame you for anything. If he asked you not to tell me, you did what a friend has to do. But now I'm playing catch-up. A woman who is my daughter-in-law is living in this town, and I want to know about her. Who is she? And what does she want with DeShawn?"

Jonathan exhaled his relief that Bobby wasn't there to be confrontational. As a pastor, Jonathan was used to dealing with interpersonal drama. Other people's drama, that is. Since Bobby had called yesterday to make the appointment, Jonathan had been anxious. He'd even asked his wife to pray as they met today.

Jonathan explained what he could. "Mariana became active with a group ministering the gospel to men's and women's prisons and visited Kentucky State Reformatory for the first time about eight years ago. She met and corresponded with DeShawn for about a year and a half before she began visiting him outside of the ministry. Another year and a half after that, they got the warden's approval to get married. I performed the ceremony, and Kesha and the warden were witnesses."

"Hmm, let's see about the details," Jonathan continued. "Mariana is a nurse in Louisville. She lives with her mother there, not here in Faircourt. Her mom has been seriously ill for the past two years, and I believe she's in the last stage of a terminal diagnosis. Mariana has a couple of brothers, but they're somewhere out of state. Not local. She's a lovely woman – a natural caretaker. Before her mom got sick, she stayed with our kids a couple of times so Kesha and I could get away. Our kids love her. What else? She's three years younger than DeShawn and me. Oh! I have a picture. Would you like to see it?"

Bobby nodded enthusiastic affirmation. He wasn't expecting to get to see what she looked like. Jonathan retrieved a picture frame from among a grouping on his massive desk. It was a picture of DeShawn's wedding day: DeShawn in his prison uniform smiling from ear to ear, Jonathan wearing a suit and holding a Bible, the warden in a short-sleeved button-down shirt and no tie, and a pretty young woman with long dark hair in a white dress holding a small bouquet.

"She's white!" Bobby exclaimed.

"Hispanic, actually," Jonathan corrected.

Bobby stared at the picture. "He didn't mention his wife was whi...Hispanic," Bobby corrected himself and set the picture on the table. "Are there any more surprises? Anything at all you can think of that might set me back on my heels?" he asked, rolling his eyes and mouth agape.

Jonathan laughed out loud. "It's been a lot lately for you, I know."

"Do you, now? Do you know how much it has been?" Bobby asked rhetorically without malice and picked up the picture again for further inspection.

"You asked what she wanted with DeShawn," Jonathan reminded him. He had Bobby's attention again.

"If Mariana doesn't love DeShawn for who he is, then I'm no judge of character. She convinced me she loved him five years ago and every day since. She told me she always wanted a godly husband and was as surprised as anyone else that she found him in a prison. Mariana says she forgot to stipulate in her prayers for a husband that he not be wearing a khaki shirt with a number stenciled on it. I heard she took a lot of heat from her brothers for it. Didn't stop her."

Bobby's eyes welled as he listened to Jonathan speak. "Is that a fact?" he said.

"So, just how curious are you about this woman? Your daughter-in-law?" Jonathan bounded up from his chair and over to his desk, giving Bobby space to compose himself.

"Huh?"

Jonathan scrolled through his cell phone, wrote something on paper, and then held it out to Bobby. It was a phone number with Mariana's name written above it.

"Call her. Introduce yourself. Invite her to dinner," Jonathan suggested.

Bobby took the paper, a smile spreading across his face.

"Yeah. I could do that. I could ask my son's wife to have dinner," the idea was taking root. "Ha!" he laughed. "I'll have dinner with her before he does! Weird." He stood up and shook Jonathan's hand.

Bobby opened the office door and noted that Ava was still at her desk.

"Ava! If I go home this happy and try to hug Rover, he'll scratch my face off. So, you're my safer option!" he prodded her.

Ava stood smiling, happy to rejoice with and hug the neighbor she once dreaded facing. They'd both come a long way since last summer.

Chapter Sixty-Two

"El, June, do either of you feel like a walk to the big cemetery? It's not too cold out, and the sun is nice. We could stroll," Marie tried to recruit female company after lunch. Grant was in their room watching an old golf tournament, and she wanted some space and fresh air.

"Sorry, can't. Cal has a doctor's appointment in an hour," June begged off.

"I can! But I don't want to," Elodie answered with sass. "I need to figure out a Plan B for dinner. I was gonna use the two bags of shrimp the Normans brought over and insisted we keep. But now they're defrosted and look a little funky - slimy. Don't want to chance it."

"Were you going to make your delicious Peanut Butter & Jelly Shrimp Pasta?" Marie asked woefully.

"Sure was. Since I have everything else for it, maybe I'll go to the store and get fresh shrimp."

"Want me to come along?" Marie offered.

"Go get your fresh air. I might dilly-dally at Dollar Town after the grocery store," Elodie replied.

"Alright then," Marie took her wool, powder-pink swing coat from the closet and headed out the front door. She pulled ivory leather gloves from the coat pockets and put them on.

"It's at times like these that I miss having a dog to walk," Marie mused,

heading down Cedar Street. She still intended to walk to Faircourt Memorial Cemetery – what she and Ava called 'the big cemetery' as opposed to the much smaller one around Grace Fellowship Church – even if she were going alone. But she'd go by GFC to get there, taking the route she walked with Ava before Ava started working. She had just passed the church building when she spied a figure in a fur hat standing near the back left-side corner of the little cemetery.

"Has to be Christine Williams. Who else?" Marie figured. She'd been waiting for a chance to meet this surly, elusive neighbor for nearly a year. And Marie approached her with no plan but the impulsive, bold example of G-Lu.

"It's a pretty little cemetery," Marie remarked, coming up behind the woman.

"It used to be," Christine answered, keeping her hands in her cashmere coat pockets without bothering to turn her head and identify who spoke to her.

Marie stopped next to her and stood, both of them facing a broken headstone bearing the name 'Clarkson Dean W' on the part that lay flat on the ground and 'illiams' on the remaining piece still attached vertically to its base.

"I'm Marie Renniger. I know who you are. My mother-in-law, Louisa, visited you at Thanksgiving. I'm sorry about your husband's headstone. I imagine it has to be like losing him a bit all over again," Marie speculated.

"Can you imagine? I see your husband taking regular evening walks, albeit quite abbreviated. He looks reasonably healthy," Christine answered dismissively.

"Lord, You know I am unprepared for this woman today – at such a spiritual low. Give me the wisdom and kindness I lack," Marie prayed in silent desperation.

She turned to face Christine. "Where is it written that your husband has to be dead to grieve him? Or that the death of a mother or child isn't as painful?" Marie challenged. Then she softened and explained, "Grant is not my first husband."

"I see," Christine replied in a lowered tone. "At first, I thought you meant there was trouble in paradise."

"I'm not going to lie. At the moment, there's that too," Marie admitted with candor.

"Fix it," Christine instructed sharply.

Her neighbor's abrupt tone did not put off Marie. She rarely met someone who skipped the conversational fluff and went straight to their point, and she appreciated it because she related.

"I've looked that man over pretty thoroughly and have not yet located the 'fix it' button," Marie responded.

At last, Christine turned and made eye contact with Marie. "I didn't say 'fix him.' But if you're convinced there's a button to remedy the problem, why not find yours?"

"Hmm, good question. I guess the answer is because my 'button' would be more like a detonation plunger. In order to fix the problem, I need to blow up wanting to control some sensitive areas of my life. You seem like a woman who enjoys a certain amount of control over her life. Could you blow it up?" Marie wondered aloud.

"And you seem like a woman who makes quick assessments about people they've known for less than five minutes," Christine dodged the question with an accusation.

"Perhaps that's true. But I have lived across the street from you for almost a year and observed. And let's just say your reputation preceded our meeting."

"No doubt," Christine chuckled, which Marie mirrored with a smile.

They both turned to face the broken headstone again and stood silent.

"No. I could not blow up my desire for control," Christine answered the question at last. "And that has something to do with what lies before me on the ground. Unless you think you'd be happy facing your husband's tombstone or could at least stand before it with no regret, then fix the problem before it's too late."

Marie hesitated and replied, "I hear what you're saying. I would never be happy to stand before Grant's tombstone. But the ship of no regrets sailed a long time ago. I don't think two sinners can be married for more than 24 hours without regrets on both sides. We're all that bad."

"We're all that bad." Christine raised an arched brow as the surprising words found their mark. She believed others saw themselves as good. More than that, these good people looked down their noses at the bad they saw in her – the bad she knew drove Clarkson to his grave. She marveled at Marie's intriguing perspective and felt a thin connection to her. It lightened her mood.

"A new monument has been ordered. It's not modest and will make people talk about me all the more, and I don't care," Christine declared brightly, changing the subject.

Marie laughed. "Not modest, huh? Well, 'go big or go home,' as they say!"

Christine smiled. "I'm going big, and I'm going home. I'm tired."

They walked together to the sidewalk in front of the church, where they parted ways.

"Marie!" Christine called after a few steps.

Marie turned around.

"You are a tolerable woman," Christine admitted.

"Likewise," Marie smiled back.

As she continued her walk to the big cemetery, she remembered to say: "Thank You, Lord."

CHAPTER SIXTY-THREE

Marie taught the fourth and final lesson in Ruth on Sunday morning. She confessed to Ava afterward in the empty classroom, with brimming eyes, that she felt like a fraud since she was distant from Grant and God.

Ava asked, "Did you say anything you didn't believe or knew to be false?"

"No," Marie sniffled.

"Okay. It's a good thing we don't have to stick our finger in some Spirit-O-Meter to register our spiritual temperature before we do ministry. How many Sunday School classes would go untaught or pulpits would go unfilled on any given Lord's Day if we required a particular level? Besides, we're worthy before God because of Jesus' works, not ours. And, I believe, God is pleased when we're faithful to our obligations despite having a low tank of resources."

"Thanks for the encouragement," Marie managed a small smile that widened. "Don't tell Elodie about the Spirit-O-Meter. She'll want it for her spiritual grading scheme."

"You're right, she would," Ava laughed. "But as long as you're accepting encouragement - and I say this as someone who's depended on it myself over the last year-plus – please talk your issue over with Grant. Your silence will not resolve it. You know that. Even if he owns all the responsibility, you bear some if you refuse to obey Ephesians 4:31-32.

Let all bitterness and wrath and anger and clamor and slander be put away from you, along with all malice. Be kind to one another, tenderhearted, forgiving one another, as God in Christ forgave you.

"Forgive as God does? Okay. Does God forgive the unrepentant?" Marie asked in response. She didn't wait for an answer but walked to the classroom doorway and turned off the light, leaving Ava to stand alone in the murky echo of the question.

***

Silas came into the junior/senior high boys' Sunday School class ten minutes late, so Chase had to wait until after class to talk with him.

"Hey, man! Did your dad get the Nashville job?" Chase asked eagerly. He'd spent a long week waiting and worrying about Aunt Shelby. He was certain that she was unaware of Will's out-of-town interview.

"Not yet. But he has a second interview this week. It's a video interview, so he doesn't have to travel there again," Silas answered brightly.

"Oh," Chase responded dejectedly. He would have to wait longer for an answer.

The boys walked down the stairs and into the foyer. Chase saw his aunt walking through the open sanctuary doors where Will was seated. She sat down next to him and began a conversation that involved giggling. Chase felt a wave of anger rising in his chest. He wondered how the mailman had the nerve to lead his aunt on.

"Hey, boys!" Will caught a glimpse of Silas and Chase and waved them over to his pew.

Silas went over and sat on the other side of his dad. Chase turned and walked out of the church, heading for home. He decided he'd rather eat pancakes with his own dad and Lovie than watch Will break Aunt Shelby's heart. Chase knew his dad would ask why he had come home instead of staying for the service and planned his answer as he walked. He'd say he needed medicinal pancakes because he skipped breakfast and felt terrible. Both would be true.

Christine Williams was almost knocked over by the young man exiting the church just as she was about to enter. The massive white-painted wooden door flew open and clipped the toe of her designer shoe.

"Young man!" she called after him, expecting he would stop to receive her sharp chastisement.

But Chase kept his pace, head down and lost in his thoughts.

"Well!" Christine exclaimed aloud to the only witness – herself. "Apparently, they don't teach manners in this church!" she followed up, muttering this time. She fluffed her tan cashmere coat, walked through the doorway, and marched to the front pew where she sat.

Christine selected the first Sunday of the month as her attendance schedule to meet the minimum requirement for maintaining her church membership. She preferred to sit in the front row so the pastor could not miss her monthly appearance. Also, she timed her arrival for exactly 10:45 am to coincide with the opening prelude.

However, today Beth-Ann Sharp, the church pianist, was delayed by a phone call giving her an update on her daughter's labor progress at the hospital. Seeing an opportunity in the lull to greet her un-greetable neighbor, June wanted to approach Christine Williams. However intimidated by the prospect, she enlisted Elodie to come with her for moral support.

"Come on, El. Please do this with me," she pleaded.

"For you, not for her," Elodie answered, rising from her seat and following June to the front row.

"Hello, I'm June Sherman, your neighbor, and I, I just wanted to introduce myself," she stammered as she seated herself on the edge of the pew, Elodie standing behind her.

"And now you have. Goodbye," Christine replied tersely.

June's shoulders fell, and her smile disappeared. She rose to take her leave.

"Oh, no, you didn't!" Elodie jumped into it, her inner-city Columbus upbringing activated. Realizing she was standing at the front of the church in everyone's view, she took the seat June had just vacated and lowered her voice.

"What trailer park charm school did you flunked out of? My girl, June, was tryin' to be nice to you. So, I suggest you check the pockets of your fancy coat and see if there's any fancy manners in 'em you might put to use. My name's Elodie Ford, F O R D," she spelled it out and continued. "And I live right across the street from you. Don't forget either of those facts!" Elodie stood, remembering again where she was and adding with more composure, "Well, have a nice day."

"I was going to invite her to our Sunday School class," June whispered to Elodie as they returned to their previous seats. "Guess we can forget that for a while."

"Or forever," Elodie whispered back. She had not entirely calmed her spirit.

At last, Beth-Ann Sharp began the prelude. As she played, Christine remembered her condemnation of the manners of the boy rushing out of the church and juxtaposed it against the one she'd just received for her own. They'd happened within five minutes of one another, and it was impossible, even for Christine Williams, not to see she would be measured with the same measure she judged others. She could think of no reason it should not be so.

Chapter Sixty-Four

Bobby agonized over which restaurant would be the optimum location and ambiance for his dinner with Mariana. He considered Gary's Dogs, a Faircourt hot dog joint on the edge of town where you ordered your food at a counter and took it to one of eight small booths if one was available. If the place were full, you'd have to take the food to your car and eat it there. That was the downside. On the upside, if things went south, you didn't have to wait for a server to bring your check. It offered a quick getaway, but Mariana might think him cheap.

He also considered a chain Italian restaurant. Bobby didn't enjoy going there alone and loved the Chicken Parmesan, which was both the pro and con of the place. If he ate Chicken Parmesan, he'd need to find a bathroom quickly. The stuff pushed right through him.

He mulled several other options before settling on Dos Loros in La-Grange. The food and service were good; it wasn't too cheap or expensive, and he knew Mariana was familiar with LaGrange. He wasn't sure if she'd ever stepped foot in Faircourt.

Bobby also fretted over what to wear because making an excellent first impression was essential. Blue jeans and a turtleneck were out. A sports coat and tie might be too formal and intimidating. He chose khaki casual slacks, a green plaid button-down shirt, and a coordinating green sweater.

Nervous as a cricket in a chicken coop, Bobby arrived at Dos Loros fifteen minutes before the agreed time. He noted his reflection in the front doors as he approached and berated himself. *"I look like Mr. Rogers without the tennis shoes."*

He was seated only a minute or two when the waiter set a basket of chips and a small carafe of homemade salsa in front of him. Bobby ordered two glasses of water with lemon. It'd be nice to have something waiting for her when she arrived.

As he waited, he recalled his phone conversation with Mariana. He'd felt a jumble of nerves, and she, not expecting his call nor caught off-guard, seemed relaxed and friendly. She said she'd looked forward to meeting him and would love to join him for dinner. He told her the where and when, and that was the extent of it. He wondered why he hadn't planned more conversational talking points or been more spontaneously curious.

Bobby began nibbling at the chips when his cell phone dinged, announcing a text message. He checked the screen and saw the apology from Mariana: "I'm so sorry. Running late. Should be there in 20 minutes." He frowned, poured some salsa into a tiny bowl, and dug into the chips. *"Hmm. She doesn't seem concerned with impressing me,"* Bobby thought.

Thirty minutes later, a sympathetic waiter led Mariana to Bobby's table. She wore an unbuttoned black wool coat over a powder-blue dress, and the top of her wavy black hair was pulled back from her face while the rest hung loose down her back. But the two things that arrested Bobby's attention were the white gold wedding band on her left hand and her red-rimmed brown eyes. She'd been crying.

Bobby stood to greet her. "Hello, Mariana. I'm so glad to meet you," he said, extending his hand to her.

Mariana shook his hand firmly. "I'm so very sorry I'm late and completely mortified," she apologized without explanation. She removed her coat, tossed it with her purse to the far side of the empty booth bench, and sat down.

"Are you okay? Is something wrong?" Bobby asked, acknowledging her obvious distress.

She took a sip of her lemon water before responding. "It's been a stressful week," she answered.

"Is there anything I can do to help?" Bobby asked, paternally concerned and forgetting his previous annoyance. He realized that her effort to dress up and do her hair indicated she was, after all, concerned about his impression of her. She also didn't immediately spill her problems or make excuses.

"That's very kind of you to offer, but I'll have to deal with this myself," she answered, dabbing the corners of her eyes with her napkin.

Bobby said nothing to see if she would fill in the silence. She did.

"Sometimes life comes at you all at once, doesn't it? My mother, who's been ill for the past few years, passed away two days ago. My brothers flew into Louisville today, and our meeting with the funeral home director took longer than I expected," she explained.

"Oh, Mariana! I'm so sorry for your loss. You should have called to cancel with me. I certainly would understand."

"That's the last thing I wanted to do. My brothers are bossy and difficult. They're already pressing to sell Mom's house. I looked forward to our meeting as a welcome reprieve from their demands – unless you don't like me. In that case, I'll bury my face in a plate of fish tacos and be on my way. The fish tacos here are divine."

Bobby smiled and motioned to the watching waiter. "Two plates of fish tacos!" he ordered.

"I hope you'll find I'm friendly, undemanding, and a relaxing break from your brothers. I'm going to guess you know lots about me from DeShawn, but I know almost nothing about you. I want to say, 'Tell me about yourself,' but that sounds like an interview question. You already have the daughter-in-law position," Bobby added his signature smile and a little laugh at the end of his comments to ensure it didn't sound snarky.

"I'm sure that was quite a surprise for you. I hope you're not disappointed. One of our marriage's best days was when DeShawn told me you'd reached out to him through Jonathan and wanted to visit. I was so happy for him, for both of us, really. My mother's illness was a long goodbye, and we realized the end was near. It was kind of the Lord to give us back our last remaining parent at just the right time," Mariana returned a genuine smile.

And in that moment, all of Bobby's anxiety for himself faded into the background, replaced by a concern for the welfare of this kind, vulnerable young woman. He would be her dad, too, because at some level, in her mind, he had been for the past five years.

"Perhaps there is something I can do for you," he suggested.

Mariana raised a quizzical eyebrow.

"Let me accompany you to your mother's calling hours and funeral. We'll be a united front against the bully brothers. I don't want you to be alone."

"I'd love that. Thank you, Dad," Mariana responded.

The fish tacos arrived, and Bobby agreed with his daughter-in-law's assessment: they were indeed 'divine.' As they were finishing, Mariana confessed:

"I drove by your house while you were in Florida. Now that you're back in DeShawn's life and he'll be released soon, I just had an itch to see where you lived and where my husband grew up. It's a lot of change, and I'm trying to ground myself, if that makes sense."

Bobby rubbed his chin with his napkin and asked the question that had just popped into his head: "I don't mean to overstep, but since you need to find new housing, could you see yourself and DeShawn living in that house with me?"

Chapter Sixty-Five

It was just past 7:30 AM when Grant emerged from the bathroom, shaved and showered, wearing his blue/black plaid flannel shirt and black jeans. There was a 9 am starter's meeting at Grassy Fields Country Club to iron out the schedule for the upcoming season, and Grant was happy for the opportunity to advocate for the days he wished to work instead of finishing out the preferred schedule of the starter he replaced last summer. It had been a long winter made longer by recent weeks of Marie's unhappiness with him, and it cheered him to return to the golf course.

He saw his wife sitting in her recliner at the end of the bed, coffee in hand and a mug of tea with honey for him on the Victrola table, and raised his eyebrows.

"For me?" he asked, gesturing toward the tea.

Marie nodded and smoothed some wrinkles from the lap of her royal blue satin bathrobe. "Do you have a minute?" she asked.

Grant sat in his matching recliner, picked up the mug, and blew gentle puffs over the steaming top.

"I don't know where to begin; it's gone so long. Too long. I realize that's my fault. I guess I'll begin with, 'I'm sorry.' I was angry with you and punished you instead of working through it. And even when the anger subsided, I wallowed around in self-pity, and that was immature and toxic." She began twirling the gold-chain bracelet on her left wrist as she spoke.

"I've disrespected you, Grant, and I'm truly sorry. I've also embarrassed myself and functionally denied Christ by my behavior. I've asked God to forgive me, and now I'm asking if you'll forgive me, too."

"I forgive you," Grant whispered the unembellished words through throat muscles tightened by rising emotion.

Marie set her coffee down and stood to hug her husband, but Grant raised his hand to indicate she should stay where she was. He needed to say more. Marie understood and complied with his silent request.

"I hurt you and I'm so sorry," she began confessing again.

"I forgive you," Grant repeated with a stronger voice, cutting her off. "But I also need to learn from this. We've never gone weeks without resolving disputes. As painful as these weeks of distance have been, I want to know why so this doesn't happen again. I never want to do this again, Marie."

Marie skooched forward in her chair until she sat on its edge, closer to Grant.

"Why did I behave like a brat? Is that what you're asking? I wish I could tell you. I'm not proud of it. Sin, I guess, is the ultimate answer, but not the one you're looking for. I know we've never left things to fester, but I just want to apologize. I'm afraid that trying to give you the explanation you want will muck up my apology and sound like excuses," she reasoned.

"I want your explanation," Grant assured.

"Well, you know I was angry because you spoke your mind with the kids, and the whole week was tense and ruined in my mind."

"I understand that's how you felt about it. I acknowledge that after all these years, I'm still prone to letting my mouth off-leash, which causes us embarrassment. I believe the things I meant to say to the kids were right, but not how I said it – without love and sounding like gongs and clanging cymbals. I'm sorry, Marie, and I hope you'll forgive me for the hundredth time."

"I do forgive you, dear."

"You said your anger subsided, yet you maintained the distance out of self-pity. I've never known you to be a self-pity kind of woman," Grant commented, still trying to make sense of what had transpired between them.

Marie lowered her head and thought for a moment before speaking. "You were right. After a few days, I realized you were right about the kids. I saw the same things you saw: Andie's irresponsibility with our grands, the immodesty and disrespect of Georgia and Grant, and worst of all – because we raised them – David and Daniel's rejection of church and meaningful faith in Christ. It was all right there in my face, just like it was in yours. But you had the courage to speak, and I didn't. And when I realized all that, I just sank and wallowed. It was easier to be mad at you than mad at them. The truth is, I could be mad at you and still be safe. Look what happened to Ava when stupid Mia and Marit got angry with her!"

Grant exhaled a deep breath he'd been holding while his wife spoke. "We should have talked about this," he said at last.

"You're right," Marie agreed, still twisting the chain bracelet around her wrist.

"So, you're worried that if the boys get angry with us, they'll stop speaking to us?"

"And cut us out of their lives and their kid's lives! I want to say they would never take it that far, but I would have said that about Mia and Marit," Marie answered.

"Let's sit on the bed," Grant suggested, wanting to be closer to her now.

Marie stood up and followed her husband to the edge of the bed, where they sat, shoulders facing one another. Grant took his wife's hand in his.

"Marie, I can't do it. I won't live in fear of my sons' potential reactions and allow it to mute my responsibilities as their father. Do I need to learn how to improve my communication? Absolutely! But if I don't say the hard things and risk their anger in doing so, who will? Who is speaking truth into their lives if it's not me? They don't have pastors or a body of believers to do that for them. But yes, it's risky, and there's no guarantee they won't follow the Van Zant girls' path. I guess it could happen. The question is: can we do the right thing and trust God with the outcome?" He let the question hang in the air for a moment before continuing.

"Baby Doll, when I think of standing before God, I'd rather have risked everything to bring my boys to Christ than have tidy relationships as they slide obliviously into hell. So, can you trust God? Can you trust me?"

"I will because there's no other choice," Marie answered honestly, putting her head on Grant's shoulder.

"Agreed. There's no other choice," he repeated her words as he stroked her hair.

Chapter Sixty-Six

"Enter if you dare!" Shelby responded playfully to the knock on her bedroom door. Wearing a new red velvet dress, she added the finishing touches on an updo for her Valentine's Date with Will.

Chase twisted the old brass knob and opened the door. An involuntary "Holy cow!" escaped from his mouth.

Shelby laughed. "Sweetie, that is the best compliment I will ever receive in my life. Someday, when you're older and have a girlfriend, don't tell her she looks pretty. Say, 'Holy cow!' like you did now."

"I'll try to remember that," Chase replied, embarrassed.

"Did you want to talk to me or just stand in the doorway and admire your old auntie?"

Chase entered the room, closed the door for privacy, and sat on the edge of her bed.

"Oh, a serious talk, eh?" Shelby guessed.

"You have a date tonight." Chase struggled with where to begin and stated the obvious.

"With our favorite postman, Will."

"He might be your favorite, but not mine," Chase thought. "Figured," he replied.

Shelby resumed fussing with her hair, giving her nephew the time and space he needed to get to the subject of his visit.

"You like him a lot, don't you?" he asked timidly.

"So far, so good," Shelby flashed him a grin.

"Do you tell each other everything?" Chase probed further.

Shelby gave him a thoughtful answer. "No, I don't think we do yet. I don't, anyway."

"Oh." Chase was caught off-guard by her answer. He thought that's what couples did. He pulled at one string of his hoodie while he re-grouped.

"Well, what if I knew something he didn't tell you? Would you want to know it? I mean, if it were really important?" he asked.

"If it were really important, yes, I'd want to know," Shelby furrowed her brow, suddenly concerned.

"He's trying to get a job in Nashville!" Chase spit out the words.

Shelby's face softened, and she put her brush on the bureau. Then she sat next to Chase on the bed.

"He told me about that, Sweetie. The company is headquartered in Nashville, but Will wouldn't have had to move there because he could work from home like I do. However, he didn't get the job."

Chase flopped backward on the bed, relieved. "I was worried!" he exhaled.

Careful not to muss her hair, Shelby laid back on the bed herself with her head turned in Chase's direction.

"I'm sorry you were worried," she whispered.

"I was afraid Will was going to break your heart," Chase confessed, turning his face toward hers.

"You did? Poor thing! But aren't I blessed to have the men in my family looking out for me?"

Chase beamed at being referred to as one of the 'men.'

"Let's sit up before I ruin my hair!" Shelby encouraged.

Once again seated upright, Shelby hugged her nephew, giving him a fabulous squeeze.

"You were missing some important facts about the situation, weren't you, Bud?" she said as she released him.

"Silas didn't tell me the part about working from home!" As soon as the words were out of his mouth, Chase regretted revealing his source of information.

"Oh, Silas, huh?" Shelby repeated the name, teasing him.

"Please don't tell his dad he told me anything! I don't want him to get in trouble," Chase pleaded.

Shelby chuckled and slowly shook her head from side to side.

"What?" Chase wanted to know what amused his aunt.

"This is just the situation your mom and I would get ourselves into when we were your age. We'd share secrets and not have the total story – one time, the completely wrong story – and then we'd find ourselves in a pickle with either our teachers or parents. It's just kind of funny to see the same thing happen with you and Silas. History repeating itself, I guess. But don't worry anymore, Sweetie. There's no pickle you'll be in. My lips are sealed." She drew a line across her mouth with two fingers, closing the invisible zipper.

"If Mom were here," Chase reasoned out loud. "If Mom were here, she'd be going out to dinner with Dad, and you'd be stuck here with Lovie and me."

"Nope! If Mom were here, she and your dad and Will and I would be going out together, and you'd be stuck with Lovie," Shelby corrected with a poke in the arm for emphasis and a laugh for love of the sweet boy.

Chapter Sixty-Seven

The Shermans had the house to themselves on the evening of Valentine's Day, a rare coup.

The Jeffersons had engaged Elodie to babysit their tribe of rambunctious boys so they could have a get-a-way dinner in Louisville. They were apprehensive about asking church members to babysit for fear of criticism of their boys' behavior being circulated in the church. But once they witnessed Elodie's power to direct the boys' energy with a simple withering glare over the rim of her glasses, they agreed there was no risk with her.

"She scares the foolishness right out of 'em, just like my daddy's mama could do to me!" Jonathan commented to his wife in Elodie's hearing. It set Elodie's shoulders a little straighter and her head a little higher to hear what she understood was a compliment.

The Rennigers and Van Zants were trying out Dos Loros in LaGrange on Shelby and Bobby's recommendations. Bobby specifically instructed: "You're fools if you don't get the fish tacos!"

"We'll take dat under advisement," was all Marcus would promise in response. When it came to Mexican cuisine, the Rennigers and Van Zants were all about the chicken fajita.

June had planned a unique Valentine's Day evening for herself and Cal, making the most of their opportunity for privacy. Although she was sure her idea would be meaningful to Cal, in the back of her mind, she feared her friends might think it silly.

June served her husband a simple supper of grilled cheese sandwiches and tomato soup at the kitchen table. Cal received it gratefully but expected something grander given his wife's considerable abilities in the kitchen. The evening was meant to be a celebration of love.

Afterward, June instructed her husband: "Now go change into your pajamas and climb into bed. Don't lie down, sit up."

"What?" Cal asked in surprise.

"I'm not taking questions. Please follow the instructions. I know that transition is a process for you, so I'll work on cleaning up the kitchen. But don't dilly-dally," she instructed with a playful wink.

She took half an hour to put away the leftover soup, do the dishes, wipe down the table and counter, and make the special creation to present to Cal. When it was ready, she went to their bedroom and found her husband had followed her instructions to the letter. He was sitting in bed and dressed in his preferred nightclothes, a gray short-sleeved t-shirt, and red/gray flannel pajama bottoms.

When he saw what she had in her hands, his jaw fell, and his eyes welled up as she suspected they might.

"A banana split with two spoons!" he exclaimed. "Oh, now I get why we ate grilled cheese and soup. I'm dense. Sorry, June!"

"I knew the banana split would remind you," she said, handing him the ice cream, kicking off her shoes, and climbing into the bed in her red-flowered tunic and leggings.

He swiped away a tear on his cheek and received a spoon from June's hand.

"We've talked about it enough over the years but never recreated it. I thought it might be nice to remember with these things," June said, moving close to her man and digging her spoon into the bowl.

"To remember our first married year when we were so broke I couldn't afford to take you out to eat supper, and we ate grilled cheese and tomato soup from a can most nights. Our big splurge was a banana split at the ice cream parlor. We had to share it because it was dear at three dollars and fifty cents. And I made you walk there, so we wouldn't spend the gas. Aww, June, you were such a trooper. You still are." He took a bite of the ice cream.

"I added the chopped nuts to decrease the glucose spike and calculated the carbs with sugar-free ice cream so you can dial in the correct amount of insulin," June noted.

A look of sadness passed over Cal's face. "Now, that's something you didn't have to do back then. Between the diabetes, the cancers, and all the other things I've got going on, I'm not the man I used to be for you."

June patted his leg. "Do you really remember our first year? I mean, all of it? It was stressful worrying about how to pay the bills. Remember I cried when the washing machine broke, and we couldn't fix it until months later? My father took pity and gave us the money – and then you didn't want to take it. I got so mad I screamed at you for putting your pride above our convenience. Do you remember how we fussed and fought – both of us showing the selfishness we hid when we were dating? And yet, all the times we've reminisced about our first year, all we ever discussed and laughed over was the endless tomato soup and the occasional banana splits – like they were the best of times."

Cal looked at the ice cream and nodded.

"That's because there were good times in the hard times, and that's what we choose to focus on. Both of us choose that because it makes us happy. Yes, these last several years have had more hard times for us because of the health challenges, but we can choose to find and focus on the good times that exist within the hard times again."

Cal said nothing but took another spoonful of ice cream.

"For instance," June intended to highlight the good she found. "We have people we love, and who love us, living under the same roof we do. We're not on our own like many people are – like we used to be. I feel like

God has put us in the cleft of a rock where we're protected and secure. And don't we get to rejoice with our friends that Grant and Marie are reconciled, and Ava and Marcus are dealing better with their unending family drama? I don't know about you, but when they're happy, I'm happy."

"Don't forget Elodie! She hasn't murdered any of us in our sleep, so there's that to be thankful for," Cal added, encouraged by his wife's words and a smile creeping across his mouth.

"As if she would ever lay a hand against you! Only the rest of us need to fear her, although her back problem makes her slightly less ferocious," June humored his silly comment and grew serious again.

"Cal, Dear, when we're in Heaven and reminisce about our life on Earth, I don't think we'll talk much about the hard parts, even though we'll understand more clearly how God gave our trials to strengthen and sanctify us. I think we'll talk about the 'banana split blessings' that delighted us, like witnessing the salvation of Chase and Shelby, the privilege of ministering to Lovie and Bobby, and...and...who knows what the Lord has in store for us yet!"

About The Author

Alexandra has been a women's Bible study leader for decades, a religion columnist for a small city newspaper, and the producer/teaching host of Christian Television Network's Scriptureology. She's melded her passion for writing and teaching into crafting relatable characters living out theological and discipleship principles in contemporary fiction.

Alexandra lives with her husband, Gary, on a small hobby farm in Kentucky, tending chickens and bees. The vegetable garden started with eager optimism each spring is usually lost to weeds and rabbits by July because, it turns out, they'd rather have adventures and cookouts with friends than actually garden.

If you enjoyed this book, please leave a review on Amazon to help others discover it. It really makes a difference.

Book Club Discussion Questions

1. The friends have differing convictions about Halloween and navigate to a consensus about participating in giving out candy. Consensus isn't always possible. How should you react when others don't share your convictions about matters of conscience?

2. Christine's hell-bent pursuit to punish her father had a devastating unforeseen consequence. What are some other reasons that taking revenge is dangerous?

3. Chase learns the difference between loving everyone and being discerning in choosing friends. Is there a friend in your life whose influence is detrimental to your walk with Christ, and what does that look like? What changes might you make?

4. Will struggles with believing his Ph.D. is useless because of his divorce, and Marcus reminds him of God's sovereignty over it from the beginning. Have your plans ever been derailed? What could be God's better plan for you?

5. Elodie devised a spiritual growth grading system to promote "structured accountability" within the Church body, which was quickly shot down. Do you think there's any way to encourage spiritual growth without it devolving into "a yolk of slavery?"

6. G-Lu tells Ava it's a tragic mistake to substitute silence for scripture when counseling suffering people. Do you agree or disagree, and why?

7. Will and Shelby's first date is a disaster, but Will gets another chance. Why? Have you given someone a second chance and been delighted that you did?

8. Marie asks Ava, "Does God forgive the unrepentant?" What impact, if any, should the answer to that question have on your understanding of the goal of forgiveness?

9. Bobby and DeShawn have both been angry with God for different reasons. Bobby can do nothing but let it eat at him. How does DeShawn handle it?

10. Grant and Marie struggle with addressing their adult children's life choices. One confronts gruffly, one evades the issue entirely, and neither produces change. How would you advise them?

www.ingramcontent.com/pod-product-compliance
Lightning Source LLC
Chambersburg PA
CBHW071405300726
48976CB00006B/1995